A Woman Called Tree

Carmen Liana Young

Copyright ©2021

Carmen Liana Young

Instagram.com/nemracanail

https://www.facebook.com/carmenlianayoung

songsofcarmen@yahoo.com

Cover painting by Carmen Liana Young

Sci-Fi Fantasy

ISBN: 9798535150246

I dedicate this book to my kids, Yael, Loic, Xeni, and Nalo; your existence inspires soul. To Leeann for inspiring me to finish this story. I love y'all.

When I looked to nature, I found who I was.

And I realized I've been perfect all along.

-Tree

Chapter One - The Encounter

Kale glanced at the register clock for at least the tenth time within the past hour. She had a little less than two hours left, but the last few hours of work always seemed like an unbearable eternity. Her restless nature was an uncontrollable habit. It wasn't the physicality of the job that bothered her; it was the stress of dealing with so many people. Kale worked in retail, and on top of that aggravating realm was the long eight-hour shifts that seemed to suck up most of her day.

Come on five o'clock or at least the last break of the day. Then, as if her prayer was answered, Kale's supervisor, Jamie a frumpy but smiley-faced brunette, walked up to her.

"Thank you, and have a nice day," Kale muttered, holding out the customer's receipt. The customer, an unnaturally thin young man, looked at Kale with a void expression. Almost as if he wanted to project his voidness onto Kale. Without a thank you, he smacked his cracked, chapped lips, snatched his receipt, and walked away. *The nerve of this anorexic punk.*

"Kale, you could show a few pearly whites," her supervisor suggested, interrupting Kale's obvious annoyance.

"I did smile, Jamie. Didn't you notice the joy written all over my face?" Kale asked.

"Well, in my opinion, you were at a two on the Smart World associates smiley level. I'm gonna need you to bump it up to at least a seven or an eight. Better yet, just get it to as close to a ten as you can. Okay, sweetie?"

Kale flashed her level-ten fake smile, and Jamie lit up.

"See! And you're so cute, too. You should smile more often, sweetie." Kale turned her head, rolling her eyes as her smile dropped just as fast as it appeared.

"Kale, you can take your break now, okay."

"Kay," Kale responded, mocking Jamie's chipper high-pitched tone as she walked away.

Jamie didn't have to tell her twice. From the corner of her eye, Kale saw another customer start toward her open register like a pond in a desert. Kale didn't even look up. She slammed her closed lane sign down, leaving the customer dumbfounded. Then she turned her head, pretending as though she didn't see him, and headed toward the entrance of the department store.

In her usual break area, the side of the building, Kale leaned back against the brick wall and propped up one foot. She took one long puff of a cigarette, closed her eyes, and leaned her head back as the smoke released into the air. Finally, a few moments of relief from Smart World's artificial atmosphere of, "Hi, how are you today?" when she really didn't care about speaking to anyone. From what she could see, most people who shopped there didn't want to speak to her either. The place was saturated with gossip and frivolous conversation. It was amazing if any true kindness and humanity still existed. Even on days when Kale was in a pleasant mood and letting a little light shine through, she'd greet her customers, and some would look at her like she'd just spoken undecipherable Cantonese. Sometimes customers slammed their money on the counter as though it pained them to treat her like a human being. That boiled her blood, especially when it was from people with faces as brown and black as her own. To Kale, as much drama as people of color have gone through, to treat each other like trash was unacceptable. And then the materialism. How could she forget? Most people who shopped there overspent on things they didn't want or need. Then they' d complain at the register like Kale was a therapist they could empty their guts to, and she'd have an answer to solve them. But it wasn't all bad, sometimes she'd get her regulars who enjoyed sharing a few sunny words. That was one of the things, besides a steady paycheck, that helped with not walking out and never coming back. She tried looking for another job, but nothing came about that fit with Kale's scheduling or good pay.

Work was only part of the stress bothering her. Living in a small town with no outlet and taking care of two small children alone drained her life's force by the day. She blew out smoke as though letting her complaints and annoyances float into the air. *Suck it up, and keep it moving.*

Kale battled negative thoughts every day; but lately, she wondered why it was getting worse. Her mother passed last year from cancer. Since then, it felt as if her whole internal world was in crisis. She just had to stay afloat, so the crisis didn't flood out to her external world. If it weren't for her mom's sister, Kale's talk-too-much Aunt Niecy, helping her with the kids, she'd lose her job.

She took one last puff from the cigarette, pulled out a cellphone from her back pocket, and saw she was two minutes over her break time. Fifteen minutes was just not long enough, but Kale knew, according to the employee of the year, Jamie, it was. Plus, she didn't want to hear Jamie's mouth. She threw her cigarette down, put it out with her boot, and rushed back in, not caring if she reeked of smoke. Kale resumed her position and, by habit, started counting the minutes until they reached the five o'clock mark to her freedom for the day.

#

Kale rushed to the timeclock and swiped her badge. The tension in her shoulders eased a bit as she dropped them away from her ears. Tensing was a bad habit she had tried to break numerous times. Throughout the day, she always caught her shoulders in the same tight position. After grabbing her purse from the locker, Kale headed through the grocery section and grabbed a few TV dinners, a two-liter soda, colorful cereal, and a couple of apples in hopes of them being eaten by her children.

Kale didn't even know why she tried to get them to eat fruit. Sometimes her son, Hampton, would eat an apple if she wasn't too lazy to peel it for him. Her daughter, Davis, the youngest, only ate a few bites before she'd lose interest in finishing it. But at least Kale tried to get something healthy in their systems, and the TV dinners did have a little bit of broccoli, which they usually ate. She let the hopeful idea of healthy eating leave her mind and paid for the items. It was time for Kale to go and get her babies.

#

Kale drove a silver, van through the apartment complex where her aunt lived. She parked and then walked to her aunt's building where Hampton and Davis were staying. Her aunt opened the door after the first knock.

"Hey, Aunt Niecy! Are they ready?" Kale asked, walking past her aunt without looking for a response. Kale's eyes went to her children as they looked up from playing with toys on the floor.

"Mommy!" they screamed, jumping up to meet her. Kale always looked forward to the part of the day where she picked up her children. They always greeted her like star-struck groupies meeting their favorite rock star. It always fascinated her how they'd see her in the mornings before work, spent most of their time with her on her days off, but whenever she picked them up, they still acted as though it had been ages since they'd last seen one another. It was like knew found excitement every time. Maybe to a young child's mind, their parents being gone all day was likened to the eternity she felt being stuck at work behind a register. But this was an excitement Kale never grew tired of experiencing. It made her feel so good. No matter how bad her day had been, returning to her children to see their faces was a joy that made life worth carrying on.

"So, y'all were good?" asked Kale, kneeling to hug them.

"Yeah, Mommy," Hampton answered. Davis just nodded, squeezing her mother.

"They had a good day today; ate up everything you brought them, though. You need to bring more snacks for them, especially for Hampton. Baby boy can eat!" Aunt Niecy said, smiling at Hampton.

Kale started getting the kids' bags and belongings together. She looked inside the fridge to make sure she didn't leave anything. Aunt Niecy was right; Hampton ate up everything she brought. Kale didn't have to work the next day, so she wasn't planning on returning to Aunt Niecy's until the day after. But she wanted to hurry and be on her way before Auntie brought up something to nag about.

"When are you gonna register Hampton for school? He's five; he could have been in head start, kindergarten, or something, right?"

And the nagging begins. Kale blew out a breath and lowered her head before responding.

"Aunt Niecy, I want to homeschool. I've told you this."

"Homeschool? I don't remember you telling me that. How are you s'pose to do that and you work? Is their daddy gonna help you with that?"

"No, Auntie, I can do it around my work schedule as long as you help me with that. I don't want my babies in the school system. Plus, I've asked Hampton what he wants, and he wants to stay with me. School and education are two different things. I want my children educated, not indoctrinated," Kale responded, feeling the tension tightening in her shoulders. A cigarette was also starting to call her name.

"Gul, what-chu talking? Is that part of that black power conscious-mess you've been reading about? It's 2021 now, and things have changed. Having them in school can help you, like a free daycare so you can get a break and do other things. Ain't nobody tryna mess up your children's minds. Lawd, have mercy," Aunt Niecy complained.

Kale rolled her eyes, taking another deep breath so she wouldn't lose her cool as Auntie continued.

"Kale, black folks fought for the right to go to school, and you fighting to keep them out? Just don't make no sense to me. And you think naming them after them black power folks gonna make a difference? After a while, those babies gonna need to go to school and get some socialization in 'em. Can't you get in trouble for not taking them?"

The same flat expression and attitude Kale wore at

work was planted on her face. She was tired of constantly explaining her plans over and over to her pompous over rambling aunt, who obviously heard nothing. Her mother once told Kale, "You have two ears and one mouth. Listen more than you speak; you'll learn more that way." But Kale doubted her aunt had ever heard that quote.

"Aunt Niecy, what I am doing is perfectly legal. I've looked into the state laws, and I don't have to register Hampton in the state of Georgia until he is six. But even without that, I've been working with him since the day he was born. I am his first teacher, after all. And I've named my kids after powerful black folks that I saw created change and acted. What's wrong with being proud of that?"

Kale paused and glanced at her children, staring at her and Aunt Niecy.

"These are my children, and I'll see to it that they are educated in a manner that's right for our family. I don't have a problem with school if that's what someone else wants to do for their family, but I don't agree with forced learning or learning at the same cookie-cutter pace as everyone else. From what I've heard, especially 'round here, it's all about high test scores. They drive the joy of learning and exploring out of these kids until they learn to accept that their interests are just hobbies on the side and that English and math are the real learning when learning is everywhere. It doesn't end at three p.m. when the bell rings. Plus, I'll see my kids even less with my crazy work schedule. Hampton and Davis would spend most of their waking time with strangers who don't know or love them. And I like working with and teaching my own. I'm tired of preaching to you, Aunt Niecy, on this; you know I ain't—I'm not going to change my mind."

"Lawd knows you're stubborn and hardheaded just like your mama." A sudden sense of pang caused Aunt Niecy to pause, reflecting on her sister. Kale caught it and felt a little guilty for going off on a tangent. But she didn't say anything to relieve the hurt of the reminder.

"All right, Kale, I'll stop talking to you 'bout it. You sound like you know how you want to organize and build your family. But can't you at least get Davis a speech therapist. I can't understand that child's homemade sign language. Ain't she on Medicaid?"

"Auntie, Davis will talk when she's ready. She's only two." Kale took a prideful glance at Davis, who had sat back on the floor to play with Hampton.

"I have faith in her. Mama didn't talk until she was four, right? Let me go, Auntie. I gotta get home. Come on, y'all."

Kale waved her hand in a fast motion for her children to move right now. They jumped up and followed her through the door.

"All right, see y'all in two days," Aunt Niecy said.

"Bye, Aunt Niecy," Hampton said, waving as he walked out the door.

"Bye, baby."

#

The young dark-skinned woman climbed out of the passenger side of the blue car, smiling and waving farewell to the driver as he pulled off. Gently brushing her thigh-length thick locs behind her shoulders, she walked to the edge of the street, paused for a moment, and absorbed her surroundings. Tilting her head to the sky, she sucked in deep breaths of air, and slowly released them. The young woman sensed an unbalancing darkness rising, even though the sun shone brightly, and the weather was pleasant and calm. Also, she knew something was drawing her to stay in this small town so that she could share her light.

She felt eyes upon her and turned around. A few elder men were sitting in a dilapidated car repair shop at a fold-up table, holding onto playing cards. Instead of their eyes on the cards, their eyes were glued to her as though she was a newly landed Martian. She met their gazes with a slight nod and smiled. They nodded back with expressionless faces; one lifted his hand and gave a stiff wave. The woman turned away and decided to walk down the road. There were no paved sidewalks, just road where its edges dissolved, meeting dirt and grass. So, she just walked along the right side, noticing the houses and plant life. Some of the houses were run down from the effects of age, abandoned with boarded windows and trash. A few with well cared for lawns exhibited touches of creativity from the neat trimmed hedges to blooming wisteria and roses.

She kneeled to touch some wild dandelion growing on the side of the road. Even though she sensed light malice in the energy around, she felt a oneness flowing through her from the plant. Something wormlike moved under her dark smooth skin and made its way to her palm as she flipped over her hand. A thin, leafy green vine broke through the flesh of her hand, spiraling toward the dandelion until it wrapped around its stem, creating a feeling of connection. This feeling excited her; it was the feeling of life. She gave a silent thanks. With a simple thought, she retracted the vine back within her hand like a snake sliding into a hole. Her flesh sealed afterward as though it had never been broken.

She heard a car coming down the street behind her. Standing, she glanced at the female driver in a van and children in the backseat, eyeing her with pointed fingers as though they were viewing an oddity in a circus. They passed and continued zooming further down the road. She saw the van pull into a driveway a few blocks down from where she stood. She continued walking in the same direction.

"Mommy, that lady has huge snakes in her hair!" exclaimed Hampton.

Hampton tried to get Kale's attention as soon as he saw the slim woman standing by the road. Kale had already noticed the woman kneeling, then standing, as she drove by. Then Kale gazed over the massive hair that seemed to swallow her tiny frame. Kale could have sworn she saw a flash of golden-green light surround the strange woman. She looked through the rearview mirror and didn't see any light, just a simple woman with thick hair. Kale wondered if it was a wig as she continued toward her house.

#

Lionel walked in the entrance of his home from the bus stop on the corner. He ran into his room and shut the door. Slinging his bookbag on the floor, he sprawled out on top of his bed, and stared at the ceiling. Thoughts overflowed his young mind, but he was trying his best to clear them. He had a rough day at school dealing with some of the other students that wanted to give him a hard time. Whenever he was not skipping, his arch-nemesis, James, was all over him with his two compadres, Mike and Lucas. James mostly gave Lionel a hard time because he was friends with Iesha, whom James had the biggest crush on but would never let her know. For the past few years, Lionel and Iesha had developed a great friendship connection, but that didn't matter to Lucas. Whenever he saw Lionel, he had to push his weight around. Now that Lionel made it home, he didn't want to think about anything pertaining to James or school.

His eyes shifted toward the flickering ceiling light. The room's atmosphere changed as it grew dimmer, as he felt a soft breeze blowing through his cracked window. A breeze would be something he would normally ignore. But within it, he thought he heard his name being whispered. He sat up, looked around his room, then toward the window but saw nothing. He continued to feel the breeze surround him as he laid back down and glanced at the light again, thinking he'd ask his grandmother for another lightbulb later. Lionel took a deep breath as the breeze stealthily entered his nose. Then there was nothing. For a short moment, all thoughts left as Lionel's brown eyes fluttered and rolled to the back of his head. His eyes flashed blood red. He blinked, bringing them back to a normal state, shaking the feeling that something else was in the room. Lionel still laid on his bed as he watched the light grow brighter. His grandmother, a thick and strong-voiced woman, burst through the door, startling him.

"Lionel Bernard Johnson!" she shrieked.

As soon as he heard his full name exiting her mouth, he knew it was time to brace himself to be chewed out with another lecture. He had deep respect and love for his grandmother, but she still got on his last nerves with all that nagging.

Besides dealing with bullying at school, he'd only skipped a few classes. He didn't think it was that serious because he still managed to get his work done. He only skipped days or classes when an assignment wasn't due. Lecture days were torture for him. Just sitting for an hour listening to the same thing he had already read on his own, plus understood, seemed like such a waste of his time. And they didn't even cover the entirety of the textbook!

His grandmother complained about how he wasn't applying himself and that he needed to calm his smart mouth when he talked with his teachers. *Why should I be the one to humble myself when I'm smarter?*

She continued until she came up with another issue she felt he was delinquent in. Lionel felt his grandmother was adding on issues that she was making up or he thought wasn't that serious. She was being a real drama queen again.

Lionel moaned in annoyance and rolled on his side away from his grandmother, facing the window.

"Lionel, don't you turn away from me, boy!" he heard his grandmother shriek at an even higher octave.

Lionel stared out the window, ignoring her. He blinked once, and the pupils and whites of his eyes became blood-red as though rivers would flow down his face. He closed them for a few seconds, then faced his grandmother with normal eyes accompanied by a sinister expression. A voice that sounded like his, but was not his, spoke from his mouth.

"Bitch, why don't you shut the fuck up and get your old fat jelly ass out of my room!" he snapped.

Lionel's grandmother stood with her face twisted in quiet shock and horror at what her grandchild spewed at her. Never in his thirteen years had she heard Lionel say anything so vile. Even he could not believe the words that just came from his mouth toward the one who raised and loved him unconditionally. Not even his parents were there for him like she was. But some force or urge inside of him had taken over his tongue. He tried to scream to his grandmother how sorry he was. But the more he tried to speak, the more venomous language shot from his mouth. His grandmother began slapping him, hitting him any place she could lay hands on him while screaming and cursing the devil for getting inside of him.

"I!" Slap.

"Don't!" Slap.

"Know!" Slap.

"What's gotten into you, Lionel!" More slapping continued.

"But I rebuke your demonic ways in the name of Jesus!"

As Lionel's grandmother slapped him like a ragdoll, his eyes became blood red. He shifted his ungodly gaze toward her. Piercing deep into her own, stopping her hand in midair. She screamed in terror, knowing this was something more than a thirteen-year-old exhibiting rebellious behavior. This was something not of this world.

"Who are you! Leave my baby! Leave him! Oh, Lionel!" she cried, easing away from him.

With his eyes locked on his grandmother, Lionel's mouth opened and released a forceful gag. His jawline dropped to a large inhumanly proportion, releasing a scream of dissonant voices. His small frame shook as though it could barely withstand the exertion. The force of the noise pushed his grandmother against the wall. She held her arms across her face, attempting to block danger and shield the fear from her grandson's deadly eyes. Through parted fingers, she couldn't help but stare like a frightened little child. She slid down, crouching into a ball as Lionel rose from his bed, moving toward her. It was as though he glided with every step he took. He kneeled in front of her and cupped her trembling chin with his skinny fingers. Tears streamed down her face as she shut her eyes.

"Grandma?"

She heard Lionel's voice, innocent, sweet-sounding, not the evil from within. She opened her eyes in hopes of seeing just him. His eyes were normal again, and she smiled.

"Oh, baby, is it you?" she asked while her eyes scanned his face for the truth.

"Yes, Grandma, it's me. You have to do what he says."

"Who, baby? Who's making you act like this? I have to find you some help. The-the Pastor, Pastor Samuel can help you."

Lionel's grandmother grabbed his hands, hoping the demon inside was gone.

"No, Grandma. No one can help. He says he and the others will spread the darkness here, j-just do what he says!" Lionel pleaded.

"Who, baby? Who?"

Lionel's grandmother burned with a yearning to know who or what was controlling her grandson. Now she held both sides of his face, looking deep into his teary eyes. Lionel's face formed into a distorted malevolent expression as a single tear rolled down his caramel cheek. Her grandson tried to reach her, but something more powerful took charge. A voice spoke from his mouth. This time, it was not his in neither speech nor sound. It dragged long, low, and rumbled like deep thunder.

"Mmmmwongo!"

Lionel's grandmother screamed; Lionel's mouth opened large enough to swallow a football. With eyes bulging, he roared a force within his grandmother's mouth, causing her scream to stifle; and then, she collapsed.

#

Kale grabbed her groceries to take inside, the children followed. Once inside, they zoomed past her like racehorses to get to their room to watch cartoons. Kale didn't bother to stop them. She always needed a moment to relax after a long day of being on the plantation, as she fondly thought of her job.

Kale put the two TV dinners she'd bought earlier in the oven for Davis and Hampton, then put up the rest of her groceries. She went to her bedroom to fall back on the bed. Kale stared at the ceiling fan, listening to the kids' cartoons through the walls.

She missed her mother. Her mother was the one who kept Kale grounded and reminded her of her own strength she sometimes forgot. Her mother helped Kale keep a positive outlook on life and always told her to never give up on love, that it was everywhere and within. Kale tried to keep her mother's words in her head throughout the day, especially when things seemed to get tough, but she still carried much anger that was hard to release. Her mother had only been gone a year, but Kale was still upset because she felt her mother had left her too soon. She felt alone, abandoned even; she still felt anger toward her mother for refusing any more treatment, letting her talents go to waste, being a wonderful artist, so many paintings unfinished.

Although Kale's eyes became shiny puddles, she refused to let a drop spill. *Crying is for the weak.* And she wasn't weak. She remembered her mother always telling the story about when Kale was five years old and told her mother not to worry about her because she was strong. And she still meant it to this day.

Kale shook her head as if she dissolved her thoughts. With her eyes now dry, she rose and decided to check the mailbox. As she walked through the front glass door, the numerous wind chimes her mother had hanging along the roof's edge on the porch rattled in the wind, producing a magical sound Kale grew to love. She saw four furry black paws stretching out from the shrubs below, and then, her mother's temperamental cat, Tora, popped up her head. Tora was a bushy long-haired cat that rarely let anyone pet her. Sometimes Kale thought the sheer presence of people annoyed Tora. Whenever Tora encountered a brave or naïve being that wanted to rub her between the ears, most of the time, she attacked with a lightning swipe of her claws or a warning bite. Even Kale had a few scars from affections that lasted a little bit too long. Kale's mother named her Tora, a Japanese name meaning tiger, because she looked like a miniature black tiger with tan stripes and because of her aggressive nature. Her mother named her right because Tora held the spirit of a wild solitary tiger.

Kale thought Tora had grown mean because she wasn't allowed to birth any kittens. Her mother had her spayed by the time she was six months old. Years later, her mother came to regret that decision. Before she passed, she concluded, "Who am I to not let Tora create life?" Before that realization, all she thought of was that she didn't want a bunch of cats swarming around her house. At least she was proud of the fact she never had Tora declawed. Although Kale questioned that because Tora was half-wild, half-domesticated, and she'd come and go out the house as she pleased. She mostly came in to eat, where her bowl was kept in the kitchen, then leave. She stayed outside most of the time, which Kale preferred so that she wouldn't take a swipe at the kids. As mean as Tora was, Kale thought there was at least one benefit of having her around, fewer rodents, snakes, and large bugs.

"Tora," Kale called. Tora sat up and looked with large curious green eyes.

"Are you going to let me rub your beautiful fur today, or are we gonna have some conflict?" Kale asked, joking.

Tora gave a big yawn and turned her head, laid back down, and ignored Kale.

Mean old cat.

"I wish I could lounge like that all day for just one day," Kale said. She lived in the house her mother left her, the house she grew up in. It was old with a lot of work that needed to be done. Thankfully, it was paid for. It was just maintaining the bills that were a headache.

Kale walked to the mailbox, noticing the grass she had been stalling to cut. It was beginning to look like a wild kingdom, and knew she couldn't ignore it much longer. Maybe she'd work her way to the yard today. Opening her mailbox to a pile of worthless sales papers, she grabbed them already having decided they were automatic trash. As she slammed her mailbox shut, time seemed to slow down. From a short distance away, she felt eyes staring at her and turned her head to see the skinny woman she saw by the road earlier while driving home.

Kale felt an unnatural calmness rush toward her like a flowing presence as if the air just shifted. The young woman approached Kale with a warming smile like the sun. Her skin was as flawless as smooth dark chocolate with perfect teeth glowing like stars. As magnetic as her presence was, she dressed plainly in a pale pink t-shirt and baggy ankle-length brown harem pants. She carried a large olive-green bag over her shoulders, appearing handmade, and wore sandals with black rubber thin soles held together with shoelaces. Her only jewelry were golden hoops, hanging from her earlobes, and a green gemstone stretchy bracelet. She was extraordinarily beautiful with regal features despite her seemingly homely clothes. But what was eye-catching about this newcomer was her hair. Kale had seen what she heard called dreadlocks before worn by quite a few men and boys in the neighborhood, a few women included. But she had never seen the kind this woman adorned. Her dark brown locs were as thick as her wrists, hanging from a thick shaft of tightly coiled afro roots, reaching to her thighs and almost to her knees. They swayed as she walked as though they were alive as a separate entity. As she came closer to Kale, she saw the woman's rich textured hair better and wondered if it was rough or soft to touch. And strangely, she looked familiar, but Kale couldn't place her.

"How are you, my sister?" she asked with a deep mature voice as smooth as her skin.

Kale stared for a few seconds too long. She was somewhat taken aback by being called sister by this stranger. Who greets people by calling them sister these days, except a hippie? Kale snapped back to herself, realizing how silly she may have appeared from staring.

"Uhm, I-I'm sorry." Kale smiled, mildly embarrassed. She looked down, then back up, gathering herself.

"No need to apologize; I realize my looks are a little different from the norm around here. I saw you when you passed me down the road earlier and now here, so I thought I'd introduce myself."
She held out her hand for Kale to shake.

"My name is Tree."

"Tree?" Kale repeated.

"Yes. Tree. I was given this name by a dear teacher and friend when I renounced my days of sleep and made a pact with the sun. Plus, at the time, my locs resembled the branches of a tree when they began sprouting from my head. Well, at least to him."

Kale just stared, confused, not knowing what Tree meant.

"That's interesting. Um, where are you from, Tree?"

Kale added a tad of sarcasm to the sound of Tree's name. She thought Tree's hair looked more like snakes but kept that comment to herself.

"I'm from everywhere because I'm connected to all things. But right now, this place pulled me here. I'm not fully sure why as of yet; but wherever I go, I go to share my light."

Kale saw Tree lower her hand. She'd been so mesmerized by Tree's strange presence that she'd forgotten about hospitality.

"Oh, I'm sorry," Kale said, holding her hand out this time.

"My name is, um, just as unusual as yours; I'm Kale."

The word Kale wanted to use was weird. She had no idea why her mother wanted to name her after a green she ate. She would have preferred a regular name like Keisha or Pamela, but her mother decided to name her after a leaf. Tree flashed a gorgeous smile, causing dimples to sink in both of her cheeks. She shook Kale's hand.

"Honored to meet you, Kale; I think your name is wonderful."

Kale felt a force like a pulsing wave move from Tree's hand to hers, then up her lower arm. She looked at Tree's eyes and could have sworn she saw the same golden-green glow she saw earlier flash around Tree's body. Kale became light-headed as she let go of Tree's hand.

"I feel dizzy."

Kale rested her hand on the mailbox to steady herself.

"I don't know what happened. I just became woozy all of a sudden."

"Maybe it's my aura. It affects others who encounter me in different ways. It's like taking a wheatgrass shot for the first time or going through a strong detox. I am the one who should be sorry. I sometimes forget when meeting new people."

Tree held out her hands as if she were bracing to catch Kale in case she fainted.

"Do you need to sit, Kale?"

"I think I'll be all right. That was crazy. I thought I

saw something," Kale looked to Tree for confirmation that she knew what she was talking about but dismissed it.

"It's nothing, never mind."

Kale tried to laugh it off. She became increasingly cautious of this mysterious young woman. All day, she'd felt fine, and then all of a sudden, she almost passed out. *Maybe this woman drugged me through the air? Is that possible?*

"Energetically, I'm a healer. We all are, in a sense, but some of us embrace it fully or lose connection with our healing capabilities because of numerous kinds of distractions. My aura naturally promotes cleansing, so in no way do I mean you any harm; I mean you, life."

Kale eyed Tree as she stood straighter.

"What do you mean by distractions? That everybody's aura can potentially make others go queasy?" Kale asked, joking.

"Distractions are anything outside of yourself that blinds you to the truth of who you are. My teacher once called this blindness the waking dream. This waking dream can be illusions, fears, desires, mental noise, or forms."

"You sound like one of those new-age artsy people my mother started listening to before she passed. That kinda stuff really isn't my thing. Personally, I don't think I'm blind to anything. I keep my concentration on reality and all I need to do to keep my job, live and take care of my kids; that's pretty much it. So, um, do you have family here, in Neville?" Kale asked. Tree smiled within, noticing how Kale became uncomfortable and switched the subject.

"Family is everywhere. But if you mean relatives, no. No family in that sense here. I just thought stopping in a place such as this would be a good way to slow down to breathe, to remember."

Tree talked with a twinkle in her eyes and a slight smile. Kale wasn't interested in hearing Tree's mystic mumbo jumbo talk, but she was as magnetic as a snake charmer and kind of entertaining. So much so that Kale couldn't contain her question.

"Remember what?" Kale blurted. *Damnit*, she chastised herself.

"Well, it's more like a reflection period than a remembrance for me. When we slow down, we remember that we are all source-connected. Our ancestors used the word Neter. Some call it God, Great Spirit or Chi. I love the use of the word Force or the Divine. Some even say it's nameless. But it is the source that connects us, to show us our purpose. So, we may shine regardless of the distractions of this world."

Kale raised her eyebrows and stretched her eyes,

incredulous to Tree's mini monologue.

"Ok, that sounds like a beautiful dream, but ..."

"Meow."

Kale looked down to see Tora watching Tree with intense curiosity.

"She's a beauty," Tree commented in awe. She kneeled to rub Tora's fur.

"Tree, be careful. Tora has a mean streak."

Tree smiled, ignored Kale's warning, and continued rubbing behind Tora's ears. Tora purred in ecstasy, burying her head deeper into Tree's hand for a stronger rub. Tree ran her hand down Tora's back to the tip of her bushy tail. Kale stared with her mouth slightly opened, then caught herself before a bug flew into it. She had never seen Tora take to someone so quickly, ever.

"You have the magic touch, Ms. Tree."

"No, my sister, your feline friend is the magical one. Cats are special. They are said to be bringers of good luck, and they are powerful protectors."

"Mommy."

Kale and Tree shifted their vision to see Hampton leaning out of the front door.

"I'm hungry."

"Oh! I forgot your dinners!" exclaimed Kale. She

turned back to Tree, who was still scratching Tora.

"It has been nice chatting with you, but I will have to talk to you later. I think I've just burned my children's meals."

"No problem, Kale. Do you mind if I sit with your feline friend a few more moments before I'm on my way?"

"Um, no problem. I guess that's fine."

Kale rushed into her house, leaving Tora to receive a rare cat massage. Kale felt a ting of jealousy that Tora was fond of Tree, a stranger, right off, and she, being her mother's daughter, now owner, was still trying to get used to her temperament. But she shrugged it off while she pulled the kids' dinners out of the oven. They weren't burnt, but in that state before burnt. In Kale's mind, they were just slightly overcooked.

"Hampton, do y'all still want these?"

"Yes, Mommy, we're hungry," he answered. Davis shook her head so hard she looked like she would knock herself off balance.

"You're always hungry little man," Kale joked, giving Hampton a light Pillsbury boy poke in his belly.

"Mommy?"

"Yeah, baby?"

Kale sat each of the hot dinners on a plate on the table

with silverware.

"Was that the lady with the snakes in her hair?"

"Baby, that was that lady's hair; it's locs. Remember, like that Bob Marley picture I showed you?"

The kids took their dinners off the table and headed to their rooms. Hampton turned back toward Kale from the kitchen doorway before walking off.

"Looks like snakes to me, Mommy."

Chapter Two – Strange Things

After the kids finished their meals, they raced outside, eager to play. They went to their usual area by the large circular trampoline outside, near the side of the house, toward the backyard. Kale checked on them every few minutes from her bedroom window and kept it open so she could hear them. She was about to wash dishes and see what other cleaning tasks she could sneak in after taking another glance. This time, she didn't see the kids on the trampoline. She saw them standing, watching something. Her gaze followed theirs toward the backyard. She saw the woman called Tree. Kale's eyes stretched as she stared at what her children's eyes were glued to. Tree stood on her hands with her toes pointed to the sky as still as a statue. Her majestic ropes of hair draped down on the earth-colored mat she stood on. Kale walked out of her room to the front door and circled the front corner of the house, closer to where her children stood. She looked in awe at how Tree held the pose without an ounce of struggle or imbalance.

"Mommy! Look!" Hampton shouted.

"I see, baby, "Kale responded, smiling at his excitement. Davis walked away from them and sat down in the grass, closer to Tree's mat, to stare at her face.

"Davis, baby; please, don't get too close. I don't want an accident." Kale looked worried.

Davis sat cross-legged, propping her elbows on her thighs, leaning her face into her palms. Her large brown innocent eyes stared toward Tree's closed ones, watching her breathe. Tree's clothes drooped, exposing toned abdominals and calf muscles. Kale watched in wonderment as Tree remained fully engaged. Tree opened her eyes to meet Davis' curious stare. Playfully she winked, causing Davis to smile brightly. Then, as if floating to the earth, she gracefully lowered her feet until they simultaneously landed between her hands. Tree remained for a short moment in a folded position, then slowly rose, uncurling one vertebra at a time. Her large locs swung back, exposing her heart-shaped face. Tree held her hands to her side at attention with her shoulders peeled back. Her hands rose toward the sky; then, she gradually brought them down together in a prayer-like position with her eyes closed.

"Ase'," she whispered with a nod. Tree opened her eyes with a smile similar to the one Davis gave her earlier.

"Whoa, that was so cool! I wanna do it!" Hampton exclaimed.

"Hey, I don't know if you can do that just yet, Hampton," Kale said, not trying to get his hopes up.

"All it takes is practice and discipline. But most importantly, breath and a steady mind." Tree said. "Over time, anyone can do it."

"What is that? A kind of martial arts?"

"It can be. I have been a practitioner of yoga for many years. It has helped tremendously with bringing peace and connectedness to every aspect of my life. You should try it. I can tell you would like it."

"I don't know, Tree. I'm like the stiffest person on earth. I know I need to exercise beyond just going to work and working around the house. I guess I'm just lazy. I'll leave the physicality to you and the kids," Kale said, shaking her head against the suggestion.

"Maybe one day, sister, you'll be open to it. It's an amazing practice. It strengthens the immune system, helps you to focus, and relax. It can help with that stiffness you feel. But most of all, it just helps you feel so good," Tree said, trying to convince Kale.

Kale smiled at the thought. "Maybe. It sounds interesting, but I don't think I'll be standing on my hands anytime soon. But I do have a question for you that's off-topic."

Tree raised her eyebrows as she waited for Kale's question. "How, I mean, how did you get your hair to grow in the manner that it does? Don't take this the wrong way, but I don't see any women with what I've heard called freeform locs. Usually, guys wear them; I mean, they are beautiful, just different."

Tree smiled, then glanced at Hampton and Davis. They had lost interest in their mom's conversation and climbed onto the trampoline, laughing and bouncing like jumping beans. She looked back to Kale, realizing that she didn't understand like a lot of other people. Tree didn't get her hair to do anything; it just was.

"My hair naturally formed this way. I mean, this is how it grows. Like I mentioned before, since I renounced the waking dream, I have never manipulated my hair or forced it to form into a manner it did not naturally want to go. All I do is wash it when needed, and I do not use products. It is just the most natural, simplistic way my hair forms. You could easily grow them." Tree said, nodding toward Kale's relaxed hair that was pulled back into a bun.

Kale looked incredulous and smiled within. She didn't think she could ever grow her hair like Tree's. Plus, it wasn't as thick, but she was growing tired of relaxing her hair. Her mother always thought when Kale was young, she would look cute with her natural hair. But going to school back then, dealing with her peers, plus the fear of being the only one in class with a knotty head, was too much to deal. She wore her hair natural until she was about thirteen but gave it up during middle school and hadn't worn her natural hair since. Strangely, she was proud of who she was; she just never thought deeply about how she wore her hair. It was just a habit by now. But lately, she thought of the message she was sending to her kids. She didn't want Davis to think she had to change herself to be beautiful, especially after naming her after the iconic afro wearer, Angela Davis. She just didn't know yet what she wanted to do with her hair. It was inspiring to see this woman before her completely unapologetic in her acceptance of herself, no matter how strange she seemed. She was a type of beauty that Kale rarely saw put on display in the world. But it wasn't just her physical beauty that made her alluring, it was her absolute comfort in being. From what Kale saw, Tree carried all of herself with full worthiness. She continued to listen to Tree without becoming too agitated with her philosophical meanderings.

"The coils and spirals of your hair are synonymous

with the spirals of all of nature. It is like a spiraling journey that leads you back to the source or divinity within you. In ancient times, it was said that the wearer of hair like this bestowed one with wisdom and knowledge, delving on to the supernatural. I've never thought of whether my roots are freeform or any other manmade title. I've heard they are called Jata by Indian mystics and also Dada by African shamans. I'm sure you're aware of the term dreadlocks, but I do not connect to the word dread, even though I understand others see that word as meaning dreadful fear of the holy or fear of God. My take on that is, why would you fear the divinity of who you are? Wouldn't you want to be one with the nature of all? Why do you have to fear the Creator to show praise, respect, and the desire for good? I'm in awe of the power of the Creator every day. I do not fear it because it is me. It is nature. It is you. It is all around us. It is the source."

"My hair is just an extension of that great Divinity. Anyone can choose to lock their hair, but there are no other people with hair like this; hair that grows tightly and easily toward the sun, uncontrolled, constantly twisting and wrapping around itself. My hair is completely free, and I embrace its differentness. I've always found it funny that I'm always asked about my hair growing as is. Why is it like this, or how did it get this way? How long have you been natural? But no one questions why someone chooses to be unnatural? Is it truly for style, or is it because someone has been influenced in some way? But then again, we have the will and the right to wear our roots as we wish, and everything is about vibration, so I do not judge. All I ask you, my sister, is to question everything." Kale stared for a moment, then raised her eyebrows and nodded in admiration.

"That was an eye-opening handful. Interesting. I've never thought of my hair as being unnatural or divine, for that matter. I guess if you're a spiritual being, anything can have special meaning. You've given me something to think about." Kale responded, watching Tree reach down to roll up the mat and slide it inside a shoulder bag. Kale felt a strange awkwardness from not knowing of anything else to say. She was used to being alone, especially since she broke up with her children's father, Jay. And she didn't make time to hang with old friends. She was either working with her children or visiting her aunt.

"It's getting late. I'm gonna get the kids in and finish up some chores before I relax, maybe google a few easy yoga moves before I go to bed tonight." Kale said as Tree stood back up.

"I'm glad you're at least interested in trying. Always

find ways to improve your quality of life, my sister. Rest also calls me, so I'm going to find a place to recharge for the night as well. It has been a long journey here."

"Do you have a place in mind? I can help you find a hotel if you like?" Kale asked.

"No, my sister. I will be fine, but thank you for your kindness. It has been an honor to meet you and your children today."

Kale chuckled. "O-kay. Well … take care, Tree. It was nice to meet you, too." Kale looked to her kids. "Hey, guys, time to go inside."

"Aw, Mommy," pleaded Hampton while Davis continued bouncing, doing clumsy baby flips, rolling over and over.

"Don't 'aw Mommy' me! Come on, y'all! Let's go!" Kale ordered. "Davis, you're gonna get dizzy! Come on, baby!"

Tree slung the bag over her shoulders. "Take care, sister." Tree waved at the children; then she walked away toward the front of the house and into the road.

#

Kale grabbed Tora's dry cat food out of the kitchen cabinet and walked to the back door to where her bowl was sitting.

She opened the back door and glanced outside through the screen door, scanning the backyard area. She saw someone walking through the alley, then veered off, stepping into the bushes across from her yard. Then disappear into the overly grown thicket, which resulted from nature swallowing the area after an old house was torn down. The only other thing past the area was a railroad track. It appeared to be Tree. Instantly, curiosity clouded Kale's brain.

"What in the hell is she doing?" Kale whispered.

Kale remembered she had already locked the front glass door when she came into the house earlier. The kids were now in their room, looking at picture books. So, she decided to see what was going on. Kale set the cat food down, then pulled the heavy back door up and carefully closed the screen door to keep it from slamming. Stepping through her backyard, she crossed the alleyway to the opening in the bushes, where Tree appeared to have entered. Moving through the tall grass, the thought of snakes crept into her mind, but her desire to know what Tree was up to overruled the fear. Kale saw Tora a few minutes after attempting to break her way quietly through the bushes and branches slapping at her. Kale paused in her step upon seeing Tora's stillness. Tora stared at something which made Kale frown, squinting to focus through the branches more intensely. Tree undress completely and place her clothes in the shoulder bag under a nearby bush. Kale's eyes became large saucers as her thoughts confirmed what she'd expected. *Something is wrong with this woman. She must be a lunatic undressing in the bushes like this or some sort of pagan devil worshipper.*

Tree leaned her back comfortably against a nearby tree trunk, and her head followed with eyes closed. Her hands stroked her thick ropes of hair draped along her sides, covering her body. She remained still for a moment, breathing deeply. Kale grew tired of watching, she had no interest in whatever ritual Tree was involved in. As she decided to slip away, something began to happen. Tree's smooth dark skin formed into a rough bark-like texture. Her locs lifted away from her body and suspended in different directions in the air, becoming immobilized, hardening, forming into branches. Tree's petite form merged into the flesh of the tree, and then she was gone.

Kale stared, unmoving from her hiding spot for about five minutes after Tree disappeared before her eyes. It was as if she was glued to the ground while her brain was still trying to process what she saw. Was what she saw real or a hallucination? Kale felt there had to be an explanation for what she'd just seen. She hadn't been getting proper sleep the past few nights. Maybe that was it, a waking daydream if such a thing existed. But she could vividly describe everything she saw like she'd just seen it with her own eyes because she had just seen it with her own eyes! Kale wanted to walk back to the house, but her feet wouldn't budge.

"Meow!"

Kale jerked so hard she almost kicked Tora.

"My God! My God!" she breathed heavily, holding her chest with one hand and holding herself up against a nearby tree trunk with the other.

"Tora, don't you ever scare me like that again, girl! I almost killed you!" Kale snapped in anger. Then lowered her voice, fearing Tree might have heard her.

She released a couple of more deep breaths to steady herself, then squinted hard at the attentive tiger-like cat.

"Did you know about this?" Kale asked, accusing the feline.

Tora sat back on her hind legs and crooked her head to one side as if to say, "Woman, are you crazy? The lady just turned into a tree?"

Kale thought about how silly it was to ask Tora that question and shook her head.

"Sorry, old girl, but you two did have some type of connection thing going on."

Kale looked back at the tree that Tree merged into and thought about walking up to it to touch, only she was afraid that maybe Tree's eyes would open. Kale wasn't sure if she was supposed to keep this a secret or tell someone. But who in the world would believe something like this anyway? They'd take her children and lock her in a nuthouse. Maybe Tree wasn't as nice as she appeared to be. She certainly seemed unusual, but Kale didn't sense any malice in the woman. Kale had more questions that she needed answers to.

After building enough courage to remove herself from the spot she stood in, Kale walked out of the thicket and crossed the alley back through her yard. Once she reached the house, Kale looked back at the untamed mini-forest expecting to see some sign of Tree, but there was nothing. The sun was beginning to set, and she imagined Tree being out there all night stuck inside of a tree. But there was nothing she could do. Kale opened the back door and let Tora inside to get to her bowl, and she followed in behind her.

#

Jay dialed his cellphone, hoping his baby mama would pick up.

"Hey, Kale, this you?"

"Who else would it be, Jay?"

"Look, don't get all stank with me. I just called to see how you and the kids are doing."

"We're fine," Kale answered.

"Can I come over?"

"To pick up the kids?"

"Naw, just to visit. You know where I live. I don't want the kids hanging over here."

Kale paused for a few seconds. "Why don't you ever spend time with them? It's like you only call just to get on my nerves or cut the fool. You could take them out to the park for a few hours if that's better than being at your place."

"I want to see you and the kids, Kale," Jay interjected.

"Well, you can't see me and the kids. I have things I need to do, but you can come pick them up if you want and bring them back in the morning. I don't have to work tomorrow, so it's whatever works good for you."

"Why are you trying to get rid of them? You got a man coming over or something?"

Kale released a loud sigh, "Damn, you are impossible. Your children miss you. and you're concerned about corny shit like that?"

Jay didn't respond.

"Look, man, don't call me unless it has something to do with our babies. I don't have the time nor the energy to deal with your foolishness. Are you coming to get them or what?"

Jay hit the end button and stood still for a moment, feeling surges of heat through his face. Unable to control himself he threw his phone into the wall, then stared at the cracked screen on the floor. Jay didn't understand why Kale couldn't see that he still loved her—that he still wanted to be with her. Yeah, he cheated on her a few times and wanted to go out with friends a few weekends a month, but it didn't mean anything. It had been over a year since he cheated, and Jay hadn't been out with anyone else. Before they broke up, Jay admitted all he did wrong so that he could right it and be there for her when her mom died, but Kale still wasn't willing to hear him out. It was her who wanted to keep Hampton when she became pregnant. Having children at a young age was never in his plan. But they came, and he loved them both; but he wanted her as well, the whole package. Shit, he'd even marry her if that's what she wanted. Jay really couldn't imagine her being with someone else, and that racked his brain. It just felt like she was still his.

So, don't let her go, a foreign voice said. "No, I can't give up," Jay whispered.

He looked out his apartment window and glanced at the project buildings across the street, then down toward the passing cars. Sunlight was gone, and only the traffic lights and the liquor store adjacent to his apartment gave any illumination. His vision moved from the streets past the parking lot to a dark figure standing on the sidewalk by some of the units near his apartment complex. He recognized some of the people walking past the project fencing, even some of the people near the figure, but he couldn't make out who this guy was. All he saw was a black silhouette, standing still as a statue. Jay heard a voice once again. *I can help you win her heart once more.*

Jay couldn't tell if he was talking to himself or just out of it. Maybe he had drunk a little too many Buds earlier today. When he and Kale were together, she'd always complain about his daily ritual of a few beers, commenting on how it made him smell or sleep too deep. He brushed away the memory and looked back out the window. As unrecognizable as the figure was, Jay felt as though it was staring directly at him. This time, the figure appeared closer to the building but still stood in the same position. And even though it was closer, Jay still could not see good enough to distinguish this mysterious person.

Jay heard a knock at the door, which made him

looked toward it. Cursing in annoyance, Jay then glanced back out of the window before he moved to answer. He didn't see the figure anymore, which he thought was weird. Looking up and down the street, whoever it was, was gone. So, he let it go. It was a waste of time trying to figure it out when he couldn't clearly see who it was anyway. Hearing another knock, Jay wondering who'd come to his apartment without calling first. His thoughts went back to his busted phone lying on the floor. How could he be so stupid, losing his temper like a little kid?

"Who is it?" he asked. There was no response.

"Who the hell is it?" he repeated, dropping extra bass in his voice but still no answer.

"Damn! I don't have time for games."

Jay rushed over to the door. Without looking through the peep hole, he unlocked the door and flung it open. No one was going to make him feel uneasy in his own home. He expected to see a homeboy, whom he fell out with earlier in the week because he owed him fifty bucks, but no one was there. Confused, Jay stepped outside the door but didn't see anyone. He was relieved a bit because he didn't have the money he owed. Yet he was sure he'd heard knocking. Maybe his drinking and weed smoking was finally catching up to him. He could hear Kale's voice now saying, "You go off into the highest clouds, speaking that philosophical shit when you're high. When are you going to come back to earth?" He stepped back into the apartment and closed the door.

"Hello, Jay."

Startled, he felt his heart jump inside his throat from hearing a whisper so close to his ear. He spun around and didn't see anything but was seriously spooked by now. Turning back around, Jay looked across the living room toward the kitchen entrance. The area seemed even darker since he had his lights off. Jay chastised himself for sitting in the dark earlier, moping, and reminiscing about missed opportunities. Only the traffic lights from outside his window shone through the darkness. Squinting he saw something there. It was the dark figure from outside; the more he focused his vision, it appeared to be the shadow of a man. Jay became paranoid, wondering how this person, whatever or whoever it was, had gotten inside. His eyes shifted around to see what make-shift weapon was accessible, since he didn't have a gun.

"Wh-who are you? How did you get in here?"

"I am one who can help you reach your desires, plus have a little fun. You have just the right body chemistry I need for me to fester and grow."

Jay wrinkled his nose, smelling a foul stench permeating throughout the room. It was coming from where the shadow stood, and for a moment, Jay was glad he'd left the window open. Ironically, the open window was probably how this dude got inside. But how could he get from the street, through the parking lot, and inside his apartment so quickly? Jay lived on the second floor, and he couldn't wrap his mind around how. All Jay knew for sure was that he wanted whoever this spook was to leave and take his filthy stench with him. Now Jay knew how Kale felt with his beer odor filling up the room when he came home from hanging out. But, damn, he wasn't this bad; this dude was a walking cesspool.

"Man, what the hell you talking about? I don't know who you are, and you don't know nothing about my desires, but you're gonna have to get yo' stanking ass up outta my place!"

Jay walked to the front door to open it, but the knob would not turn. He used both hands, and still, the doorknob would not budge. He grew frustrated and glanced back at the shadowed silhouette standing in the kitchen entrance. His frustration took control. Without thinking twice, Jay hurried across the room to find out who was messing with him. He wasn't going to let this smelly spook scare him.

"Man, I don't know who you are and what this is all about but get the f …"

Jay froze in motion. His eyes caught, unblinking in a hypnotic headlight of darkness. Red rose from the bottom of his eyes and filled to his lids until they were bulging with blood. Jay whimpered like an injured canine. His veins popped and pulsated as he used every muscle in his body to try and move, but it was useless. He was held in mid-movement by fear and an unseen force. He felt his mouth being forced open and the cracking pain of his jawline dropping to accommodate an unnatural entry. The shadow began to slither inside of his mouth like thick sludge crawling, bubbling, and oozing until it was fully inside of him. Jay lost consciousness and collapsed onto the floor.

#

Tree's eyes gradually opened as she woke from her deep sleep. Her raised bark-like skin lowered, then smoothed out to its original human texture. Her body eventually morphed back into her slender frame. The extended branches from her head lowered as the leaves shrunk within them, transforming back into fluffy dark wool. Feeling renewed, Tree gracefully rose as she detached from her symbiotic partner she'd shared the night with. Looking at the tree, Tree could see it was as renewed as much as she with its vibrant green leaves. Tree grabbed her hidden belongings and dressed. Then slung the bag over her shoulder. Tree placed a hand on the tree she shared the night with. "Thank you, my friend. You will produce plentiful pecans come next season," she whispered before walking away.

As she moved out of the thicket, nearing the alleyway, she was aware of eyes watching her but continued as though she didn't notice. Walking back toward Kale's house, Tree saw two men walking through the alley in her direction.

"Damn, man! Look at them wicks!" One of the men exclaimed.

"Them shit's hard right there!" said the other.

"Hey! Hey! Miss Lady," the first one called, catching up to Tree.

"Where you from, Jamaica?"

"How can I get my hair like yours?" joked the second one.

Tree paused, then turned toward the young men. Turning her head, her thick locs gently slung around her, stopping the young men in their tracks. A strong force emanated around her. Tree noticed the combination of apprehension and awe across their faces. With a slight smile, she nodded, breaking the ice. Tree didn't want to invoke fear but held their gazes with a bewitching stare. She gazed upon the first guy who spoke to her. He was tall and slim but a toned, light-skinned man with a low-cut fade.

"Wherever the creative force is, that is where I am from. And so are you, brother, if you look deep enough." Tree responded with a sly smile.

There was a silence. The two young men gave each other quick questioning looks and curious smiles, then looked back toward Tree.

"And you, brother," Tree said, shifting her gaze to the other young man with a cute smile but pants straddling his knees made him appear childish. His thin, locked hair looked as though it suffered from over twisting. "See these plants and trees all around you?" The young man's eyes followed from Tree's hand to the nature around that she pointed to.

"As individualistic as they grow is how different your locs would be from mines. No set is ever the same; even when one tries to control how it grows, the spiraling of creation will try to free itself to coil in its own wild way. You should leave your hair alone to form its own power to connect you to the cosmos. Its crowning glory will amaze you."

Impressed by Tree's words, the locked-haired young man smiled with light in his eyes, then nodded toward his friend in confirmation. The light-skinned, tall one spoke again. "Yo' that was deep? What's your religion? Are you like a Rastafarian, Five Percent, Muslim, or something?" he asked.

Tree closed her eyes, drawing in a deep breath. Then opened them with sparkling wonder, releasing a full-extended breath. "See that, brother? That is life; my religion is life."

The two men looked at each other, not really sure what she meant, but Tree could tell it had their brains desiring to know more. How could life be a religion? It just didn't sound as heavy as they'd thought it should; it was too simple. They expected an answer a little more extravagant, some mystical title that she called herself or her spirituality, something they could grasp in a book or look up to study. Life could be anything. They waited for Tree to elaborate a little deeper into what her answer meant, but all she gave them was a smile.

"You mean like ... meditation?" asked the tall one.

"Yes, that's part of it. When life is your religion, you realize the greatest subject you will ever study is the study of self. Therefore, everything you live and express is sacred.

You take time out to notice the breath flowing through you, which is the source of your power. You then realize you can call yourself any title you want, read all the books of the world you want, and see goodness in that. But their purpose is to lead you back to yourself, to your life, your inner world. And it is only then that you will discover the secrets of the universe." Tree gave the young men a moment to soak in what she said. "My brothers, my name is Tree. I'm glad we have met today. What are you both called?"

Tree held out her hand, and the light-skinned man shook it. For a moment, he forgot what to say. With a puzzled expression, he stared into Tree's eyes; then he looked away, taking a second to regroup his thoughts.

"Um, um, I'm Kinte, and this is my cousin Tahj," he stuttered, laughing a bit. Kinte thought he was just stunned by Tree's answer explaining her religion or maybe her mesmerizing presence. He wondered why he was at a loss of words to the point of almost forgetting his name. Kinte moved to the side so that Tahj could shake her hand. But as Tahj came closer, he eyed Tree's hair instead. Tahj reached out, trying to feel one of her locs.

"Aye, yo'! I don't mean no disrespect, but how you get them joints so big? They must be heavy as hell!" Tahj asked excited.

Before Tahj could land his fingertips in her hair, one of Tree's large locs moved like a snake, slithering into a hiding place behind her. The young man jumped back with a yelp, bumping into Kinte, almost toppling him over. Tahj fell to the ground with his pants dropping to his ankles. Tree chuckled to herself, watching Tahj crawl back on the ground with a fright.

"Man, what's wrong with you?" Kinte snapped embarrassed.

Tahj quickly jumped and yanked his pants up twisted, well above his waist. He looked at Tree with shock.

"D-Did you see that?"

"See what?" asked Kinte.

"Her hair's alive, man! It moved!" Tahj shouted, pointing to Tree.

"Man, are you crazy? Fix ya damn pants and stop worrying about the lady's hair."

"Kinte, man, I ain't crazy. I'm for real. It moved like a worm. She got something alive in her hair!"

"Brothers," Tree interrupted the two young men's arguing. They simultaneously quieted and looked at her. "I bid you good day."

Tree smiled with a nod, adjusted her shoulder bag, then walked through the alleyway toward Kale's backyard.

Realizing how silly he looked, Tahj straightened his pants and followed behind Kinte, still trying to convince him of what he saw.

Chapter Three – Sun Traveler

Kale pulled herself out of bed, intending to use her Weed Eater to finally tackle cutting the grass. After showering and getting dressed Kale still felt tired. Witnessing what happened the evening before, she couldn't sleep well. Kale looked in on her children, and they were still sprawled out over their beds from staying up a little too late. Good. Letting them sleep would allow a quiet moment. Kale went to open her front door to let the sunshine in and saw Tree sitting in the tall grass with Tora beside her. Tora meowed as though she was communicating some weird cat language only Tree could understand. Kale stared through the glass with apprehension, trying to decide if she wanted to close the front door back and pretend Tree didn't exist or muster up the nerve to confront her. In silence, she counted to five and chose the latter option.

Kale walked outside to the edge of the porch and cleared her throat.

"Good morning."

Tree turned around, flashing a bright smile.

"Good day, Kale. Tora is highly entertaining. She says this is her house, and you are her human." Tree laughed.

"Ah, I see," Kale responded, raising her eyebrows.

"Did you sleep well, Kale?" Tree asked, noticing Kale's uneasiness.

Uh, mph, I slept okay. Did you … sleep … okay?"

Kale felt stupid for even asking. Do trees even sleep? But she wanted to see what Tree would say because she obviously did something a little more than sleep.

"Oh, yes, I had a wonderful night of deep rest. I was quite tired after my journey arriving here, so rest was much needed."

Kale didn't say anything. She fiddled with her fingers as she watched Tree begin to rub Tora between the ears.

"I," Kale started, then stopped as she felt nervousness taking control. *Speak ya mind, baby,* she heard her mother say. Her mother always encouraged Kale to be her full self and express her thoughts no matter what. Now was not the time to shy away from a subject such as this. What could this Tree woman do, make her grow grass out of her ears?

"I – I saw …" Kale's words came out in a strained whisper as Tree focused on Tora. Kale raised a hand to her mouth and touched her lips as if permitting herself to speak.

"I saw you change last night," she blurted.

Tree stared at Kale. Relieved that she got her words out, Kale realized she couldn't retract them. *Hopefully, I won't be turned into a mulberry bush.*

"You changed into, um, a ..."

"A tree," Tree answered for her.

Kale stood still, startled by the fact that Tree answered truthfully. She was surprised that Tree's face remained calm.

"You saw one of the physical capabilities I have. I told you before that many years ago, I made a pact with the sun."

"What are you?" Kale asked.

"I am a sun traveler, a healer, a cosmic being totally charged by the sun and sent forth to inspire and show others the way back to their true selves. My purpose is to share light."

"How did you become this way? Are you human? Why are you here? I don't even understand what I saw."

Kale's words poured out like water from a faucet. Tree held her hands up, stopping Kale's overflow of questions. Tree stood and walked to the porch near Kale.

"Kale, how I came to be this way is a long journey

that's really not that important now. But, yes, I am human, just evolved or, more correctly put, returned. Like so many others, I used to be in a waking dream, neglecting this beautiful earth we rely on, neglecting others, and even this vessel I reside in. Through the trials of life and with the guide of a great teacher, I started to trust the visions my first eye was showing me. My teacher helped me not to be afraid of the vibration I came to this planet with. And once I accepted myself, not just intellectually, not with ego, but with deep internal compassion and love, I could face great responsibility. My being began to evolve, and it changed my physical body along with it. My teacher was the same, different in gifts, but the same light he carried is the same within me. And just like it pulled him to me, I feel it's pulling me to you."

Kale held an incredulous look and, for a moment, couldn't find words to say. This seemed crazy. There was no way she was interested in turning into a tree and wandering around like an aimless hippie.

"Look, Tree, I think you must be mistaken in what you call your vibes or this calling? I appreciate the natural beauty thing and getting healthy, but I am in no way, like you, nor want to be, no offense. My son probably would think it's cool to be able to shape shift into a tree, but my calling lies with my two children I'm raising. I have a job, bills, and frankly, no real talent and not much support. I don't have time to save the world by turning into a plant. I- I'm just not feeling that idea."

Tree laughed.

"Kale, your evolution is not mine, and mine is not like yours. We are different expressions of the same light. All people are. It is just that some are meant to guide humanity to a deeper level so that others can easily connect to that light within and bring forth their purpose. Creative forces are sent to share that light in different individual ways. It is up to you how you decide to let it shine through. But what you have to challenge is that rising fear, convincing you it's real or you have no talent because you do."

"Honey, you don't know me." Kale rolled her eyes and crossed her arms.

"No, you don't know yourself because if you did, you'd see how amazing you are and realize the keys to all you need are already inside you. Don't let the waking dream blind you with the mundane of this world, keeping you from the beauty of discovering your purpose."

Kale was about to protest against Tree's words, but she held her tongue for a moment. Tree wouldn't understand. She didn't have any responsibilities, no children, and no job and didn't seem to be looking for one. She just seemed to wander around pretty much doing nothing as far as she could see. Kale decided to do what she always did when a conversation was not going to her liking, change the subject.

"Tree, if you're human, how long have you been like this? How old are you, if you don't mind me asking?"

"Honestly, I've been on this path since birth but didn't know it. I'm forty-three if it's that important for you to know."

"Forty-what?" chuckled Kale.

"I've existed in this body for forty-three years, but I don't think about my age until someone is curious about that number. Spirit is ageless, so age doesn't matter a whole lot to me at this point in my life."

"I would've knocked at least thirteen years off of that. I'm twenty-three. You look closer to my age, but you're closer to my mother's age. She would have been forty-eight in August this year. Damn, now I feel old and out of shape."

"That feeling can change when you study self and move into alignment with nature and the cosmos. Your self-love grows, affecting your aging process, how you eat, your emotions, how you deal with others, and the world. The power is within you, and you can either ignore it or face it. But this power, this light, must shine through whether it's in this life or the next."

"Kinda figured you'd say something mystical like that." *What she's saying sounds so hard. I just want to lose a few extra pounds.* Kale thought. "Why can't I just stay my comfortable regular self without all the metaphysical themes? Growing old is going to happen, and terrible things are unavoidable sometimes. Unlike other species, we have to pay to survive. Life is hard enough as it is, and I've found my way of dealing with it. Becoming a new age light being or sun traveler will just be more work for me to deal with. I haven't even completely dealt with the death of my mother."

Kale's thought of her mother brought a wave of anxiety within her. She reached in her shirt pocket for a cigarette and pulled it out, looking at it between her fingers. Somewhere between pulling it out and staring at it, the desire to puff went away. She saw Tree glance toward the cigarette then back toward her. Slightly frustrated, Kale shoved the cigarette back into her pocket.

"Did you do something? Use your plant magic on me?" Kale asked.

"No, I did nothing, but maybe my aura did," Tree said, displaying a mischievous smile. "It vibrates a good several feet away from my body."

"Was it a green glow?" Kale asked.

Tree nodded.

"Oh, Lord, help me! How did I know that?" Kale whined.

"It's because of the light." Tree answered, remaining calm.

"Did you know I had a cigarette in my pocket?" Kale stared at Tree, raising her eyebrows.

"I could kind of sense that's what you desired before you pulled it out. Plus, your aura became a bit duller, and you looked as though you were getting agitated. I can tell you are going through a lot. Sometimes we feel the easiest thing to do is numb, even though it doesn't change the reality of the circumstances. Thank you for not harming yourself. I've heard from other smokers that the temptation can be really strong, almost unbearable for them. But I've also met others who have quit cold turkey and never smoked again. Placing it back in your pocket is a testament to change."

"Strange, it's like I can't smoke right now for some reason. It's like the feeling was there and completely left me," Kale said. She really wanted to enjoy that smoke. Kale thought maybe because she was standing near Tree, she was the reason the feeling left her. It would probably return when she left.

"People usually can't smoke around me or near my

presence; over time, they eventually quit."

"Probably all that clean tree oxygen energy you give off; it's like a scented oil or something. Well, maybe that's one benefit of knowing you. When I get ready to fully quit, it will be pretty easy. But I just don't think I can be this light-bringer. I definitely don't have that calling," Kale said, shaking her head.

"Kale, only you can walk your journey of life and decide whether you want to stay comfortable in your waking dream or evolve from that. Just make sure you're the one truly living your life, and nothing is controlling that living through you. Don't lose yourself in survival living and limitations just to grow old and never realize the gift in you that makes your light shine. Who you are has no boundaries, and yes, this body will grow old and change. But let it age with grace and joy. Let it carry out and perform its earthly tasks that will allow you to share your light with all of humanity."

Tree's words caused Kale to feel a lightning chill race through her spine. She sounded like Kale's mother before she passed, always encouraging her to get out of her own way and not make the same mistakes she did. But Kale seemed to follow almost every step her mother took regardless of the advice. Like her mother, she was stuck at a dead-end retail job, not committed to the father of her children and choosing someone too immature to take on the role, smoking, and thinking she was a superhero that had everything handled. Kale's eyes shifted back tears from just thinking about it. She crossed her arms and looked up toward the sky. The clouds darkened and unnaturally moved as though they were waves on an ocean.

"What you're saying, Tree, it makes sense, but I'm good where I'm at in my life. I just don't have it in me to do what you do. But I have a question for you. Why are you here? I know it's not just to grow plants and preach peace on earth. This little Georgia town is dead as a desert, and you could be somewhere like New York finding like-minded people."

"I feel needed here, and it's not where like-minded people are, but where the lost ones are is where my message is needed. Plus, I sense something else beyond your potential as a sun traveler. There's an energy here that's come to make sure no one sees beyond the waking dream."

"An energy. What kind of energy—like something evil?"

"In a way, it's more like an imbalance of energy, swaying more toward the negative like yin and yang energy, out of order."

"I don't get it."

"Kale, it just sounds confusing to you now, it won't always. You think in terms of form now, the inner you feels what I speak."

Kale sensed great sincerity in Tree, even though she still felt lost at some of the things Tree talked about. Kale didn't feel as much fear around her as she did a few moments ago. Strangely, she felt a calmness. Something in her knew Tree didn't have malevolent intentions. She didn't know how, she just felt Tree really did care for humanity and helping all who came in contact with her.

The sky crackled with thunder, and the two women looked up to see lightning dancing across it.

"The weather looks like it may be getting bad. You wanna come in for a bit til it blows over?" Kale asked. She didn't want to be this sun traveler Tree talked about, but at least she could share kindness, even if the woman did turn into a tree.

"Thank you, sister, for your generous offer. For the moment, I must decline. Maybe later. I have a calling elsewhere right now. But I do have a gift."

"A gift? What?"

Tree reached into her shoulder bag and pulled out three large plump mangoes. They were so exquisite it looked as though they were fine pieces of crafted art.

"Where did you get these mangoes? I know not from here. It's sinful how bad they look at the store where I work. But these look so delicious!"

"They're just gifts from the sun. I always have fresh quality fruit to share; it gives me joy to share something so valuable."

Kale smiled at Tree's ever-sounding mystical talk, thinking it was ironic that she was offering a gift from the sun on a day the sun was hidden behind the clouds. She decided to accept the mangoes and took them from Tree's hands. There was a knock coming from the inside of Kale's front glass door. Kale and Tree turned to see Davis standing inside.

"I'm sure that's my cue for, Mommy, I'm hungry."

"Well, my sister, you have the perfect breakfast to share in your hands."

Tree waved toward Davis, and she raised her small hand and waved. Tree smiled, then her attention went back to Kale.

"Good day, Kale." Tree started to walk off.

"See ya, Tree. Also, I wanna know why my aura is dull next time I see you."

Tree chuckled, then turned, walked through the yard,

and headed down the road. Her long huge locs swung behind her. Kale expected to see some other form of strangeness, but nothing happened. Tree simply walked away. Kale decided she would serve her mangoes as breakfast, then clean up her yard as much as she could before the rain decided to fall.

#

Lionel sat on the porch consuming an apple. He felt relaxed, listening to the rumble of thunder above him and the creaking of the old rocking chair he sat in. He gazed down the road to the nearest intersection, then simultaneously paused both the chewing of his apple and the rocking of his chair. An unusual woman with long, almost knee-length hair casually walked up the intersecting road. She emanated powerful energy without him even seeing her face. All he could see were massive ropes swinging around her tiny frame. He felt threatened by her clean, bright aura. His sharp gaze flashed red with a single blink, then back to normal when his grandmother walked outside, disturbing his thoughts. He resumed chewing his apple.

"You want something to eat? I –I can make you something," she said, looking nervous.

Her dragging voice stuttered as though she was sick, sick from fear. She moved as though she was in a trance.

"You see me eating, do you not?"

Lionel's eyes pierced deeply into his grandmother as he slowly rocked. He took another unnaturally large bite, swallowing a thick piece of apple that could easily choke a child of his size and age.

"Sorry, baby. I just thought you needed something heavier than … than that."

His grandmother was looking at the barely-there apple that looked like a wild animal had devoured it. She dropped her head down like a sad puppy and turned to walk inside.

"Yes," called Lionel.

His grandmother stopped in her tracks, but she didn't turn to look back at him.

"Yes, my dear grandmother, make me something," Lionel requested with false politeness.

"Yes, baby," his grandmother answered and walked inside the house, letting the screen door slam behind her.

As his grandmother went inside, Lionel turned back, searching the road for the woman he'd seen. She was gone, but he wanted to know who she was. She felt wrong to him, untouchable, like an illuminating light he couldn't see into. This feeling rising deep inside him was disturbing and had to be eliminated. He heard a voice inside his head weeping as his eyes stared off in space.

"The more you cry, the more I feed on your soul," he whispered.

"Please, just let me speak to my Grandma."

"Shoosh," Lionel's shoosh was long and cold, cutting off the voice inside.

"You no longer have a grandma; you have no life; you are nothing, and soon, you will be gone," Lionel spoke.

The crying faded. Lionel threw the rest of his chewed apple on the ground, rose from his seat, and walked inside to get ready for school.

#

Tree walked through the streets of Neville, admiring the rich, plentiful plant life all around. But she understood what Kale meant when she called the town dead. There were hardly any sites to explore on a materialistic level, and quite a few of the buildings in the downtown area on the west side were abandoned or closed. A few retail stores and businesses were opened, but she had no interest in purchasing anything. Tree passed a gas station on the major street, and further down, she passed a courthouse. Soon, she came to a doctor's office district and decided to walk through it. Tree reached a nearby park clearing with a pond and a gazebo not too far behind one of the office buildings. Noticing a family of ducks floating across the pond's water, she walked up to the pond to get a better look, kneeling to appear less intimidating to them. Not impressed, the family of ducks floated farther away, keeping their distance. Then the sky rumbled, continuing to threaten chances of rain. Tree looked to the sky, watching the spreading darkness, and knew she didn't have much time. Leaving the ducks, Tree walked away to sit down onto the thick grass, crossing her legs with ease into a lotus position. Tree placed her fingertips down in front of her, digging through the grass until her palms reached the coolness of the earth. Then she closed her eyes.

Whispers began to rise in her ears. Voices on top of voices grew louder and louder until they blended enough so that she could distinguish them. As she peeled her eyelids open to reveal bright chlorophyll glowing eyes, a green glow surrounded her hands.

"What is this dark energy I feel? It's like a slow swallowing that's consuming this place," she murmured.

"Oh, Green One." Soft voices spoke in unison from the grass. "A being arrived here not long before you came accompanied by two other fleshless ones. They have come to further tip the balance to this already weakened place. The consciousness here is in a deep sleep, and the dark ones are here to make sure no one ever wakes up."

The green spirits sounded deeply worried.

"Who are these beings? And are the fleshless ones able to become flesh?" Tree asked.

"Green One, through the winds, the dandelions have told us that they have already chosen flesh bodies to reside in. The original beings are held as prisoners inside their own bodies until the fleshless ones can fully consume them."

Tree lowered her head, mourning for the innocent lives trapped by the fleshless beings. The thought of them suffering and unable to communicate the help they needed, greatly disturbed her. Tree knew she had to locate them to be able to free them. But first, she had to find out who they and the fleshless ones were. As if reading her, the green spirits responded to her pain.

"To find out how to stop them, you must find the old Mother Oak at the edge of the cemetery west of here, near the edge of town. Being the oldest elder here, it is her, whose roots reach the deepest and widest. Mother holds the wisdom of several hundred years; only she can tell you more about these beings. The cemetery is near a place where humans sell their goods."

"Thank you, my friends. Your help is greatly appreciated."

"It is our honor to help you, Green One. We want

balance brought here as well. The light is dimming here, and most people in many other places don't see the connection between nature and themselves. Stopping the fleshless ones will help others awaken to their light to create change."

"Good day, my friends."

The voices from around Tree faded as if blown away in the wind. Her chlorophyll eyes blinked back to their dark brown shade; she looked toward the pond where the ducks had walked onto land, still careful to keep their distance. Tree lifted her hands out of the grass and placed them in prayer position at her sternum. She nodded her head toward the ducks, then held her hands out to the sides as though carrying a humongous beach ball. She closed her eyes, willing plants to pushed through the ground's surface, rising through the grass with a green glow that seemed to pull them from the earth. They formed at an extraordinarily fast pace until they matured into large droopy sunflowers, dropping seeds into piles. The ducks approached Tree, heading toward the sunflower seeds on the ground.

"Hello, my shy, beautiful friends." Tree smiled, rubbing the ducks' fluffy white and grey feathers as they surrounded her, trying to get to the seeds. "This has been a short meet and greet, but I must leave you now and continue on my journey."

One of the larger ducks quacked toward Tree.

"Well, Sir, it is my pleasure. I enjoy sharing my gifts."

After giving the large duck's feathers an extra rub down his back, Tree rose with as much ease as she sat down and used her hands to swoop back her thick locs. She adjusted her shoulder bag, spun away, then walked to the edge of the park, headed back toward the major road.

Chapter Four – Darkening Skies

Lionel strolled into English, his last class of the day, ignoring the boisterous chatter of the other students while sitting down at his usual desk in the center row. Iesha seated in front of him with long, cornrowed braids turned around, revealing a cute, playful scowl.

"I tried to call you yesterday to see what you chose to write your essay assignment on. Why didn't you answer?" she asked, waiting for his response. Her fingers played with some of the wooden beads on the ends of her braids. Lionel's face was expressionless, then his brow furrowed, returning to his serious gaze.

"Assignment?" Lionel asked.

"Miss Sable gave us like five different topics we could choose from. I did mine on should students have more freedom at school."

Lionel rolled his eyes as though he could care less. He ignored her and looked out the window.

"You didn't write anything," Iesha commented,

which was more of a statement than a question. Lionel continued to stare out the window.

"Hello, earth to Lionel. You okay?"

Lionel turned back to focus on Iesha.

"Don't worry about me, Iesha. All is fine."

"What?" Iesha wrinkled her nose, eyeing Lionel.

"All is fine? What's with the proper talk? Who are you, and where is my best friend?" Iesha asked, teasing.

Someone passed Iesha's desk, ramming into Lionel's shoulder, almost knocking him out of his seat.

"Dang, James, you don't know how to walk straight? So, freaking rude!" exclaimed Iesha.

James plopped down at a desk in the back of the room. Lionel straightened himself up and glanced back with hard eyes toward James, then turned back to face the front of the classroom.

"Shut yo' ass up before I pop you in the mouth," James snapped.

"Whatever, you're walking like your goofy behind needs a cane. You want me to ask my grandma can you borrow one of hers?" Iesha laughed, causing others in the class to snicker.

"Lionel, you don't have to take this mess." Iesha cut James the evil eye. Lionel continued staring out the window at the darkening clouds forming across the sky, seemingly oblivious to her and James' spat.

"Yes, he does have to take this mess, and maybe you do, too, since you got jokes and talking your smart ass smack," James responded, licking his lips, and grossly extending his tongue toward Iesha.

"Whatever."

Iesha feigned a gagging motion toward James, then rolled her eyes turning back toward the front of the room. The classroom teacher, Ms. Sable, walked in as James stood, attempting to move back toward Lionel and Iesha's desks. Upon seeing the teacher, James eased back into his seat. Ms. Sable, a middle-aged woman whose heavily lined features reminded the students of a turtle, sat down at her desk, and began taking attendance. As she was doing so, she ignored the occasional snicker of the students imitating her slow, draining voice.

"Okay, young people, you were all given an assignment to write with the freedom to pick the topic of your choice out of the five titles I gave you. I will come by and receive your papers now. Iesha turned back to glance at Lionel, but he remained calm, without an ounce of worry on his face. When Ms. Sable reached him, he reached into his bookbag, pulled out his paper, and placed it on his desk.

"Thank you, Lionel. Glad to see you could make it today," Ms. Sable commented as she took his paper.

Ms. Sable was one of the classes whose lectures Lionel always tried to avoid. Lionel looked up at Ms. Sable with cold, deadly eyes. She became uncomfortable under his gaze, pressing her lips together as she continued to the next student. Iesha glanced back at Lionel, sensing something wrong. He gave her an unusual smile, and she could tell from his eyes it wasn't real. She glanced back, seeing Ms. Sable reaching James' desk. James fumbled around, struggling to find his paper in his book bag.

"Mr. Thompson, you didn't do your assignment?" Ms. Sable asked, dragging her words.

"Yeah, I mean—yes, ma'am. I put it—I mean, I wrote it last night and put it in my bag. I don't know what happened," James replied, pulling all his items out of the bag, desperately searching through it.

"I will give you til the end of this period to rewrite your paper. And since you cannot type it, I will count ten points against your grade."

Ms. Sable gave a slight grimace toward James grateful eyes and shook her head, walking to the next student. Lionel looked back at James and smiled. James shot a look of deep hatred in return, then pulled out his pen and notepad to rewrite his paper. Ms. Sable finished taking up essays and went in front of the class in her boring slow manner to begin lecturing for the day.

"This is gonna be a good nap," said a student seated near the back of the class. Some of the other students snickered at his remark.

After fifty-five minutes, the bell rang, alerting half of the sleepy-eyed students in the class that their sentence of boredom was over. All rose and left the classroom except for James. He approached Ms. Sable's desk and handed his paper to her, satisfied that he was finally done. She looked at the paper, then raised the droopy hoods from her eyes. Her vision shooting back angrily towards him.

"Is this supposed to be funny, Mr. Thompson?"

James looked confused as Ms. Sable handed the paper back to him. James thought that was the fastest he'd ever seen any part of her slow turtle-like body move. He grabbed the paper and looked, reflecting the shock Mrs. Sables formerly held.

"Ms. Sable, I- I didn't write this!" he exclaimed.

"You gave me this filth. It has your name written at the top. Who else could have written it, little gremlins inside your desk? I thought I was being polite by giving you another chance to complete your assignment when I specifically said papers would be due at the beginning of class. This will require detention for one whole week, starting Monday."

"But, Ms. Sable, I swear I didn't write this. I wrote on my favorite quality about myself!"

"Well, obviously, Mr. Thompson, according to this so-called paper you claim you didn't write, you do not think very highly of your qualities at all. Now leave my classroom! Detention starts on Monday."

Ms. Sable pressed her barely-there lips together in a tight line and turned her head. She began working on paperwork on her desk, ignoring the pitiful look on James' face. He hung his head in defeat with his paper in hand and walked out of the classroom. He went down the hall to his locker to meet his friends, Mike and Lucas.

"Man, what's up with you? Iesha didn't want to snuggle?" asked Lucas.

"Don't play with me! I wrote this paper for Ms. Sable's class, and I think somebody went in my backpack and stole it."

James was convinced someone went into his backpack and took his paper, but he just couldn't figure out how. His backpack was either with him or locked in his locker. He looked back at the paper in his hand, not believing what was written for two full pages. His hands began to quiver as he dropped his paper and looked at Lucas and Mike with confused eyes.

"What the hell is wrong with you? You shaking like a chihuahua on crack, man!" Mike shouted. His tone was a combination of worry and annoyance. Lucas laughed.

"My paper, man!" James exclaimed, ignoring Mike's insult. "The paper I just rewrote in class. I wrote it and handed it to Ms. Sable. It was filled with two pages full of fuck you's!"

Mike and Lucas burst into laughter, falling over one another.

"Oh, man, I wish I could've seen the look on turtle lady's face when you gave her that," Mike laughed.

"I bet her old ass wishes someone would do that to her!" Mike exclaimed. He and Lucas filled the hall with even louder ruckus.

"Nigga, will you shut the hell up! That ain't the point. Look at the shit now!" James snapped and grabbed the paper off the floor, holding it out for them to read.

Lucas took the paper and saw it was written in James' handwriting in regular essay format.

"My favorite quality about myself, man, you an arrogant nigga." Lucas laughed, reading James' essay.

James smacked his lips, annoyed with Lucus' mental slowness, and snatched the paper from his hand. He glanced down the hall and saw Lionel and Iesha walking out the double doors, heading toward the bus ramp. A burning hatred rose within James.

"I don't know how he did it, but I bet that skinny punk Lionel had something to do with this. His ass was smiling at me when I was looking for it in my bag. It's like he enjoyed seeing me struggle to find it."

"You're always on that nigga. He's too scared of you. Why would he have the balls to mess with you like that?" Mike asked.

"I don't know. Maybe he's getting the balls now. He had a funny look in his eyes, though, like he was playing with me."

"Like he likes you like that?" asked Mike with a look of disgust.

"Hell, naw, fool! You crazy?" snapped James, rolling his eyes at Mike. "I'm gonna get that dude for this. I got one week of detention with Miss Turtle Face for nothing, and if I got to pay, he's got to pay."

Mike and Lucus glanced at each other, shrugged, and then looked back at James. They didn't understand all that was going on. But like sheep, they felt they were meant to follow along, and so they did.

#

Iesha sat by Lionel on the bus from school. Lionel was usually more talkative. But ever since Ms. Sable's class, he'd barely said a word. As a matter of fact, he hadn't said too much of anything since the bus ride to school that morning. She stared at him with curiosity as he looked to be mentally miles away.

"What's wrong with you? You're acting strange," she blurted.

Lionel rolled his eyes toward her; then, like before, he ignored her and kept staring out the window at the cloudy skies.

"You haven't said nothing all day. Are you okay?"

"I'm fine, just thinking," Lionel answered, not looking at her.

"About what?"

"Nothing that concerns you, Iesha."

Iesha became aggravated with his short answers that didn't do any justice in explaining his behavior. The bus was approaching the first stop near the Sunrise Projects. Lionel's eyes were fixated on the Hadley Grove Apartments across the street. Iesha remembered her dad saying how nice those apartments were back when he was a kid, but that was not the case today. Iesha had classmates who lived there, and she heard the stories about the nightly shootings, the block parties, gambling, and selling drugs. Iesha wasn't allowed to go there nor visit her friends that lived there. Iesha and Lionel read online once when they were studying for a black history project that Hadley Grove used to be an institute for black students helping the community in the late eighteen hundreds up to the early nineteen sixties. It was started by Lucius Hadley, a bishop and an advocate for the education of freed slaves, who dedicated his life to the upliftment of colored people. Mr. Hadley would be turning over in his grave at the state of Hadley Grove today, filled with people now lost to the knowledge and richness of this history and themselves.

The bus was still in the southwest part of town, so they still had a few miles to go before they reached the stop in their neighborhood. The bus door opened, and Lionel rose to get off.

"Lionel, why are you getting off here? where are you going?" Iesha asked out of concern.

Just as her parents didn't want her to hang in the projects or Hadley Complex, she knew Lionel's grandmother didn't allow him to either.

"Do you mind!" Lionel snapped. "I have business to

attend to."

Hurt stung Iesha's eyes. She had never known Lionel to be short and cold to her. He stared at her like she was a stranger. Then he rolled his eyes, turned away, and got off before the bus door closed. He stood on Sunset Projects sidewalk until the bus pulled off. Iesha's watery eyes glared at him through the window. Lionel glanced back at her with bloody cold eyes, then blinked them back to normal. Iesha stared in shock, not believing what her eyes saw. Her focus remained unflinching as the bus drove away.

Lionel crossed the street and walked through the parking lot into Hadley Grove Complex. The main side across from the Sunset Projects usually attracted some form of rowdiness where mostly young folks would hang out drinking, playing loud music, and socializing. Sometimes an occasional fight would break out, but it was mid-early afternoon, and only a few young guys were out loitering. They looked at him with suspicion, then ignored him. Lionel came to the nearest building by the parking lot and walked inside the foyer, taking the stairs to an upstairs apartment. He went in as if he knew where he was going; then he reached Unit 9-B and turned the unlocked knob. He eased into the dark and dingy place, noticing the horrid sour smell that wreaked throughout the trashed unit. He stepped through the living room area over paper cups, trash, clothes, and junk sprawled over the floor.

"I see you found a clean young piece of flesh."

Lionel turned toward the voice coming from the darkest corner of the room near the kitchen entrance. A man that seemed to be in his mid-twenties stepped forward. He was just as dingy and sour-smelling as the apartment he resided in. His light brown complexion around his eyes was gray and sunken, but his eyes bulged as though fresh blood had been poured into them to the point of bursting. He was a decent-looking young man. But at this point, he looked like a hungry starving sickness and Lionel knew it was not for food.

"And I see you've found an older dirtier piece of flesh to spread your filth in. You're jealous, Ugonjwa?" Lionel asked, smiling.

"Me? Jealous of your puny child's body? Mwongo, don't flatter yourself. But I must say what you picked is perfect for your lying trickster nature. This body, however," Ugonjwa extended his tongue, which was twice as long as a human's tongue. He licked his face. Then his tongue went inside his nose, pulling out black mucous-type sludge, which he pulled back inside his mouth while closing his eyes in pleasure as he shivered.

"This body feels so good to be in."

"Better pace yourself, or you will wear that body out quicker than your last," warned Lionel/Mwongo.

"No, I don't think so. This body is a strong one; he didn't pollute it too much. Still has good use, giving me enough time to do what I want until I decide to leave it to rot." Jay /Ugonjwa smiled with thick saliva running down his mouth. "Have you had word from Isfet?"

"No, no word, but the darkening of the sky tells me it is here," Lionel/Mwongo answered.

"Well, until it reveals itself, I will do what I do best and spread my uncontainable affections to these already toxic people of this community. Also, I can access a few of this body's memories. He has people he cares for that I may visit." Jay/Ugonjwa began looking desperate to move.

"Do what needs to be done and spread what you will, Ugonjwa. I will do the same until Isfet comes."

#

Lionel only had one more block to walk before he reached his grandmother's house. He made an early turn, cutting through a back alleyway to reach there quicker but was stopped in his path. James stood before him, blocking the way. He turned around and saw Mike and Lucas blocking him from behind. Instead of running away like he would usually try to do to avoid a confrontation with James, he smiled, smoothly crossed his arms, and raised his chin. James scowled at the seemingly newfound confidence exuding from Lionel's puny frame. They were the same age, but James was at least five inches taller, and he was bulkier. If he wanted to, he could crush Lionel like a cockroach, but he took his time playing with him like a mouse caught in a trap.

Lionel heard Mike and Lucas snickering like two hyenas, moving in for the kill, making sure to stop him in case he ran. But today, Lionel made a choice, and running was not it. He kept unflinching eye contact with James, ready to take on anything thrown at him.

"Little nigga, I know what you did!" James shouted, grabbing Lionel and jacking him up by the collar. "You stole my paper, playing some kind of trick on me. Admit it!"

"Well, playing tricks is what I do best," Lionel said, smiling without struggling in James' grasp.

"I'm gonna knock that goofy-ass smile off your ..."

As James' fist rose in midair, intending to meet Lionel's jaw, James' voice stopped and found that he couldn't move any further. His muscles were locked, and he couldn't speak to say what was wrong. Mike and Lucas looked on with perplexed stares, wondering what was going

YOUNG /A WOMAN CALLED TREE / 90

on. They were eager for a beatdown and a good laugh.

"James, jack that little nigga up!" Lucas yelled, "What the hell you waiting on?"

"Yeah, man, you having a seizure or something?" Mike followed.

James' hand, instead of hitting Lionel, moved down to caress his arm. He couldn't break his stare as he started to speak. Through the voice, what he heard from his mouth sounded like his and felt like his, but it was not his.

"I thought you liked me!" James shouted.

Mike and Lucas' mouths dropped open. Their eyes widened in unbelievable shock. They shot each other confused looks then looked back toward James, revealing a secret neither one of them had any idea about. As much as he complained about Iesha hanging with Lionel and trying to bring her attention to himself, this was a complete surprise to the utmost level.

"I've always liked you, and no matter how hard I tried to get your attention, you always ran. But today, I had to let you know how I feel. I- I just couldn't keep it hidden any longer," James spoke with intensity with tears streaming down his face. James' screams within went unheard as he listened to his own voice spew out embarrassing lies. He strained to take control of his own voice, but it was no use.

"Answer me now, Lionel. Do you want to be with me?"

Lionel threw his head back in laughter. His eyes rolled back, showing only the whites as they began to bleed over and fill with red like ink staining a paper towel. James begged, *Please, somebody, help me!* But he couldn't convey it to Mike and Lucas.

No one can save you! He heard a voice say inside his head. James, now with tears in his eyes, began to feel himself do the unthinkable. He leaned in, intending to kiss Lionel, but Lionel planted his hand over James' face, blocking him. Lionel pushed James with enough force to send him flying into a nearby trashcan, crashing onto the ground.

"Dang! exclaimed Mike, "You let that lil' boney nigga throw you like that?"

"Man, this is wack! I ain't' dealing with this sugar ass nigga no more, let's go." Lucas stated, waving his hand in dismissal and walking away.

James struggled in pain but managed to roll over, turning his tearful dirt-stained face in Lucas and Mike's direction. His whole body ached as he tried to lift himself.

"Wait!" he yelled, finding he had control over his own voice again.

"Help me! This dude is a demon! It wasn't me! I ain't

say all that crazy shit!"

"Naw, you just a punk ass!" Mike yelled back, following behind Lucas.

James clumsily gathered himself and staggered to his feet. He saw Lionel still staring at him but now with normal eyes. Lionel began walking toward James. As he came closer, James stepped backward, trying to get away from him.

"Get away from me, man!"

Lionel continued stepping closer in silence, keeping his focus on James. Hidden behind a fence, Iesha watched the boys, holding her breath. She couldn't get the vision of Lionel's eyes and the way he'd been acting all day out of her mind. She had planned on speaking to his grandmother since she didn't think Lionel would tell her what was going on. But on the way there, she heard a loud noise as though something had rammed into a trashcan. She kept hidden until she knew what was going on and was shocked to see James appearing afraid of Lionel, trying to back away. Usually, it was Lionel scrambling to get away or running to avoid James, but Lionel wasn't Lionel. She didn't know what he was anymore, but she knew he wasn't her best friend.

James walked back until he reached the fence and couldn't go any further. His eyes darted around to see if there was anyone who could help, but it was only him and Lionel. He began to regret all the times he gave this little punk hell. Lionel stood only a few feet away from him when his jaw cracked with a loud pop; he opened his mouth large enough to swallow James' head. James shook out of control as his voice released a high-pitch he had never reached before in his life. As the sound of James' scream left his throat, it was pulled into Lionel's mouth, drowning the sound away. James grasped his throat as the pulling sensation began to tighten.

Iesha held her breath, shaking as James' life force was sucked away, leaving an empty shell. James' dry corps fell over, hitting the ground. Iesha blinked in silence while tears streamed down her face. Through the cracks in the fence, she saw Lionel's glowing red eyes as he retracted his jaw back into place. He lifted his head in her direction and began walking around, circling the fence to where she was hidden.

Lionel walked behind the fence. He heard slight movements but thought there was nothing beyond a bushy cat crossing into the next yard. He had seen that cat before and always thought it looked like a miniature tiger. The cat looked back at him, releasing a hostile hiss before it disappeared behind a nearby house. Lionel's now normal colored eyes returned the level of hostility. Cats had always rubbed him the wrong way. Since ancient times, they'd always been able to see beyond the façade of the body he wore. He turned the opposite way and continued back home as if nothing had happened.

#

"The water dragon rose from the depths of the deep, exploding through the ocean's surface, outstretching its massive wings to rise high in the sky, gearing for battle against the demon hoard sent to steal his ..." Kale's descriptive body language and animated tone trailed off while telling a fantasy story to Hampton. She was making something up off the top of her head because he claimed he was bored from reading the same books they had at home over and over again. He thought his mom created way better adventures, anyway. They sat on the porch sofa while Davis sat on the ground in front, making dirt pies and playing with her dolls.

Kale saw Tree walking down the street toward the house. It was late in the afternoon, and she decided to wrap up story time.

"Mommy, are you going to finish?" asked Hampton, eager to know what was coming next.

"Yes, baby, but later. It looks like we have a guest coming, and I gotta make you guys something to eat. Okay, what would you like?" Kale asked, glancing at Tree walking toward her yard, nearing the mailbox. Tree saw her and waved.

"French fries!" Hampton said. Davis' face lit up when she heard Hampton. She left her toys and skipped up on the porch beside Hampton, expressing excitement to her mom.

"Okay, do y'all want burgers and fries?" Kale asked.

"Yeah," they responded.

"Okay, kiddos, go on inside and wash your hands. Hampton, help your sister, and I'll get everything ready." The kids hurried inside. Davis leaned back through the glass door and waved at Tree. Tree smiled and waved back.

"So, you did some exploring around this boring town? Find anything?" Kale asked, watching Tree walk up to the porch.

"Yes, I did some meditating and listened to spirits speak. I see why you are bored with the energy of this place on a certain level. But if you use your first eye vision, you can see the magic it holds," Tree responded, looking around.

Kale burst into laughter. Tree smiled, wondering what was so funny.

"I'm sorry. You just sound so much like a character in a story I'd create for my kids, this run-downed city, magical? That was funny. I guess I have too much going on to see the reality in that," Kale said, holding back her laughter.

"Well, most stories of fantasy and magic are rooted in reality. Magic exists because we create it. There is some historical greatness, even in this neighborhood you live in. I can sense it. Also, spend more time outside; the magic of nature will fill you with endless ideas for your creations. Tora has hinted that you spend too much time indoors," Tree stated.

"You and that mean old cat have a weird kind of relationship. I'm going to let that go. I've tried for years to connect with her. But she's too bitter, and I'm tired of getting scratched. And with being outside, it's too many bugs and gnats. But, please, tell me, what did the spirits say? Did they give you positive affirmations to share with us small-town folk?" Kale was eager to hear about Tree's escapade through town.

"I only asked about the dark energy I feel that is starting to take deeper roots here. It's something I do not want to worry you about now. But tomorrow, I will find out more. Then I will explain everything to you so that you will understand better."

Kale was a little let down by not getting the details

of Tree's full purpose of her visit but, she'd try to be patient enough to hear about it later. Tree felt that Kale took to her transformation of becoming a tree pretty well, but telling her of a dark energy taking over someone's form would be too much in one day. She'd wait until she knew exactly what she was up against before informing Kale of all the details.

"Well, I'm about to prepare the kids some burgers and fries. You want to come in for a little bit and talk, rest, or whatever? Like I said before, I'm not usually into the whimsical metaphysical type of things. My mom was heavy into it the past few years of her life, but I did really want to know why you said my aura was dull," Kale said, trying to convince Tree to stay. She didn't understand why she was beginning to want this mysterious woman around; maybe it was curiosity. Maybe she could actually become a friend. Kale didn't hang out too much since becoming a mother and sometimes missed adult conversation. Tree's conversations were different but still interesting.

Tree's attention went to the windchimes' light clinging and then to the dark sky. Tree kept in mind the words of the green spirit guides but knew it was just as important to slow down and share light with Kale and anyone she came in contact with. She nodded, displaying a slight smile.

"I don't think of myself and what I do as new age. Because what I speak isn't new, and it applies to any age. Maybe it's new for you, my sister, but I'm just me. But, for a moment, it would be nice to sit and talk."

Kale returned a smile and opened her glass door to allow Tree to enter. Tree untied her sandals and left them on the porch steps, and walked inside. Entering Kale's home immediately brought a sense of coziness. Inside was a balanced combination of spacious and warm energy. The dark hardwood floors felt cooling to Tree's feet as she mindfully stepped into the front room. She looked to her left, seeing the living room area furnished with a small couch, computer, and a few African masks and paintings on the walls.

"My mother painted those," Kale said, turning back to see Tree looking at them.

"Beautiful, your home is beautiful," Tree stated. Kale smiled with pride. Tree locked in on a painting of women of different sizes, complexions, and hairstyles standing around a bowl of fire on a table filled with fruit. All the women wore different cat masks ranging from tiger, lion, panther, leopard, lynx, cheetah, and even a house cat.

"That one she named the Secret Feline Society. It's what she called herself and a group of friends she used to meet with when she lived in Atlanta. This was before I was born. It was like a women's support group or sister circle."

Tree just looked around, admiring the paintings and art in awe. "Your mother was a great woman."

"Yeah, she was. Come on in the kitchen and sit." Kale enjoyed sharing memories of her mother, but she couldn't dwell too long on them; it was too painful.

Tree continued behind Kale to the kitchen area, seeing the kids playing in the room across from them. Tree smiled. Hampton walked up to the room entrance, studying Tree. He looked at her and then glanced toward her hair.

"How did you get those big snakes to grow from your head? Are they heavy?" He asked.

"Hampton, that's rude. I told you they are locs, like Bob Marley, remember? Now go to your room until I'm done," Kale scolded.

"No, it's fine, Kale. I love snakes." Tree laughed. "My little brother, in certain old traditions, hair like mine did represent snakes and snake power. Only the wisest and magical people could handle wearing them. Many people today consider snakes evil because some people fear what they have no knowledge of. But in a lot of ancient indigenous cultures, snakes were a symbol of great wisdom and intelligence. Snakes were also animals that represented healing, mystical things, immortality, and beauty because of their colorful and unique patterns. So, I do not get bothered by others thinking my hair looks like snakes. I've been told that many times before. It's actually an honor. Also, my hair texture is soft and cottony, making my locs spongy. It's not heavy at all, my little brother."

"What is e-emor-tail-li-tee?" Hampton asked.

"It's the ability to live forever," Tree responded. Hampton's eyes lit up. And he smiled.

"That's crazy! Like a vampire?"

Tree laughed. "Well, a vampire deals with death; snake energy deals with eternal life, although it does have the power to kill. But snakes prefer to be left alone. I will go in greater detail for you later," Tree answered.

"Okay," Hampton said, returning to his room after seeing his mom's face.

Tree turned into the kitchen area to see Kale reaching in the fridge to pull out some items.

"Sorry about that," Kale said to Tree.

"Kale, it's fine; that's how one learns is by asking questions. And he's a wise one, I can tell. He's a lot like you." Tree smiled at Kale.

Kale raised her eyebrows in agreeance. "Yeah, I know. Because now I want my question answered." Kale smiled, staring at Tree. "This is crazy. Well, maybe not crazy, but there's a bright green light I see around you sometimes. When I first saw you down the road and when I shook your hand, is that really an aura?"

"Yes, it is. Other highly sensitive beings can sometimes see it and can tell what color it is. Most people can feel it. It is like your vibe or frequency. Sometimes frequencies intermingle easily and sometimes not. You know, when someone steps into the room, and you feel the energy change? That's the aura of that person. Sometimes auras shine brightly and expand when one is in tune with themselves, and sometimes it's dull or small when one is in a lost state." Tree answered.

"I've experienced that room-changing thing. I felt it strongly before you approached me. It was like the energy shifted. Are all auras green or just yours?"

"Beings emit different colors, mostly in the range of the chakras, the circular energy centers within you which consists of shades of reds, oranges, yellows, greens, blues, indigo, and violet. I have also seen grays, white, black, and browns as well, and they all have different meanings. My aura is mostly green and gold. I think it's always been that way for me because I've always had a calling to serve this earth or share something with humanity. I've also had an affinity for natural things and nature, so the green in me grew. The gold enhanced as I became the person you see today. I am loyal to the light."

"I think my mom has a book left on our bookshelf about chakras. I'll have to check it out later. You said mine was dull, how? Am I in a lost state? And what color is it?"

"You are internally going through something. I can tell you are in pain. But it's understandable. The world seems to be closing in on you, and you lost your closest support. Also, you're mostly alone from what I see with your children. You're smoking and not taking time out to concentrate on your wellbeing. That's one reason you should try yoga or any other healing modality. It will help you calm the mind and bring you back in tune with your natural state of who you are. Your aura does not have to stay dull, and I think you already have a sense of what your aura color is," Tree said, smiling at Kale. "You're more powerful than you think."

Kale stared at Tree, oblivious as to how she would know what color her aura would be.

"Try, Kale," Tree suggested, nodding toward her.

Kale's puzzled face looked away from Tree; then she brought her palms up to observe them. Glaring at her hands, she concentrated hard but couldn't see anything. She dropped her hands by her side in defeat and looked back toward Tree, but Tree just nodded, indicating for her to try again. Kale took a moment to scan the feeling throughout her body and noticed the tension she always carried in her shoulders. Kale closed her eyes, taking in a deep breath, and released it. She began to let the air flow through her evenly. Then relaxed her shoulders, melting the tightness away. Kale became aware of the sensations throughout her body then slowly opened her eyes, bringing her palms up once more. A rich blue began to fade into view around them, the color of the clearest sky. Kale flipped her hands over then flipped them back, studying her aura. Kale then looked up at Tree with shining eyes meeting her smile.

"This is amazing! Blue. It's blue. One of my most favorite colors." Kale said in awe.

"Blue! You are meant to use your voice to speak words of power to teach and help others; your intuition will guide you. The pain you feel now for your loss is a resistance that will take time to accept and that is normal. The nurturing love of a mother, ah! It is one of the most magical loves one can experience. Just think of the joy she had in loving you, her child. The pain may never go completely away. But just remember, your mother is within you, an ancestor, helping to guide you on your physical journey in this realm. All of your ancestors are here. You are never alone, my sister." Kale's eyes began to glisten as Tree spoke. No longer watching her aura, she turned away, grabbed the food she had taken out of the fridge to prepare, and wiped the tears away.

"As you come more into your own, your aura will grow, and you will come to see the aura of others. It doesn't ever remain dull. It's like the waters of the ocean, everchanging, reflecting the circumstances of our lives." Tree continued. She became quiet, sensing Kale's increasing sadness.

In silence, Kale opened up the packages of food and placed them all on pans to warm in the oven. After she was done, she seemed to come back to herself.

"Tree, um, you're welcome to eat with us. You seem to walk everywhere you go, so you must be tired or needing something to eat or drink."

"Thank you, my sister. But I'm fine; I won't be needing anything." Tree answered.

"You sure? Have you eaten anything today?"

"I do not eat." Kale stared for a few seconds, confused at Tree's answer.

"Huh? What do you mean?" Kale asked, shaking her head.

"I gain my nutrients directly from the sun. I sometimes drink water, but I haven't eaten solid food in years."

Kale dropped a bowl. Then she bent over to pick it up, glad that it was made of plastic. She stood, thinking she had never heard anything so crazy in all her life.

"You mean you function like the plants—like the plant biology I learned about in class?" Kale smiled. "How? But you said you're human. Do you store chlorophyll in your body, too? This is unbelievable! When was the last time you ate?"

"A little over a decade ago. As I grew from my waking dream, my melanin evolved with the rest of me; it functions very similarly to chlorophyll. I could sense my darkness was something pretty powerful, naturally absorbing the energy information from the sun, but I began to notice I needed extremely large amounts. Taking in the light, as I do, not only in my skin but also throughout my body, began to enhance my ability to transform darkness to light. I found that I never felt hungry anymore. By that time, I was a pure juicearian which had already raised my vibration and long evolved from being a fruitarian, vegetarian, and what most now call vegan. I found that I only needed water and light to be nourished. I had never felt so amazing in all my life and still do today. Once my abilities awakened, the sun enhanced my skin and overall health for the better. The sun, and all of nature, is the reason I am what I am. I remember, early on in my youth, remarks about how my skin was hated, feared, or discriminated against. I was told how sad it was that I was not only just black but too black, sometimes from our own people. Like in school, work, or shopping, most things we do require us to stay in buildings all day away from the sun when it is known we need sunlight, air, and earth for our health. We are not taught in everyday living that to eat plants, especially anything green, is taking in sunlight power and that sunlight power can heal us." Passion sparkled in Tree's eyes as she spoke. It was as if whatever she went through, she overcame, and nothing from the outside could affect her any longer. She was at total ease with herself.

"I'm brown-skinned. But I've always considered myself dark, though I was never teased like some of our deep chocolate folks. It always made me angry like it was an insult to me, ya know? Tree, your skin, your darkness is your superpower then. But why you? Why are you the only one like this? How come other people as dark as you haven't changed or developed superpowers if that's what one wants to call it?"

"Others dark as I am do have superpowers. Some just haven't tapped into what it is because they have been kept from seeing it. Whether it's through societal illusions or other's imposed opinions from family or friends, or their own internal lies, they hear repeatedly. The darkness feeds off of it all, deepening the belief that someone like me has nothing of value to contribute to this world; that dark skin is not beautiful. That I am nothing, it's all pure lies of the waking dream.

I am not the only one. You are one if you accept it. We are all a superpower with many different gifts and abilities to bring to the collective. It may be through art, writing, nurturing, or simply through acts of kindness in everyday life. But if you mean as someone with all of my exact abilities, I know of no one except the ancient myth of Ausar, as my teacher once told me. He was known as the perfect black and the green one. Which is what my green spirit guides fondly call me. Sometimes myths are based on experiences of reality, so maybe there was another sun traveler who inspired the story of Ausar."

"Wow, this is so fascinating. And to me, you are the perfect black. Your skin is utterly flawless, and you shine like gold even without your aura," Kale said. Tree smiled and nodded.

"You are definitely inspiring me to want to better my life and health, but I know it will be a gradual process. The no-eating thing will never be my goal. I love to eat! I'm still struck by hearing that. What is that called breatharianism?" Kale joked.

"Yes, actually, but I don't call myself that. I'm just simply a sun traveler. Kale, just remember to always do your best for yourself; you don't have to become a breatharian, or this, or that title. All that is required of you is to be your greatest self and live your purpose. Once that is in process, share it. Never forget to share your light."

The sound of thunder boomed through the house. Kale looked out the kitchen window to see the rain falling. Hampton and Davis ran out of the bathroom area into the kitchen.

"Y'all are just in time! Foods almost ready. I'm about to take everything out of the oven. Did the thunder scare you guys?"

"Yeah, Mommy," Hampton answered. Davis just held Hampton's hand, staring at her Mommy with brown doe eyes.

"Okay, then. Sit down. I'll fix you guys a plate."

Tree rose from her seat as the children sat down. Davis rubbed Tree's hair with her tiny hands as she moved around her. Davis laughed as Tree's loc wrapped around her fingers and moved away.

Tree chuckled. Her locs usually moved behind her when someone tried to touch them, but she felt the pure energy of innocence coming from Davis. Plus, she and Hampton had just washed their hands.

"You're leaving already?" Kale asked.

"Yes, I must rest. I have plans for tomorrow. Maybe you can help me if you are free," Tree suggested.

"Well, I have to work, but I'm free after six o'clock."

"Okay, thank you, my sister," Tree said, nodding.

"I'll walk you out," Kale said in the middle of preparing Hampton and Davis's plate.

"Thank you."

"Yeah, no problem. Be right back, you guys, hold tight," Kale said to her children.

Tree turned to Hampton and Davis and bowed. Hampton returned Tree's bow with a nod, and Davis smiled, waving goodbye. Tree followed Kale back to the front door and walked outside to slip on and retie her sandals.

"You're sure you'll be okay in this rain?" Kale asked, looking out into the dark sky. Tora raced past her as she held the door opened. Kale knew she was heading for her kitty bowl. She forgot to fill it, so Tora would probably have an attitude when she walked back to the kitchen.

"I'll be just fine, my friend. Good night, Kale."

"Okay, be safe."

Chapter 5 – Darkness Strikes

Heavy rain poured, beating onto the roof of Kale's house. It was getting closer to her yawning time. She was tired from the busy day with the kids, and not getting enough rest the night before didn't help. She had finally accomplished her task of cutting the grass earlier, as well as doing a lot of reading, watching learning videos, and story time with Hampton and Davis. They were now in their room playing with blocks. Kale had wanted to take them to the park, but the weather had been looking suspect for days; now, it shown its true intention.

Lying on her bed, she barely paid attention to the movie playing on the television, thinking mostly about her conversation with Tree. She held up her hands, still amazed that she could see the blue glow. She smiled before hearing a beat on her glass door. Wrinkling her face, Kale wondered who had the audacity to come to her house beating on her door in the middle of this weather. She walked outside her bedroom toward the front door.

"Who is it?" she asked.

"It's me, babe, Jay."

Tree stomped her foot in silent agitation and shook her head, releasing a hard breath. Telling herself to calm down, Kale thought she'd just get rid of him as soon the front door was opened. She unlocked her glass door, peering out at him so she could hear him better. She stared, wondering what was wrong. He looked terrible, as though he was sick. He didn't look this bad when she saw him a few days ago.

"Jay, what are you doing showing up here like this, in the rain, without calling me first?"

Jay stared at her for a few seconds, not saying anything. He looked as though he was just trying to catch his breath.

"Dude, what the hell is wrong with you? You need to be in the bed."

"S-s-sorry, babe, I was in the neighborhood seeing one of my boys down the street. I just thought it would be all right to just visit y'all for a minute. Can I come in and see the kids j-just for a little bit?" Jay asked.

Kale glared at him. She didn't want to be bothered with him since he looked terrible. But she also didn't like not letting the kids see their dad. She knew how that felt as she didn't have a father in her life. Hampton had been asking about him, but Jay just looked way too sick today. And she didn't want to risk the kids catching anything from him. She had to go with her instincts, even if that made him angry.

"Jay, I know how much you miss them, and they miss you, too. But you're gonna have to wait til you clean yourself up. You don't look well."

"I'm fine!" Jay snapped.

Kale stiffened from Jay's quick response which confirmed her instincts even more. He had to leave. Jay paced in a circle on the porch for a moment, then looked back at Kale with pleading eyes.

"Kale, I'm sorry. I know I look messed up. I've had a hard week, and I just haven't gotten any rest. I started a new job at-at-at that chicken place in Vienna. Um, um, what's it called?"

Jay snapped his hands as though commanding his brain to remember the place he was talking about. Kale knew he had to be on something and grew impatient with wanting him to go.

"Tyson," she answered for him.

"Yeah, yeah, Tyson."

He paused for a moment and walked closer to the door, where she leaned out from. The stench that lingered from him took over Kale's nose. She gagged and shut her eyes before opening them again, which was more confirmation that there was no way his stanking ass was coming up in here.

"Jay, just come back tomorrow or in a few days. You need to head to the hospital; you look really sick, man. I don't want the kids to catch nothing."

Kale could no longer hide the aggravation she felt. Jay's face hardened. Kale could tell he was going to give her a hard time about leaving. Anytime she expressed herself to him on decisions he made that she thought weren't the best, he always felt she was going against him. But she always felt he handled things somewhat immaturely and didn't consider the family's needs as a whole. His needs always came first, and then when he'd mess up and realize what he'd done, he'd come crawling back, trying to make it right. Kale was tired and wasn't in the mood to argue with him today.

"But I want them to catch something, and I also want to give you something as well."

"Huh? Jay, go home."

Kale dismissed him and leaned back inside her door to shut it, leaving Jay outside with the rain. But the door stopped before she could close it completely. He put his foot in the doorway, holding it open.

"Jay, I'm gonna tell you one more time, leave, and

come back later. Now move!"

Kale tried to keep her cool but felt liquid fire bubbling under her skin. She knew how stupid drinking made Jay, but this was something different. He either was on something harder, or he was crazy from sickness. A mix of fear and fight entered her when she looked into his eyes. They looked unrecognizable. She didn't want to call the police, but she would if it meant protecting her children.

He leaned in, holding the door with his hand, and moved his foot away. She pulled on the inside door handle to snatch it back from him. But even though he appeared to be weak from sickness, she was no match for his strength. He smiled when she tried to snatch the door away, and thick black sludge slipped from his mouth as he leaned in closer to smell her. Kale jumped back, letting go of the door to keep Jay from touching her.

"Baby, what your gonna do, huh? Nothing. Let me see them damn children, and let me have some fun with you." Jay laughed.

His slimy grin grew wider like a Cheshire cat as he walked into the house with hunching shoulders, dripping rain, and slob onto the hardwood floors. Kale backed away with fear; her stomach ached in disgust. Outwardly, she remained calm and alert. All she could think about was getting the kids to safety, hoping they would stay in Hampton's room and hidden in the back of the house.

"You wanna play with me, baby, huh?"

Kale didn't answer.

"Answer me, Bitch!" Jay yelled, causing Kale to shake.

Hearing the noise, Hampton ran outside his room.

"Daddy?" he called, staring in fright at his dad's inhumanly shaped face.

Kale glanced behind herself at Hampton, then back to Jay. Jay lunged to attacked. They fell back onto the floor with Jay on top.

"Hampton, get Davis and run!" Kale yelled as Jay held her down.

Kale held onto him as well to keep him from going after the children. Hampton took off like lightning, doing exactly as his mother instructed, and zipped through the kitchen out the back door into the rain.

Jay pinned down Kale's arms as he lifted his head to peer into her eyes. His were bloody red and bulged so hard Kale thought they'd drop blood on her; instead, tears streamed down his cheeks. He lowered his face, glaring his teeth like a wild beast. Kale freed one of her arms to block herself as Jay leaned in, sinking his teeth through her flesh, causing her to scream in agony. He held the bite, enjoying her screams before lifting, laughing in pleasure as Kale's blood and thick mucus ran down the sides of his mouth. Jay paused, disoriented for a moment as his eyes blinked back to normal.

"Kale! What happened? Oh, God! Baby, did I do this?" he screamed. "I-I-I don't know what's happening to me!"

Jay leaned back further in shock with tears flowing down his face. Kale struggled to get from underneath him with her strong arm, but his weight was too heavy. He was about to move to release her, but something else within took over.

"No! No, not that easy!" Jay snapped, giggling. His eyes glowed again, and he leaned in to take another bite of her.

Kale heard a fierce cry as a blur of blackness flew over her and jumped onto Jay, attacking his face, clawing, and hissing. Jay screamed in agony, falling backward as Tora fought him, allowing Kale to wiggle free. She slid back on her strong arm, wincing in pain, then felt hands wrapping around her, helping to lift her.

"Tree!" she exclaimed, looking back.

"Go to your children!" Tree commanded. Her eyes

looked hard at Kale, then at Jay, fighting to pull Tora away from him.

Kale scrambled up and rushed around Tree, running to the back of the house. Jay finally caught a grip of Tora's fur and ripped some out as he slung her into a wall. The adrenaline inside made her hop back up on her paws, wild and, hissing, ready for war. Tree held up her hands, causing Tora to pause and hold back. Jay's eyes flamed red through his fingers as he gave Tree an evil glare. His ragged breathing pushed through the palms of his hands as he watched Tree move closer to him. He sensed something different about her; she wasn't a normal human. She smelled extraordinarily pure. He shivered with the desire to infect her pureness. He released his pain-filled face and glared, showing his deep scratched distortion. Then he rushed her.

Tree's eyes glowed bright green as he came hurrying in toward her. It was as if time slowed; her locs lifted and moved with lightning speed. They seemed to grow longer as they surrounded her. Jay stopped upon contact as one of Tree's locs hardened like a broken branch with a sharp end, piercing into his shoulder. Tree walked closer, never once taking her eyes away from him.

"Who are you, fleshless being?"

"Fleshless?" Jay laughed through his pain, coughing

up a bit of mucus. "Can't you see I am not fleshless; this is my body!"

Tree, ignoring his obvious lie, looked hard at him. "Let the human go. His body is weakening and will be of no use to you. Let what's left of his body go free."

"And go where? Will you give me your body instead? You are powerful. We could have a lot of fun together."

"I don't think we have the same idea of what fun means. Tell me who you are, and maybe we can figure something out. You give me the human, and I let you go. Maybe I can heal you and this body."

"Never, pretty one." Jay snickered. "I am sickness itself. Nothing can cure me, nor do I care to be!"

Jay snatched his body off of Tree's branch and jumped through Kale's glass door, shattering it into pieces, running through the rain into the darkness of night. Tree's branches softened, shortening back to their original length at her thighs. Tree walked closer to the spot where Jay stood, dropping sludge and mucus onto the old wooden floors. Then kneeled with bright green glowing eyes, willing the sludge and mucus to lift into the air. Holding out her hand to let it rest in her palm, Tree let her vines cover it. Then retracted the vines into her hand and watched the mucus thin out and dissolve. Tree knew what Jay was up to. She stood to look for Kale and the others.

#

Perry and his wife, Shae, were sitting and eating their meal in front of the TV when someone began beating on their front door. Shae worried, looked toward Perry. He waved his hands, motioned for her to stay put, then rose to look through the peephole.

"Help! Please, help us!" Kale yelled as she beat again.

Perry recognizing Kale opened the door. She staggered in with Hampton and Davis behind her. Perry caught her and saw her clenching a bloody arm against herself.

"Shae, call nine-one-one!" Perry yelled.

Shae hurried out of her seat, grabbing her cell phone off a nearby wall table while Perry helped Kale to the sofa. Hampton held Davis close to him and stood by where Perry caught their mother; both watched through teary eyes. Kale saw their fear, hating they had to see their parents in that situation. But glad she got them out unharmed. Now she just had to take care of this excruciating pain from the bite mark. She finally took a deep look at her wound, scrunching her nose because the smell emitting from it was terrible. The same smell came from Jay; she was scared he may have infected her with whatever was wrong with him. The puncture holes in her skin oozed blood and thick yellowy mucus. Just looking at it made her stomach cramp, and Kale thought she was going to throw up.

"The police are on the way," Shae said, putting the phone down. She looked at Hampton and Davis and walked up to them.

"Y'all, babies, come on with me. It's all right, Mommy's gonna be all right. Perry, get Kale some bandages to clean up her wound, and I'm gonna get y'all cleaned up before this rain makes y'all sick. I have some of my grandbabies' clothes in the back y'all can use."

Hampton stared at Shae, not saying anything, then looked to Kale. Kale nodded, giving the approval that it was fine for them to go with her. Hampton followed Shae to the bedroom, still keeping his arm wrapped around Davis. Perry had walked away and returned with a clean cloth and bandages. He sat beside Kale and guided her damaged arm toward him. Kale lifted her other hand away from the wound to let him take a look. She shivered, feeling extremely cold.

"What happened, Kale? Who did this?" Perry asked, looking shocked at the large amount of mucus forming from her wound.

Kale hesitated, not wanting to talk about it because she knew that no one would believe her if she told the full truth. And even after all she went through, she honestly believed Jay didn't want to physically harm her. Jay could turn into an immature idiot when he'd drink sometimes. But in the six years since she'd known him, he'd never been violent. Something else did this, and those eyes that she looked into when he attacked her told Kale that. She thought about Tree's words that something had come here to make sure no one sees through this waking dream. Whatever it was, it had gotten Jay and almost killed her.

"I was attacked," Kale started and paused, feeling dizzy. The room began to spin.

Perry waited for Kale to say more, but he saw the flashing blue lights reflecting on the picture frames on the wall behind her. He got up and walked to the door to open it for the officers to come inside.

#

Tora meowed, calling from the floor where she lay. Tree sat down beside her, saddened from seeing her in pain. Tree held her hands over Tora's body, moving them in slow circular motions, creating heat, and guiding it into Tora. Tree could tell Tora had a broken rib from the impact of hitting the wall. Tree held her hands in one position, took a deep breath, closed her eyes, and then opened them as they glowed bright green. Small vines broke through Tree's palms and lengthened, wrapping around Tora's torso. Tree held her position, unmoving as a pulsing light traveled from her hands down the vines to Tora's body. Tora meowed and placed her head down to rest. When Tree could see Tora was deep enough in sleep to promote the healing she needed, she retracted the vines into her hands, and the glow from her eyes faded. She scooped up Tora and walked through the shattered glass front door. Seeing flashing blue lights coming toward the house, she walked the opposite way, keeping Tora near to shield her from the pouring rain. She moved around the side of the house, running to the back, then across the yard into the thicket across the back alley. She hid behind a large pecan tree, levitating her locs into the air, letting them interlock together, forming a mesh of branches to protect Tora from the rain. Knowing Tora would be back to normal in the morning, she just had to protect the both of them until then.

Tree hoped she could find Kale before it was too late. Looking at the excreted mucus from Jay's body, she could tell it had the potential to spread and cause great sickness, possibly death if held in the body for too long. Tomorrow, she would find the Mother Oak that the green spirits spoke of. She had to find out who all three of the fleshless ones were. And to find a way to stop the spreading of this darkness that had begun.

#

Kale opened her eyes in panic, almost knocking over the IV stand next to her bed. A blond nurse wearing a face mask turned around, holding her hands out to calm Kale.

"Where are my children?" Kale asked.

"They are with your aunt. She told me to tell you when you woke that she'd picked them up from your neighbors. They are fine. Please, lie back down and rest."

Kale looked confused. The last thing she remembered was seeing Jay with this wide distorted grin, attacking her, and running to the Reeves' house begging to be let in. She eased back down on her bed.

"My things—can you tell me where my cellphone is?" Kale asked, desperate to speak to her aunt to confirm what this nurse said was true.

"All your things are there on that table, but I didn't see a cellphone. Maybe your aunt has it. She was here when you were first placed in the room."

"What? I don't remember even getting here."

"Yes, the ambulance had to bring you in because you fell unconscious from shock."

Kale shook her head and looked at her arm where Jay had bitten her. The blood had produced dark stains that shown through.

"How long have I been here? W-What time is it?" Kale asked, looking around the room.

"It's after four."

"What! Oh, hell! My job is gonna fire me," Kale snapped, rising again to scramble through her things, checking to see if her cellphone was amongst it. She was frustrated that she couldn't remember any phone numbers, except her mother's.

"Ma'am, please, calm down."

An older masked male came into the room as the nurse tried to get Kale back into bed. Feeling weak, Kale took a deep breath and sat back down. He slid his mask to his chin revealing his caramel-colored face as he looked at her with kind eyes.

"Hello, Ms. McCray, glad to see you are finally awake. I'm Doctor Anderson."

Kale looked at him with suspicion but didn't say anything. She nodded and slid back on the bed, resting her back against the pillows. She wasn't at her job right now, so she didn't feel a need to put on her fake customer service persona. But she did have a few questions.

"When can I leave here? And why is this bite oozing this gunk? Am I infected with something?"

"Well, Ms. McCray, we want to keep you here a little while longer for observation until we know exactly what this is. And, yes, you are infected with something. Your body is severely congested with large amounts of mucus and inflammation within your lungs and in other parts of your body; the amount is strangely increasing at a fast rate. The test will be in soon, and we will know more, hopefully, by tomorrow. But it's imperative that you simply rest and don't strain yourself. We don't want it to increase in production."

"I don't know if I have the patience to sit here and do nothing, but I have no choice. I am so freaking tired."

Kale began coughing and heaved in a strained breath. She began coughing again, causing dark thick mucus to land on her hand. The nurse grabbed some napkins from beside Kale's bed on a table and pulled several sheets out so Kale could wipe her mouth and hands clean.

"Ms. McCray, just try not to concentrate on anything but your wellbeing right now. I will be back to check on you," Dr. Anderson said.

Kale nodded and leaned back in frustration. Dr. Anderson and the nurse left the room. She hated being away from Hampton and Davis. Plus, she was scared but wouldn't tell the doctor or nurse that. Her health was important to her. Kale had to take care of herself to be able to care for her children. And with Jay being taken over by something she couldn't explain, he definitely couldn't protect them. She remembered seeing how distraught he looked for a short moment. He seemed to come back to his senses, then as quickly as it came, the real Jay left, and something had taken a deep hold on him. Whatever it was inside him was ruthless and would have killed her and done only God knew what to their children.

Kale felt her nose running and sat up to go to the bathroom for tissue instead of using the rough napkins beside her bed. Wanting to wash her hands in soothing warm water, Kale stumbled around the bed into the bathroom area and peered into the mirror. She looked terrible. It had only been a day, and Kale had dark circles under her crusty eyes. The mucus running from her nose was extremely thick and sludgy. Her right nostril, which was the most mucus forming, was closed shut. Kale couldn't even blow that side of her nose a tiny bit. Wiping the mucus away as much as she could, she then ran the warm faucet water over her hands. Feeling as though she'd faint, Kale cut the water off and went back to the bed. Her hospital phone rang on the side table, and she answered.

"Hello?"

"Oh, baby! I'm so glad to hear your voice! How ya feeling? What did the doctor say? I tried to stay longer, but they wouldn't let me," Aunt Niecy blurted.

"Auntie, I'm okay. I just feel like I have the flu with the snottiest nose ever. How's Hampton and Davis?"

"They are fine, just worried about you, naturally. I'm so glad that Shae 'nem helped y'all; they talked to the police because as soon as they walked in, you passed out. I hadn't spoken to Shae in a while. But luckily, she still had my number. They called me to see how you were doing earlier this morning, but you were still out of it then. What did the doctor say, baby?"

"Aw, they don't know what the hell this is. They're waiting on tests to come back and told me to rest. All I know is slimy shit is coming out of my throat and nose, and from looking at this bandage, it looks like it's still leaking out of this wound. It stinks, Aunt Niecy. I can't stand sitting here not doing anything, but I'm weak as hell. I was supposed to work today. I hope I haven't been fired for a no call/no show."

"Don't worry, Kale. I called them. I spoke to that chipper girl. What's her name?"

"Oh, yeah, Jamie. She's so fake. What did she say?"

"She said she'd relay the message to your manager, but you should be fine."

"Oh, cool. I hate that place, but I can't lose my job—not right now at least."

"Well, you'd find another one just like you found that one. A job ain't nothing but a J-O-B. Just Over Broke. All that matters is you getting better. I will try again to see if I can visit you later. It's strange; it's like they were trying to keep me from coming to see you."

"I have no idea, Auntie, unless it's this mucus thing I'm excreting. It stinks like it's from the nastiest sewage or garbage disposal system in the world. They wore masks when they came in here, probably because I smell so bad. It's embarrassing. I noticed the same odor on Jay before he attacked me."

"That's who attacked you!"

"Please, Auntie, don't tell the police or anybody!"

"What! Are you crazy? Lawd, my niece done lost her natural-born mind. Why are you defending this nut? He could have harmed the kids if he got to them. He damn near gnawed your arm off like Cujo. Please, don't tell me it's because you still love him, girl!"

"Auntie, if you just calm that motor down, I'll explain."

After a few more "Lawd's" and "Have mercies," Aunt Niecy quieted down. Kale took a deep breath as she was beginning to feel more strained.

"I don't think it was Jay that attacked me."

"You just said ..."

"I know what I said. How can I say this, and have you believe me? I think it was Jay's body that attacked me, but it wasn't Jay."

"Kale, do you think this sickness has you delirious? Maybe the mall is open, and ain't nobody shopping?"

"Auntie!"

"Okay, baby. I'll hush it. But mark my words if you're trying to make sense out of a crazy person, the crazier you will get."

"No. Auntie. His eyes were filled with blood when he looked at me. Jay came through for a short moment, and he damn near cried, thinking he may have hurt me. Jay's not crazy like that. He's not violent. I've been knowing him since we were teenagers. It was like he was possessed."

"Lawd, it's hard for me to believe that, baby. The police asked did you have a boyfriend. I told them no. But you did just break up with the nut a few months ago, so maybe all they are going to do is question him when they find him."

"Dang it, Aunt Niecy."

"I'm sorry, baby. I didn't know anything. All I know is I just lost my sister; I can't lose you, too."

"I know; it's okay. What's important is Hampton and Davis' safety. Please, if Jay does come through, trying to see them, do not open the door, and don't even talk to him. I think he or whatever it is inside of him infected me with something, and I don't want him getting near the kids. Maybe you shouldn't come to see me. Either; it's good the hospital staff didn't let you stay long."

"Kale!"

"No, Aunt Niecy. I'm sick as hell, and I don't know what's going on. I feel like my whole body is breaking down and filling up with this slimy shit; it's like it's taking over. My breathing has become ragged within one day of Jay biting me. I just hope this Doctor Anderson figures out what the hell is wrong with me. I have to lie down, Auntie."

"Okay, baby. You stay strong."

"Please, just kiss my babies for me."

"I will."

#

Tora lifted her head and leaped from Tree's bark hands onto the ground. Tree, sensing Tora was not with her, began shifting her skin back to its original state. Her branches lowered, gliding easily down through the air, softening back to its tight kinky texture. She didn't fully merge into a tree, so she still had her clothes on, which were now dry. Tora stretched out each of her four limbs and mouth, baring her fangs in a wide yawn. She glanced up toward Tree with her bright green eyes. Tree stood up, giving herself a full-body stretch, looking up to the sky, which still appeared quite gloomy; at least the clouds were not raging for now.

"It's so glad to see you back to yourself, my beautiful friend."

"Meow," Tora answered.

"You put up a strong fight protecting Kale. I'm sure her mother would be proud of you for keeping watch over her."

Tora stared at Tree as she grabbed her shoulder bag from under a bush, where it was hidden. She placed it over her head, across one shoulder, then slung her locs back.

"Yes, I know of your old owner. I met her a long time ago, in my younger days, before my roots sprouted from my head. She was a dear friend, but she had to go her own way, and I had to go mine. But that's another story. Now is the only thing that matters, and I must focus on finding the Mother Oak. Plus, Kale needs our help."

"Meow," Tora responded as though she agreed.

Tree climbed out of the thicket, Tora jumped out ahead of her, and gracefully landed on her paws. Then came up to Tree and rubbed her body against Tree's leg. Tree leaned down to rub Tora, then stood, looking toward Kale's house. Tree crossed over the alley and walked through the front yard. Seeing the shattered glass on the porch, Tree thought about the young man from last night. The entity within was quickly ravaging his body. It would have been easy to kill him, but death was something she always tried to avoid. Tree lived by the deep-seated truth of the value of life and wanted to save him as well as remove the darkness. Her thoughts traveled to Kale and her children. If she didn't find the Mother Oak soon, the sickness Kale was carrying would spread further.

"Meow," Tora said, interrupting Tree's thoughts.

"You protected her well, but I fear she is contaminated with something that can possibly overtake her and others. By this time, she would have been taken to the hospital here. I will go there to check when I return to this area of town. My friend, please, keep watch over your home until one of us returns and stay safe. I must go." Tree leaned over to give Tora one last affectionate stroke.

"It was my honor to help you, my friend," Tree said.

Tora walked away from Tree and darted up the steps

to Kale's porch. She turned around and sat like a regal statue, watching Tree as she walked to the road, heading west then turning north on an intersecting road. Tora watched her swaying ropes until they disappeared.

#

Tree walked straight on her path for about an hour before she came to a major street ending at a three-way intersection. She saw a cemetery across the street further down on the right. Going right was the west direction the green spirits said she should go. She saw some old businesses east of her, a remnant of a club and liquor store that looked as though they suffered from the hands of time. A few men, young and old, stood in front of the liquor store and a nearby chicken joint, smoking blunts or just passing the time away. Her eyes scanned them, and she recognized one. It was Tahj, the young brother she met who thought she had something alive in her hair. He didn't see her at first from afar, but he turned his head as he took a puff of his blunt and saw her. He looked around as if wondering why she was in this area. Tree gave a slight nod, acknowledging him, and turned the opposite way, heading toward the cemetery.

Tree crossed the street and continued down the side of the road, getting closer to her destination. Looking around she hoped this was the right place the green spirits spoke of as she needed to contact the Mother Oak. The cemetery wasn't surrounded by many trees, which sparked doubt that she'd found the right place. The gravesite was vast, and as she came closer, she could feel voices whispering. But this time, it wasn't the green spirits trying to contact her; it was souls. Their voices moved like the wind circling around her. Tree walked through the old cemetery gates named Westview and entered, making sure she stepped around the graves and not on them. Whether in the physical realm or spiritual realm, Tree held all life in high esteem and didn't want to disrespect anyone. Not able to distinguish the voices, she stilled herself and listened with her mind instead of her physical ears. With her physical eyes, Tree couldn't see their form the way they were when alive. But she sensed whether their energy was masculine or feminine, and saw the colors they radiated. Some spoke to her as though offering greetings; most ignored her and spoke as though they were in a scene in a movie. Tree passed a weeping feminine soul that vibrated with a greyish color. Tree moved closer to it, but the soul kept moving away as though it was searching for something. *I lost my baby. Help me find my baby.* Tree reached out to it, but it moved past her as though she stood within the smoke.

Hey, pretty lady, what are you looking for? You look a little lost. Tree turned around to see a soul of masculine energy vibrating a white glow.

No, I am not lost; but I am looking for something. Tree answered with a smile. Tree could tell from the soul's color that it meant her no harm. She lowered her head and sucked in a deep breath. As she released it, her own green aura extended, growing brighter. Extending her aura further into the spirit realm allowed her to communicate with her thoughts and intentions better. With her first eye, she began to see the physical remnants of a young man's form. He wasn't that tall; he had full strong features with skin as dark as her own. He exuded personal style for a soul in the spirit realm. He wore a bowler hat cocked to the side, revealing short natural tight coils, similar to the numerous balls of hair on a Buddha statue. He wore a simple button-down shirt and slacks with shiny black shoes.

Tree turned to the right, sensing she was being watched in the physical realm. But she ignored it and turned back to face the white glowing soul.

Tahj had left the store and followed behind Tree at a distance. Hiding behind a nearby tombstone, he watched her. Tahj squinted his eyes, wondering why in the world would she be walking through a cemetery in broad daylight. She appeared to be looking for someone or something and then stood still, staring into space. Tahj pulled out his cellphone to film her. Certain he was not going to be made into a fool again. This time Kinte and anyone he talked to was going to believe him. Tahj was laughed at when he talked about the strange talking woman with dreads as big as tree trunks coming to life to attack him. But this time, he was ready. No one would be laughing when he'd catch her in the act of doing something supernatural. Tahj just hoped he saw something spectacular because staring into space wasn't enough for them to believe him.

Wise soul, I am here needing help. I am looking for the oldest oak here. Can you tell me where it is located? The man smiled, recognizing whom Tree was referring to.

Oh, you mean Mother. Baby girl, she ain't here. Most trees have been torn down here in this area, and the living expanded it with all these houses in the past thirty years. You need to go southwest to the cemetery next door to the farmer's market. You'll find her there; you can't miss Old Mother sitting in the back corner of the cemetery. She's big as a house.

Tree was thankful the soul was happy to help her. *Wise soul, thank you. Please, tell me your name? And is there anything I can do to repay your kindness?* Tree noticed that other surrounding souls were moving in closer around her.

It looks like they are being drawn to your living light, baby girl. The name's Bobby Lee. Bobby Lee Buckins. Kale is my granddaughter, and her mother was my daughter. I lost touch with her mother's family not long after she was born. I was extremely young then and didn't know how to take care of things in the way they should have been handle. By the time I got the chance to reach out and look for my daughter, it was too late. Bobby Lee held his head down in shame for a short moment, then looked back at Tree with pain in his eyes. *I'll just say I missed my time, but I'll be doggone. I'm gonna make up for it in this here spirit realm. All I ask you to do is protect Kale. Don't let nothing happen to her. She's special. She don't know it yet, but she will soon.*

I promise I will, Bobby Lee, thank you.

Bobby Lee could tell Tree was the kind who didn't break promises. He smiled with radiant joy in his eyes. He looked at the other souls moving in and getting close enough to Tree to touch her. He knew it was time for her to go. It wasn't wise for the living to be hanging around in the spirit realm for too long, or they'd start to drift from their purpose in the physical realm. Bobby Lee touched his hat and nodded then held up his hand to wave goodbye.

Good day to you, my friend.

Tree came back to herself in the living world. Bobby Lee and the other souls faded from her first eye view like leaves being blown away.

Good day to you, Bobby Lee.

Tahj was growing impatient with watching Tree just standing in the cemetery, apparently not doing anything. He'd decided to watch her for a few more minutes; then, he would sneak away. This was becoming a waste of his time. Maybe he needed to just let it go. He saw a woman in red approaching Tree. He had no idea how or when she came about as he didn't see anyone walking up into the cemetery; maybe she was hiding, too. He continued to watch them, wishing he could hear what they were saying.

Tree looked around and beyond the graves before deciding to leave. But she began to see flashes of red moving behind some of the tombstones, flashing in and out of sight. From behind a larger tombstone stepped out an attractive young coffee brown woman in her late twenties wearing a red headwrap and a long flowing red dress. A sinister smile curled the ends of her glossy, wine-colored lips; but Tree didn't smile back.

"Ah, you are as beautiful as they say, and those locs, magnificent! Too bad this world refuses to acknowledge your kind of beauty," the woman said, placing a hand on her hip, displaying confidence. With elegance, she moved further out in front from around the tombstone as though she glided on air. She smacked her red-stained lips at Tree, shaking her head in shame.

"Who are they?" Tree asked, her gaze unmoving.

"Ugonjwa, you met him last night, and Mwongo saw you walking like a magnificent mythical creature through this pitiful little town. I'm sure anyone who has encountered you has been spelled bound, though they would never care to admit it." The woman in red answered, rolling her eyes up and down.

"And what is your name?" Tree asked. She could sense the coils of her locs tightening, aware of the darkness exuding from the woman in red.

"You'll find out soon enough. I am spreading through this place as we speak. This town is small, and darkness will easily overcome the balance in a matter of days. Why don't you do yourself a service and leave? You don't belong here. You're a higher specimen than these people; the energy here was filled with a certain amount of darkness long before we even came into the picture. People were throwing away their lives here on a whim with ease, the racism that will never end, and you trying to be a good

Samaritan. Girl, you'll scare all these pale folks as well as the negroes when they see you coming with all that nappy hair. This place is filled with broken wellness, a sickness that's here and yet to come, the lack of true education, the youth against the elders, the unspeakable crimes, people fighting against their own, shall I go on?"

"All issues that have the potential to heal once the seed of sun travelers born in and near this area are activated, and they heed to the call of their purpose. What you speak of is everywhere. It is the balance of light and dark, and it's ongoing. But when people remember who they are and can see beyond the illusions you throw at them, they have the potential to return to what they are, light. Then change will happen."

The woman in red burst, releasing a loud cackle. She laughed so hard she had to lean back on the nearby tombstone. She held her chest, catching her breath as Tree watched her stifle her laughter.

"Did you just hear the word you said? Potential. That's a maybe they will go to the light; maybe they will go to the dark. From the looks of the whole world, dark is so much more fun, easy, and appealing. You are the only fucking illusion I see, and everything you stand for will be erased."

The laughter ceased within the woman in red as she spoke. Her eyes, holding pure hatred, filled with blood as she simultaneously erected her hands in the air, demanding attention. Crackles of red lightning rose into her body as though she pulled it from the ground. It moved up to her arms, then she directed her hands toward Tree, sending the red lightning toward her. Within a few nanoseconds, Tree's chocolate skin shifted to midnight blackness as her locs spread, surrounding her, forming a green illuminating force shield. The red lightning hit her created shield, then Tree's locs lifted, holding onto the lightning, reflecting it toward where the woman in red stood, but she had vanished. The lightning hit the tombstone, annihilating it to dust. Tree's skin faded back to her natural dark brown color, and she brushed her locs back behind her when they came down. She hated that she destroyed someone's tombstone but had to protect herself. Tree kneeled before the grave, placing her hand upon the ground. As her eyes and hand glowed, a sprout burst from the top of the grave and multiplied into vibrant gold daffodils. Every spring from now on, the daffodils would bloom in honor of the being that was lain here. Tree closed her eyes and bent her head down in respect. She stood, still in deep thought.

This was the second violent encounter she's had

since arriving in this town in a short period. Tree knew it was only going to get worse. She had to find the elder Mother Oak. But since she hadn't located her first, she decided to check on Kale. She was worried Kale's sickness was what the woman in red was referring to as her spreading. If so, everyone Kale had come in contact with since yesterday might be at risk. And who knew where the fleshless one who attacked Kale was, causing more harm. She had to find him as well. Tree walked to the cemetery entrance and stopped. She looked toward a nearby tombstone ahead of her.

"My brother, you do not have to stay hidden. I will not harm you."

For a moment, there was nothing. Tree waited patiently, then Tahj eased from his hidden spot. Tree stared at him, noticing he moved more easily. His pants were now in place around his waist. He wore his locs pulled back into a loose ponytail. Tree watched his eyes dart around nervously. Tahj forgot his phone in his hand and shoved it in his back pocket.

"I ain't seen nothing. Your secret is safe with me." Tahj said, easing further away from Tree to run if necessary.

"I'm not asking you to keep anything secret. I'm more concerned about you being in the wrong place, putting yourself in danger. That woman you saw would have no qualms about harming you."

"Who was she?" Tahj asked.

"Not she, it. And it is wearing the form of a woman I don't know. But it can come as a man or woman. I feel bad about the body it has taken, but I could sense the original woman who has resided in that body has been gone a long time."

Tahj shifted in his stance and frowned. He wasn't sure he had heard correctly. But after what he saw, anything was possible.

"You mean something is taking bodies?"

"Yes, but only until they need another one. It is one reason why I am here. I have to stop beings like that and share my light with you and others so beings like that cannot take over. Light helps you to grow more into your destiny so you can fulfill your purpose. But darkness and beings like that can sometimes become so strong they keep you blinded with illusions in a waking dream. Tahj, I have to find my way to your town's hospital from this area. Can you direct me?" Tree asked, remembering Kale.

Tahj wrinkled his nose. There was no car or any type of vehicle nearby. He felt silly asking, but it was better to ask a silly question than let ego make him look stupid.

"Can you fly?"

Tree laughed, causing Tahj to smile a bit. He didn't think his question was that funny, being that he did just see her direct lightning with her hair.

"No, Tahj. I cannot fly. I am human, and I walk everywhere I go. But I must be on my way to help a friend in need. I must leave, my brother."

Tree walked past him and passed the cemetery gates. Tahj didn't know why, but he had to find out more about this strange lady. He prayed she wouldn't harm him.

"I have a car," he blurted. "Well, it's not mine but my cousin's. You remember, Kinte? He lives in this area. He can borrow his mom's car to give you a ride there. This town is so small you can spit in it, and it'll flood. I know you can walk. But after some demon lady tried to kill you, maybe it's safer for you to ride."

Tahj stared, assuming Tree would refuse when she didn't answer. Tree looked off down the road where she was headed then let out some air and nodded.

"Ok, let's go," she answered.

Chapter 6 – A Friend in Need

Lionel sat at his grandmother's kitchen table, gorging on the large meal he told her to make. At this point, she barely saw any glimpse of her grandson. Sometimes he would call her in a tone that made her eyes light up; those were the moments she just knew he was coming back. Then something else inside would take over, and he'd be gone again. Lionel's grandmother thought about calling her pastor over; only she was scared he'd be harmed. Still, she had to try something. There was no way she couldn't continue to go through life fearing her own grandson. Standing by the table, watching him eat, she turned her head in disgust regarding his nasty manners.

"Why are you standing there watching me? Don't you have something to do, clean, anything?"

"Whoever you are, please, let me speak to Lionel. I-I just need to know my baby's all right. Please."

Lionel's mouth was full of food as he stared at her coldly. He narrowed his eyes then relaxed his shoulders. He closed his eyes, wiping his mouth. Then opened them while sharing a warm smile.

"Grandma! Oh, Grandma, how I've missed you," he said sweetly as his hands lowered to each side of his plate with a fork in one and a paring knife in the other. Lionel's grandmother grimaced, turning her head from Lionel. He burst into laughter with chewed food showing in his mouth. She stomped away, heading out of the kitchen. She knew her grandson was there somewhere inside of his body; now, she couldn't reach him.

"Hey!" Lionel roared, stopping her in her tracks. His grandmother didn't turn around to look at him. Lionel rolled his eyeballs back as they filled with blood. He opened his jaws and sucked in air. His grandmother began holding her throat and spun around, gasping for air. Falling to her knees she gasped then slumped to the floor. Lionel came and stood over her. Looking up at him, she held her chest, trying to catch her breath with tears rolling down her face. He looked down at her in silence. He stepped over her and walked out. All she heard was the door slam.

#

Jay entered Smart World, the store where Kale worked. He walked around the front end to the registers and sat on a waiting bench for customers. Jay was aware of how bad he looked, so he wore a long trench coat to hide the wound he received the night before and a black baseball cap to hide his face. Customers passed by as they were leaving the store and grimaced, noticing a foul odor. He began to cough uncontrollably, holding his chest. Jamie, standing nearby, saw him and recognized who he was. She knew he and Kale were no longer together and figured he'd probably come up here looking for trouble. She walked to the customer service desk to speak with the manager on duty.

"Jackson, I think we are having an issue," she said in her high-pitched tone to a tall man with a small afro.

"What is it, Jamie?" Jackson asked. He was busy helping a store associate on the register.

"There is an unpleasant guest near the waiting bench, and he's scaring customers. He's Kale's ex-boyfriend. I think he's the reason why I received that call this morning," she answered.

Jackson inhaled and released a deep breath. "Okay, I'll deal with it."

Jackson stepped away from the customer service desk, mentally preparing to deal with either a complaint or an irate customer. Neither of which he was in the mood for. He smelled an odor and immediately wondered where it was coming from, then realized where once he approached Jay.

"Sir, do you need help?" He asked, leaning in to see Jay's face.

"Hell, naw, man! Get away from me! I feel like a million bucks!" Jay snapped, looking Jackson up and down, then started coughing again. He got up, standing closer to the manager, patting him on the shoulder as he cleared his throat.

"Store looks great, man; real clean, real clean."

"Thank you, are you looking for something?" the manager asked, rolling his eyes while trying to hold his breath. Jay flashed a plaque and mucus-infested smile, ignoring Jackson's question. He walked further into the store.

"Excuse me, Sir. But I'm going to have to ask you to leave; you're disturbing guests here." Jackson watched Jay walking away, coughing hard and barely covering his mouth with the inside of his elbow. He held up one of his hands to tell the manager to give him a moment when he tried to stop him. Growing impatient with customers staring, Jackson pulled out his handheld device to call security. Then Jay lifted back up, standing straight.

"Man, who you calling, the police? You don't have to do that. I've done all I needed to do. I'll go; I'll go," Jay said with a smile, clearing the rumble in his throat. Then he rushed up close to the manager and leaned on him, coughing directly into his face.

"Motherfucker!" Jackson yelled, shoving Jay then wiping Jay's saliva from his face with his hands. It took everything in him not to punch Jay. By then, security was coming after Jay. Laughing, Jay grabbed a nearby candy bar off of a display stand and ran out the door, bumping into customers coming in. He ran out into the parking lot as though he'd lost his mind. A driver backing out, struck him on impact, sending him sliding up the back of the car and rolling onto the ground. The hysterical driver stopped the vehicle immediately and exited her car, filled with fear that she had killed someone. A security officer, coming from the store's entrance, called the ambulance. As Jay lay unconscious on the ground on his back, the driver kneeled over him, crying, ignoring the horrid smell. Jay's eye popped open, then he dashed up, kissing the woman in the mouth. He held onto her, slobbering his mucus-filled tongue into her mouth before she pushed him away, which gave the police plenty of time to get to him. The woman began gagging and spitting while the cops took him. Jay was still laughing with his coat flying open, revealing his blood-stained shirt. As the cops took him away, onlookers watched as he began freestyling and spitting a rap lyric he had been repeating in his head.

"I'm all inside of you.

Now what-chu gonna do?

Crawling up and creeping through.

Yeah, you feeling me? I'm feeling you!

You can't get rid of me.

I'm quite possibly,

The most tainted-born MC.

You feeling me? Yeah, you see!"

#

Tahj and Kale stepped onto the porch of Kinte's mother's home. It was a blue vinyl house with white trimmings. The hedges and bushes were shaped to perfection, with the grass cut evenly throughout the yard. There were some puddles from the rain the night before, but the yard and house still held an organized feel. Tahj pressed the doorbell and waited, no answer. They heard music playing from around the house and walked off the side of the porch to look around the back. There were family members out having a small barbeque. Kinte was standing there, sipping on a beer, talking with some friends. Someone tapped Kinte on the shoulder. He looked to see Tahj, standing with Tree by the house. He set his beer down on a nearby picnic table and walked over to them. He didn't look too happy to see Tahj. He glanced at

Tree and looked back to Tahj.

"Man, why you ain't tell me y'all were putting meat on the grill?" Tahj asked, ignoring Kinte's annoyed expression.

"You know my mom's boyfriend, Smokey, rain, sun, snow, whatever, dude's gonna find a way to grill him some ribs. What the hell you doing here?" he asked. "Pardon my Portuguese, Sis, but I ain't in no mood to hear about how you got electrical wires in your hair or that your hair is alive from my cousin," Kinte stated, pointing at Tahj.

"Kinte, man, I ain't here 'bout that. Well, maybe. I'll talk to you 'bout it later, but she needs a ride to the hospital." Tahj said it more as a statement than a question. Kinte looked to Tree, then back to Tahj, and then Tree. He flashed a skeptical smile because Tahj was convinced she was an alien species in human disguise. Now he wanted to help her with a ride to the hospital?

"Why? Sis, you sick?" Kinte asked Tree.

"No, someone I know is extremely sick, and I have to get to her to see if she is okay," Tree answered, and Kinte nodded.

"Kinte, who are you talking to?" An elder woman came up from behind him. "Oh, hey, Tahj, and who is this?"

Kinte's mother stared up and down at Tree with

childlike fascination. Tree smiled and held out her hand.

"I'm Tree."

"Tree? How you get that name, baby?" asked Kinte's mother, taking Tree's hand, shaking it, thinking Tree was a strange name for a young woman. She shook her head, noticing a weird energy was making her dizzy. When she released her hand from Tree, the feeling disappeared.

"A teacher of mine gave me that name when I made a pact with the sun and began growing my roots, you see." Tree caressed one of her locs in her hand.

"Oh, so it's like a nickname. Okay, and you have some beautiful dreads! I've never seen the kind like yours."

"Thank you, my beautiful sister, but I do not have dreads. To have dread is to have something to fear." Tree chuckled. "Then again, some fear what they do not understand. But I walked in the light, and my roots grow in reflection of nature, protecting me, so I see no dread."

"Ohhh, okay, that's interesting. I learn something new every day," Kinte's mother nodded. She wasn't sure what all Tree meant because, to her, dreads, locs, dreadlocks were all the same, but to each his own. She smiled, brushed the loc issue aside, and turned her attention to Tahj and Tree.

"Well, y'all come on back and say hey to everybody."

"Auntie, Tree needs a ride to the hospital to visit a sick friend. I wanted to ask you could Kinte take us?" Tahj asked. Kinte shot an annoyed look at Tahj. He didn't want to deal with Tahj's mouth today.

"That's fine. Kinte, you can take them. But first, y'all step back real quick and say hey, then get yourself a plate," Kinte's mother said, ushering them all further to the back patio.

Kinte's family greeted Tahj and gawked at Tree. Tree kindly smiled at everyone she made contact with. Some smiled back; some just looked. Tahj pulled out a chair for Tree to sit once they reached a clear space at a picnic table.

"I'll go make us a plate," Tahj said to Tree.

"No, thank you, my brother. I am just fine," she responded as he stepped away.

"You're not hungry? I figured you'd be starving; you know after ..." Tahj's voice trailed off, referring to the run in Tree had with the lady in red. But he didn't know if Tree felt comfortable referring to a supernatural fight she had while sitting in the middle of a small group of family members having a barbeque.

"My brother, I do not eat food. I am a sun traveler."

"What! What! You don't eat food? What kind of thang is that? You must be a Muslim?" asked an elder heavyset man, sitting near Tree and Tahj. He, Tahj, and other family members ogled her.

"Must be fasting? Some people do that as a spiritual practice. It sometimes helps to clear the mind," replied the thick chocolate man, tending to the grill.

"Are you a vegan? I've heard of some vegans that clean their systems out like that, kinda like taking a detox. That's interesting. But, honey chile, I gots to have my meat," Kinte's mother interjected.

"You ain't lying!" exclaimed the elderly heavyset man, laughing. "Smokey, when you gone be done with them poke chops! We got a vegan in the house! She needs some meat on them bones!"

"Chile, I think I'd die without meat." Another lady sitting in their circle laughed.

"What? She don't eat meat," a young girl said to a boy coming up to stand beside her. He scrunched his face upon hearing this.

"Chops is coming, Big Chuck!" The chocolate man at the grill said, answering the heavy set elder.

"No, my brothers and sisters, I am not vegan anymore; I am a solar being. I am like a plant. I create food within myself. I drink water sometimes, but I do not eat solid food anymore."

All the family members stared at Tree as though she'd just transformed into a unicorn. Tree smiled in amusement.

"But you can die? Humans can't do that; that's impossible. Y-You need protein to live," Tahj said, breaking the silence.

"I am human. And I assure you it is possible, and humans need many more nutrients than protein to live. I am one who has returned to her original natural state. I've learned, over many years, that I need very little of anything, and one of those things is food. It was an unexpected quality that came into my life, but one that has served me well. I am no special than anyone else. Others have achieved this, but it takes many years of discipline, erasing doubt, and being one with the divine source. Also, my brother, amino acids, which you call protein, is in everything. It is why cows, horses, gorillas, or elephants eat plant foods and grow as big and strong as they do. It is not a physiological requirement for humans to eat meat; I assure you; you will not die." Tree laughed.

"I don't know if I can do that. I've been eating meat all my life, and to stop just like that, whoa, that would be hard," Tahj said, shaking his head.

"You can do anything you choose to put your mind

to. I'm not telling you to do as I say or do as I have done. You are the master of your destiny. All I ask is for you to do your own research and find out what works for you. From my understanding of nature, I have learned from it all, and animals have been and remain to be great teachers of the animal kingdom. I see no reason to eat them to sustain my life when it is not needed. I do not think they are here for that. Just as divinity dwells in you and me, it is in them as well. They love, feel, care for their young, and connect as all beings do.

Years ago, when I did stop eating them, my energy increased. But my intuition was strong, even then, and I made sure I ate an abundance of plant foods in the beginning. Over time, I naturally progressed to needing less and less until nothing. Your journey is not mine; it is yours. Always question and do your own research."

"So, you're one with the Lawd? The one who sustains you, and fills your soul, so that keeps you from feeling hungry?" asked the heavy set elder. He looked toward Tree, squinting his eyes.

"You can say it like that," Tree answered. She smiled, finding him humorous.

"Aw, shit! I still gots to have my meat!" The elder exclaimed, causing everyone to laugh. "I love the Lawd, too, but I'd starve. I'd die a painful unhappy life if I couldn't eat. Young lady, I don't know if I can believe that no eating type of thang. I'd have to keep you hostage a few days like a science project, study ya," he said, giggling.

Tree chuckled, shaking her head.

"And you have a pretty smile, young lady," Kinte's mother said, noticing Tree's deep dimples.

"She is very pretty for a dark skin girl, chocolaty," said the other seated lady.

"Gloria, you said that like dark skin ain't pretty. Member that girl, Coco? Nadine's daughter that went to school with Kinte?" Kinte's mother snapped. "Now that was a pretty girl. I remember Kinte told me that the kids in school used to tease that child bout how dark she was. But you, Tree, are a gorgeous young lady." Kinte's mother said, looking back to Tree.

"Yeah, she was pretty and very dark; she had a head full of thick long, good hair." Gloria paused for a moment. "Well, I'm ... sorry. I ain't mean nothing by it. You're a pretty girl, unique," Gloria said, trying to dismiss what she said earlier.

"Ignore her, honey chile! She ignorant," Kinte's mother said, rolling her eyes, dismissing Gloria. Gloria smacked her lips at Kinte's mother.

"Thank you, my sisters. It is an honor to be the color of the indigenous humans who populated the earth. It is in the darkness where the source of all things begins. My color allows me to absorb all forms of rays from the sun without premature aging or disease. It even shifts darker to help me tap into deeper powers within myself to share abilities to help others. It is like carrying the power of the universe every single day, and it just absorbs light, making me stronger. I thank divinity and my ancestors for this skin I am in and the hair that grows out of this scalp. My darkness and the tightness of my roots are two of my most powerful assets."

"Okay, preach on!" Kinte's mother exclaimed.

Tahj had walked back to the circle from grabbing himself a plate of barbeque. He held up a bottle of water, showing Tree he got something for her, even if she didn't want to eat. She nodded toward him.

"How old are you, Tree? You sound so wise to be so young. Where are you from?" Kinte's mother asked.

"Wherever divinity is, is where I am from. And I'm forty-three."

"Forty – what?" Kinte's mother, the elder man, and the lady said in unison.

"Damn! I thought you were a twenty-five-year-old! You only ten years younger than me! Maybe after these here poke chops, I may do a fast," the elder man said, rubbing his hefty belly, making everyone laugh.

"Big Chuck, the only fast you doing is putting them ribs fast in yo' belly! Man, you a mess." Kinte's mother laughed. Big Chuck winked his eye at her, smiling.

Kinte walked back into the circle and stood beside Tahj. Tahj looked at Tree and ushered his hand to let her know it was time to head out. She nodded and stood up with her large locs swinging behind her.

"It was a pleasure to meet all of you, but I must go." Tree nodded and bowed like a humble monk, stepping away from everyone.

"It was a pleasure and very interesting to meet you too, young lady," said Smokey.

"Yes, come back and see us again. We'll have Big Chuck eating a salad next time," Gloria joked.

"Salad! Bunny food? Woman, don't you play with me like that!" Big Chuck joked. "But it was nice talking to you, too."

Tree smiled and followed Kinte and Tahj back toward the front of the house, where the car was parked.

"Bye, nice to meet you," others spoke as Tree moved from earshot.

"It has to be that vegan food she eats; she probably

didn't want to say. It can grow your hair like that and make you look young with all those green smoothies they be drinking," someone said to the others as Tree, Kinte, and Tahj walked out of sight.

#

Kinte pulled into the parking lot of the hospital and parked near the visitor's entrance. He noticed quite a few people walking in; usually, the hospital parking lot was calm.

"Thank you both for this ride; it's much appreciated," Tree said, turning to nod at both. Her locs were swept to the side as not to take up her seat.

"No problem. While you're here in town, if you need a ride, just let me know. You have some different ways, but you're cool people," Kinte said.

"You need anything else?" Tahj asked.

"No, brother, I am fine. It's best you both leave and protect yourself. I'm afraid my friend is very sick, and what she has may be spreading. It is my job to find a way to keep it from doing so."

"What, like a virus? What's wrong with her?" Kinte asked, stretching his eyes.

"I've encountered evil since being here, and it's the kind of evil that means to destroy the goodness of people like yourself so that you can't recognize any light whatsoever.

One way of doing that is enforcing the waking dream you live every day, enhancing the lies about who you are, and another is creating sickness to not only harm you and others but to weaken you as a whole. Please, advise your family to stay home and take care of their health and strengthen their immune systems. This thing may not have spread enough to where the news or health organizations have become aware of it, so that is good. I have time to contain it to stop it here."

"How can you stop a virus? I don't know if I can even believe this. That sounds like something the government or the World Health Organization should handle," Kinte said.

"Honestly, I do not know. I've never stopped a virus before, but I will find a way. And if you cannot, believe me, I will still do what I need to do. Please, just take care of yourself."

"It's that lady that had the red dress, huh?" Tahj asked, already knowing the answer.

Tree nodded her head, seeing the worry in the eyes of the two men. She had a deep controllable faith, even though she didn't know what to do exactly. However, she knew one thing, she was going to defeat the darkness causing this and save this town.

Tree stepped out of the car and waved as the cousins drove off. She entered the hospital's sliding doors and was immediately approached by a greeter with a mask covering her face.

"Excuse me, ma'am, can you please wear this mask while you are inside the lobby?" she asked.

Tree looked at the mask she held out for her. She did not want to put it on. But she complied as long as she stood inside the lobby. She took it and hooked the rubber bands of the mask around her ears. The greeter expressed immediate relief, dropping her shoulders.

"Now, how can I help you?" she asked.

"I am here to see my friend, Kale. She is a patient here. She needs me."

"I'm sorry. But unless you have to be admitted, we cannot allow visitation at this moment. There has been a large number of patients admitted within the past twenty-four hours, and we aren't sure what is going on. So, to keep others safe, we cannot allow visitation."

Tree nodded and took her mask off. Turning away, she threw it in a nearby trashcan on the way out of the lobby. If she couldn't see Kale, then she had to find another way. Tree walked around the front of the hospital, looking at the size and height of the brick walls. There was no way she could figure out what area Kale was in, so she needed to rely on help. Walking to the back, Tree found a quiet grassy area to sit down in the lotus position. Then closed her eyes and began concentrating on her breath. Her thoughts reached out to call an old friend she knew would be watching over Kale, one who would never leave her alone.

A white glowing soul appeared in front of Tree. Tree opened her green-lit eyes and saw its bright light before her. Tree felt its loving frequency and then watched as it floated up and dissolved into the hospital walls.

#

In her quiet room, Kale lay in bed, barely moving. She was attached to a ventilator because it had become too hard to breathe on her own. The mucus that had formed throughout her body had filled most of her lungs and moved into other areas. The sludge Jay infected her with drizzled down the side of her mouth and from her ears. Her head lay to the side toward the window, watching the day darken, not only from the sun setting but also from the clouds hovering over the city. Her half-opened eyes stared at a white glow forming in the corner of the room by the window. As it grew brighter, tears began to stream down her face. She sensed a love only one could give her.

"Mama," she mouthed, not able to produce a sound from her painfully sore throat.

#

Tree stood and walked further around the hospital, studying the layout like an architect. She saw a white glow emanating from a second-story window and walked to the wall underneath the window's location. Stretching her hands out, a bright golden-green glow shined from her palm. The ground beneath her palm began to sink in as something from within was coming to the surface. A spiraling vine came out of the ground, thickening in size similar to Tree's locs. It grew, crawling the hospital wall, winding side to side until it reached the top of the window, where she saw the white glow. Tree, seeing the woody vine reach its destination, began to climb it like a ladder with ease. She reached the window and saw Kale lying in the bed alone in the room hooked up to wires and machines. Tree placed her palm on the window, sliding it open and crawling inside.

"Mama, don't leave me," Kale mouthed. Her hands began to shake as the white glow began to fade. Kale closed her eyes for a moment. Tears roll down the sides of her face then opened them to see Tree.

"Go, you'll be…come sick," her dry lips whispered.

"No, I will not leave until I help you." Tree said with a gentle look from her green eyes. She brought light back to her hands and placed them on the sides of Kale's face, wiping her tears away. Then she stood taller and held out one hand over Kale's face. Tree's skin within her palm opened, releasing a rich green liquid, dropping into Kale's mouth and onto her lips.

"The chlorophyll will help you to become stronger and release most of the mucus that disguises itself as diseases. It will take a moment, and you may go into a dream-like state. But you must remain strong; remember, you are the light," Tree whispered in her ear.

Tree detached the IV needle from Kale's hand and eased the nasal tube from her nose, then held Kale's hand until she drifted off into a deep sleep. Taking a pillow cushion from the chair by the far corner of the room, she used it to sit again in a lotus position on the cold floor beside Kale's bed. Tree placed her forearms on her thighs with her palms faced up and closed her eyes.

#

Kale opened her eyes and found herself standing in a white room with no walls. She spun around in every direction, which seemed to go on forever. She found herself dressed in her regular clothes, a t-shirt, jeans, and Converse sneakers. She felt fine, as though she never was sick.

"Hello," she called, "anybody here!"

She didn't understand how or why she was here, but she knew she wanted to get the hell out. It was as though she stood in nothingness. She walked around in a circle once and then stood still, trying to figure out what she could do. If she walked, she couldn't tell what direction she was going in to be able to find an exit. There were no walls, just a white floor and white ceiling with lights shining from a place she couldn't locate.

"You're awake?"

Kale heard a voice behind her that startled her. She spun around to see a slim boy standing there. She had seen him before. After staring at him for a few seconds, she placed him into her memory.

"You live in my neighborhood, right? I've seen you walking around before."

"Yeah, I'm Lionel," he answered.

"I'm Kale. How did you get here, Lionel?" Kale asked, staring at him.

"Something took my body. I'm trapped, and I can't get out." Lionel's eyes began to glisten. He looked into Kale's eyes. "It's made me do terrible things. I'm scared something may hurt my grandma. She's alone, and … and James, h-he's gone."

Lionel burst into tears, shaking uncontrollably. Kale

walked over to him and placed her arms around him.

"Don't worry; we will figure this thing out. I-I really don't know how, but we have to stay positive no matter what. Do you remember anything about where you were before you came here?"

Lionel calmed down and wiped his tears. He took a deep breath and nodded.

"I was in my room when I last had control over my body. It's like something came and made me say things I didn't want to say, but I didn't know how to stop it. It told me it was going to destroy me, that I wouldn't exist anymore, it, it ... I have to go! It's coming!" Lionel shouted, looking back paranoid.

"What? What are you talking about? No one else is here!" Kale said, not seeing anything around them but the same endless whiteness.

"He can hear me. I have to hide. The deeper I hide, the more I can't find my way back. Please, if you wake up, help me!"

Lionel pulled away from Kale, who was clutching his arm. She looked in the direction his eyes went to and saw a shadowy dark figure with red glowing eyes standing way off into the distance. When she looked back to Lionel, he was gone. She spun around, desperately trying to see where he'd run off to. But he'd disappeared. She looked back toward the shadowy figure. It stood, unmoving, watching her.

"Kale," called a man's voice.

She looked to her right and saw Jay. She stepped back, holding her hands up to keep him from coming closer to her.

"Jay," she said.

"Kale, I'm sorry. I love you. I'd never hurt you," Jay said with sincerity.

Kale still kept her distance from him. A tear dropped from one of her eyes as she studied the sadness in his handsome face. He wore clean clothes, his body looked healthy, and he smelled fresh.

"Well, you did. Last I remember, I was lying in a hospital because of you. I know something is in you." Kale's voice trailed off.

"Then you know I wasn't the one hurting you. I tried to control it, but I wasn't strong enough. I fear I may die in the sick state you saw my body in. I just wanted to let you know, even after all my dumb ass mistakes, that you are the one and always will be for me. I fucked up, and I humbly accept anything you throw at me. But just know, I love you."

Tears fell from Jay's eyes. He held his head down and looked back up to the direction of where the shadowy figure stood. He looked back to Kale and faded from her sight. She reached out to touch him, feeling the wind move through her fingers. She caught her breath, wiping her eyes, refusing to release any more tears, then looked to the shadow, where there were now two standing. She faced their direction. As she gathered the nerve to face her fear of confronting them, she heard someone smacking their lips behind her.

This time, Kale wasn't startled. She looked behind her and saw a woman dressed in red from head to toe, sitting on a throne-like chair. She studied Kale with a sinister smirk written on her face as though she was planning something. The woman in red rose from her seat with her dress flowing around her like incense smoke. As she moved closer, Kale kept her eyes on her with the same intensity.

"What is your name?" the woman in red asked, casually cocking her head to one side. A headwrap framed her head like a red halo.

"Who wants to know?" Kale asked.

The woman giggled, touching her lips.

"A friend, possibly, warm up a little, missy. I'm not here to cause you any harm. I'm the type of person who believes in everyone being happy and getting what they want."

"Really? And who said anything about harm? Have you caused harm to someone?" Kale asked, raising her eyebrows.

"No, no. I've just come to make a proposition. I've noticed your plant friend has been very caring toward you small-town folk. I feel it's because there are others like her or similar that will exist, or as she claims, come into the light." The woman in red said with a grin.

"Why does that matter to you? Who the hell are you, anyway?" Kale asked, becoming impatient.

"It matters because I can tell you are one of these others. I know that a certain evil plagues this place, and it will only grow worse."

"Tree said that same thing before. Do you know her?"

The woman in red smacked her lips again, "I'm aware of her; we've met."

"So, what does all this mess, evil, darkness, whatever you call it even mean?" Kale asked, holding her hands out, then dropping them back down to her sides. She glanced at the shadowy dark figures still staring at her.

"Your Jay has spread a dis-ease that will make it very uncomfortable to be in one's body. You lay dying as we speak. But I can stop it. And everything will be quite dandy as before for everyone," the woman in red said, smiling.

"Can you stop talking in circles and just tell me, what do you want?"

"I want your body." The woman in red said with a hard look in her eyes.

"What?" Kale almost laughed.

"I am not an ordinary being. I need flesh that is of quality. And this one I am now residing in, though beautiful, has run its course, and I've grown tired of it. But you— mmph, you have the potential to be a shining light for the world, which is a great responsibility to bear. I can tell it's something you do not want, right? All you want is to be your regular simple boring self, taking care of your everyday life, right?" The woman in red held an intense, hungry look in her eyes.

"Yeah, but I'm not giving you my body. That's not even possible, and even if it was, why would I want to do that? I have a family to take care of. If you are in my body, how could I be there for them?" Kale asked, crossing her arms, leaning to the side.

"You wouldn't. I'm offering you an opportunity to save humanity. Give me your body or watch an infectious virus take over everyone you love, including your family, and die right along with them. Either way, you die." The woman in red gave a cheesy smile. Her eyes began to glow, matching the red stares of the shadowy figures.

Kale grew increasingly uncomfortable, uncrossed her arms and backed away from the woman in red. She looked away as if diverting her gaze would protect her. If Jay loved her so much, why wasn't he here to protect her now? When she looked back toward the woman in red, the two shadowy beings were standing beside her like loyal soldiers. They looked almost seven feet tall with eyes cutting into her soul. Kale backed even further away when their shadowy figures dissolved like smoke, and Lionel and Jay stood in their places. They were not in the state they were when she talked to them. Lionel's innocence was all gone, and Jay appeared the same as the night he attacked her. He dripped blood from his shoulder from an unhealed wound. The woman in red leaned in close toward Kale. Her face appeared inches away, large and curved like an amusement park mirror.

"You better run," she said in a harsh raspy whisper, which transformed into uncontrollable laughter.

Kale spun and took off like an Olympian sprinter, leaving the wicked echo of the woman's laughter behind. Lionel's jaw dropped open, and the horrendous sound of a thousand voices vibrated throughout the white space. Kale held her hands over her ears. The screams shook her a bit, causing her to almost stumble, but she kept running. Jay took off after her. Sludge ran from every visible physical opening as he galloped like a beast on all fours.

"Baby, wait! I just want to talk to you!" Jay growled.

Kale glanced back and saw Jay's glowing red eyes and his wide Cheshire cat smile. Sharp teeth glared back at her. Panicking, she tripped and stumbled, causing herself to fall to the floor. With a broadening smile, Jay jumped on top of her like a lion going in for the kill. Lionel stood over her on one side and the woman and red on the other. As Kale screamed, her voice was being pulled into Lionel's unnaturally large mouth. With her neck and shoulders exposed, Jay lifted his head back and dove in, sinking a full row of teeth into her shoulder. Crying out in agony, she looked up ahead, beyond the demons, toward the ceiling. She saw a white glowing light growing closer to her. Strangely, she felt something separating her from the pain. She was losing consciousness. Then she let go.

Kale blinked her eyes, then opened them, jumping up in a hysterical fit. She looked around, expecting to see Lionel, Jay, and the woman in red; instead, she saw her mother standing before her. The endless white room was gone, and she found herself in a clearing in the forest. It was bright, sunny, and beautiful. She extended her shaking hands toward her mother's face, not believing it was real. She snapped her hands back to the sides of her own face then to her head in disbelief. Her mother nodded, smiling with tearful eyes to confirm she was there. Kale stretched her watery eyes in awe. She could do nothing but stare at her mother's face. Her mother stepped closer to her, pulling Kale's hands down from her head then wrapping her arms around her. Kale swallowed hard and closed her eyes, then lowered her tense shoulders, collapsing into her mother's arms.

Chapter Seven – The Zar

Kale opened her eyes to blurriness, squinting at the glaring lights. She tried to sit up, but her uncontrollable coughing prevented her from doing so. Feeling mucus loosening in her throat, she grabbed a cup she had been drinking water from earlier off of the side table. Retching and leaning to one side, she vomited clumps of dark-colored sludge and yellowy mucus into the cup. Mucus slid from her nose, ears, and every opening in her body. Tree popped her eyes open from her meditation and stood, racing toward Kale. It was almost as if the darkness was trying to free itself from within her. Kale coughed so hard she could barely breathe, and Tree wanted to relieve her of her discomfort. But she knew it had to continue if Kale was to release it from her system. Kale doubled over, coughing, trying to dial for a nurse, but knocking over the receiver instead. Tree caught the phone and Kale.

"You must release this toxicity from your body, or it can destroy you. My chlorophyll won't be able to release it one hundred percent at this moment. But it will take care of most of it so that you can easily do the rest. Please, Kale, stay strong," Tree remained calm as she spoke in her friend's ear.

Kale fell back, gagging, opening her mouth to make way for a large clump of mucus to emerge. As the mucus released, it slid out like a python coming out of a deep burrow. Kale's eyes rolled back as her body was going limp. With glistening eyes, Tree silently recited a prayer for the wellbeing of Kale as she held onto her. Once the sludge came out enough, Tree grabbed it with one glowing hand and pulled to force it to release quicker. She helped Kale back onto the bed, slid her other arm out from under Kale's body, and took a firmer grip on it with both hands. Numerous lizard-like eyes appeared all over the serpent sludge's form. Then it began to release a piercing scream. The noise vibrated outside the room, alerting the nurse and doctor to come. Tree, assuming the room's door was unlocked, mentally commanded the vine from the window to grow further inside. It rapidly crawled across the floor, growing like a spreading crack in a wall, reaching past them and rising up the door, wrapping and thickening around the door handle, hindering entry. The door handle shook, but it did not open. Tree continued pulling harder on the serpent's sludge, wanting to contain it before the doctor and nurses found a way to break in and before Kale lost consciousness.

Once it neared the end, Tree yanked it out, holding the beast in her hands. Kale was exhausted and collapsed sideways onto the bed. The beast violently twisted to release itself. Numerous small vines broke from all areas of Tree's hands and forearms, wrapping around every inch of the parasitic form. Feeling the burn, its flesh began to smoke from the penetration of pure chlorophyll seeping within. The sludge decreased in size, and Tree dropped it to the floor, where it further dissolved, leaving a dark puddle.

"Open the door! Ms. McCray! Ms. McCray, who's in the room with you? We have the police out here!" yelled a nurse.

Tree's glowing hands dissolved the remaining filth and retracted her vines. Tree wrapped her arms around Kale, helping her walk toward the window.

"I can't; le-leave me," Kale whispered.

"Kale, I can take you to your children. You're no longer contagious; you're just very weak."

"They'll come," Kale said, referring to the police and doctor trying to enter the room. "Please, I'm too weak. Just go check my babies w-with my auntie at Garden Pointe."

The vines holding the door entry handle were

weakening as it became easier for the outside forces to move it. She didn't use a particularly strong vine to hold it for long. Kale, realizing Tree didn't have much time and being too exhausted to keep standing, began easing herself to the floor. Tree helped her sit and Kale leaned her back and head against the wall. The floor was cold and uncomfortable, but she would be all right. She waved her hand for Tree to leave, assuring her with a whisper that she would be okay. Tree climbed out of the window, holding onto the vines, willing her skin to complement the darkness of the night with her locs resembling the woody vines she climbed on. She crawled down as the door of Kale's hospital room burst open. The doctor and nurse entered with a police officer, all seeing the thick woody vines that grew along the floor from the window.

"What the hell happened in here?" Dr. Anderson asked, looking from the vines to Kale.

The officer rushed to the window while the nurse and doctor rushed to help Kale off the floor. The officer looked outside toward where the vines led, then along the nearby bushes and trees near the parking lot. He couldn't see any trace of anything leaving the window or climbing down the vines. But then, he saw movement behind some of the bushes and the glow of two shimmery green eyes. He returned their stare for a short moment; then, they were gone. "Probably a cat," he thought, dismissing it. But why did the eyes seem so human to him?

"Ms. McCray, what happened in here? You cannot unplug yourself and leave the bed; it's dangerous in your state," Doctor Anderson said, chastising her as they placed Kale back into the bed. She ignored him and fell into a deep, restful sleep as soon as she reclined.

"How could she possibly have gotten up while this was going on? She couldn't even breathe on her own a moment ago," the nurse replied.

"She's obviously breathing now. Something or someone was in here with her. But this…," Doctor Anderson said, looking at the vines. "I don't know; I don't have an explanation for this."

"We'll find out what's going on when she wakes. Make sure to contact me," the police officer said.

#

There was light knocking on Iesha's bedroom door before it opened. Her dad leaned in, seeing her on the bed, looking at a laptop screen. She greeted him with a pensive expression and not her usual cheery smile.

"You okay, hon?"

"Uh, yeah, just finishing up some work. What's up?"

she asked, turning away. Her dad came into the room and sat beside her.

"You're not going to school today. I got a call, and they are temporarily shutting down," he answered.

"W-what?" Iesha asked confused. In a way, it was a relief since she didn't want to risk running into Lionel.

"There is a serious virus that's going around; it was announced on the local news that schools and some businesses are closing shop for a while to minimize spreading." Iesha's dad was quiet for a moment, then pressed his lips together as though he wanted to say something more.

"Dad, what is it?" Iesha asked. She was afraid he was going to say something that confirmed what she saw a few days ago. She was hoping he wasn't going to say anything else. Iesha looked down to hide her sadness then stilled herself. She raised her gaze back to her dad then smiled a bit trying to play off his concern. Then he said it.

"One of your classmates was reported missing, Jamison Hicks. But the police found his body. They, um, announced it on the local news this morning. They think it was this virus thing. The way his body was found, it was as though he rapidly deteriorated. Was he a friend of yours? Did you know him?"

Iesha looked off into space for a few seconds, then

turned away from her dad, looking back at the laptop. Her dad confirmed what she saw was real. James was gone and her best friend, or whatever was in him, was the murderer. A tear dropped from one of her eyes. She wiped it away and continued looking at the laptop screen. She didn't like James, but he was still a human being, somebody's child. Seeing him killed like that was something that would stay with her for a long time, possibly forever.

"What businesses are closing? And how long do you think this thing will last?" Iesha asked, staring at the screen.

"Honey, did you hear what I just said?" her Dad asked, sounding worried. Iesha didn't say anything.

"I don't know how long this will last. The Foundry is shutting down, but they told me I could apply for unemployment. Hopefully, that will help keep us afloat. I don't know about your mom's job; she'll be home later today. Esh, please, come talk to me if you need anything, okay?" Her dad leaned over closer and gave her a light peck on the forehead. Iesha's reaction bothered him, but he couldn't force her to talk. All he could do was just be there for her.

"Look at the shutdown as a blessing in disguise," he said, watching her blank stare. "We get to spend more time together as a family. We've been advised to just stay home and be safe."

Iesha's dad left the room. *Stay home.* A break from school was just what she needed after seeing her best friend, possessed by a demon, kill another kid. She was afraid to run into him and even more afraid to tell her dad what she'd seen. Who would believe it? Lionel was possessed with a red-eye demon. He drained the life out of James; now, she would be placed inside a mental facility if she told it.

"Dad!"

"Yeah?"

"Does this shut down mean no one can go out at all? Like I can't go anywhere?" Iesha asked.

"Honey, I'm not comfortable with you hanging over anybody's house with this thing going on if that's what you're thinking? Plus, everything is closed. So, you really can't go anywhere but to the grocery stores. Doctors don't even know what this is, but they're saying it can possibly be fatal. Just wait til we have more information on what's going on."

Iesha released a long-held breath and said, "Okay."

With the distress she felt, she'd usually go for a walk to clear her mind. Moving meditation was always a good remedy. Iesha and Lionel would always take walks while discussing the latest project they'd be working on, downloading an app to create a cartoon or the latest video game strategies. But the idea of James being gone, murdered, was a hurt she couldn't shake. Iesha decided to pick up the laptop and go online. In the search engine, she typed: demon with red eyes. All that came up were mostly art-drawing sites and photography sites of models in Halloween monster costumes. Iesha saw a site called Oude Rode Ogen or Old Red Eyes.

"A Flemish bogeyman," Iesha smirked and kept reading. Her eyes scanned the words; witnesses spoke of seeing a naked black man stealing young girls and shapeshifting into a black dog with red eyes. Iesha decided not to continue the article.

"Racist crap, not what I'm looking for," Iesha muttered.

She deleted that search and typed: possessed human with red eyes. Mostly, similar sites as before came up. But nearing the end of one page, she scrolled down and saw one site that said Zar and clicked. She read the short article. Ancient demons or spirits were said to possess humans of all kinds, to wreak havoc upon the earth in the form of Chaos, known as Isfet; Lies, known as Mwongo; and Illness, known as Ugonjwa. While inhabiting the bodies they took, they would drain its usefulness, living upon the lifeforce until death. A Zar absorbed the soul, growing stronger, then roamed the earth, searching for another perfect flesh to inhabit. Ancient myths have said the Zar were known for their glowing red eyes and bodies of shadow, which easily seeps into the body they choose. Stories of the Zar have been passed among many African and Middle East regions, and some secret cults worship them today.

Iesha paused for a moment, feeling the chill rising within her spine. Could this be what is within Lionel? But why? And How? The article said it was three demons. Lionel was only one person she'd seen this way, unless two other people were taken, so who were the other two? Although this story sounded just as crazy as the Flemish bogeyman, it did make a little more sense. Iesha wanted to go to her dad, but she didn't want to hear what he'd say. After what she had seen and read, she wished there was a way she could speak to Lionel's grandmother without him around. She decided to call his house phone and see if his grandmother would answer. She grabbed her cellphone from the bed and dialed Lionel's house phone. His old school grandmother refused to get a cellphone because she felt it was like carrying radiation in her pocket. She would always complain about young people getting new diseases because of all these cellphones and other modern technologies. Iesha heard four rings; she was about to give up when someone answered.

"Is Miss Johnson available?" Iesha asked in a weak business-like tone. The silence on the other end worried her. She was prepared to impersonate a telemarketer if Lionel answered. She just prayed that it wasn't him. After a few seconds, someone spoke.

"Yes, this is she. Who's this?" Lionel's grandmother asked, sounding weary.

"Miss Johnson, please, if Lionel is home, please, do not say my name. It's Iesha." Again, there was a slight pause.

"Oh, Pastor Samuel! How have you been? You've been keeping safe with all that's going on?" Lionel's Grandma asked.

"Yes, ma'am. I've been staying safe. I've contacted you because, well, this may sound crazy, but I think Lionel is possessed by, um, evil," Iesha closed her eyes, thinking she sounded like an idiot telling his grandma this ridiculous information about her grandson.

"Yes, Pastor, I have to agree with you there. It's a lot of craziness going on. Not much we can do about it but read the Word of the good book. You don't know if the news is telling you lies or the truth these days. It can stress you so bad where it sucks the breath of life right out cha throat, mmm mmph," Miss Johnson spoke as though a great sadness took over her.

"Oh, my god. Do you know about Lionel having something to do with James?" Iesha whispered.

"Now, Pastor, ain't nothing to be done right now but to stay home and stay safe and my grandson and I are here together. I make sure we are taken care of. I just hate the church is shutting down. I was hoping to come to service next Sunday, but God is here every day in my heart."

"Thank you, Miss Johnson."

"All right, bye, Pastor."

Lionel's grandmother hung up the phone and turned to see Lionel standing in the doorway, watching her. She gasped and took in a deep breath but didn't say anything.

"I'm going out. Don't think that Pastor can do anything to help you. I will control him just as I control you, possibly suck the life right outta his throat," Lionel said, mocking her phone conversation.

"You don't have to worry 'bout me. As long as my grandson in that body somewhere, I won't go against ya. I know you won't let me speak to him. But can you, please, just tell him I love him?"

Lionel held a stone-cold face, lifted his head, and walked away.

#

Jay was sprawled on the floor of his cell, waving his arms and hands wildly in the air. He coughed and laughed, spitting out rap lyrics. The cell guard walked up to the cell bars and banged a few times to get him to be quiet.

"Man, shut the fuck up," the guard snapped.

Jay lifted his head and turned toward him. His face was smudged with mucus. He smiled with a dead look in his eye, coughed saliva in the air, and continued reciting his lyrics.

"I spread the breath of death. Once taken in, you will never be free. Oh, best believe, it's true. Ain't nothing you can do, but breathe til the very last drop of breath is gone. Oh, no! Oh, no!"

"Nasty ass nigga," The guard remarked.

Jay rolled onto his back, laughing hysterically as the guard walked away, shaking his head. The guard seemed to get the memo that trying to control a crazy person would only make him crazy in the process. Jay stopped laughing and held his breath. He looked at the ceiling, then flopped his arms to the floor after hearing a voice in his head.

Let me the fuck out!

"You will never get out! I'm gonna drain you til you're dust!" Jay yelled.

The guard looked back at Jay, ignored him, and continued walking away.

I'll find a way to get out of this; I swear! I'll—I'll. The voice threatened.

"You'll what? Do nothing, just like you did when I bit ya girl. Crying like a lil' bitch!" Jay laughed. "Oh, baby! Oh, baby, did I do that? I didn't mean to hurt you! With the amount of venom I put in her ass, she should be dead by now. So shut the fuck up, this my head, my body now!"

Jay began writhing on the floor, fighting with himself. His eyes shifted from red to normal brown in between the twisting and jerking movements. He jumped off of the floor and slammed himself into the wall. He fell back down, aching and breathing heavily. He remained there letting his body lie limp, and his eyes returned to normal. As he crawled off the floor, he felt every pain inflicted upon his body; he stumbled to the bars of his cell.

"Please, can I have my phone call? Please. I need to go to the hospital; it's an emergency!"

"Shut up, Michaels! You refused your phone call, remember!" the guard responded.

Shit. Jay turned around, leaning his back on the bars. He scanned the room. There was no way he was getting out of here before this being or whatever it was took him back over. He heard a thud outside the bars and turned around to see if he could see the guard from where he stood, but there was nothing. He heard footsteps coming closer, like the striking of heels. He backed away from the bars and waited. An attractive woman, dressed in red from her headwrap to her shiny shoes, came to his cell. Jay stared at her, confused because he had never seen her before. She walked closer to the bars and smacked her lips in disgust.

"Tsk, tsk, Ugonjwa. You let a human soul push you into the background; you are slipping, my brother. Maybe you do not deserve to be a part of the Zar any longer?" For a moment, he wanted to turn around to make sure she was talking to him.

"What are you talking about? Who are you? Who's oo-gon-ju-waa, and what is the Zar? Please, I need to get out of here! This is a mistake!" He slowly repeated the name she said, not sure if he was pronouncing it correctly. The woman smiled.

"Ugonjwa handled this," she responded.

Jay felt himself shrinking as though he was sinking into himself. Then he was gone. Jay's eyes glowed bright red, and the Cheshire cat smile emerged. He wheezed through his chest as though he was about to suffocate.

"You're weak and careless, Ugonjwa, but you have

done well spreading the sickness. The human body you have taken is strong, maybe stronger than you." The woman in red said.

"Never, Isfet! I was just fooling around. No human is as strong as I am. You know I like games," Ungonjwa/Jay responded. He glared at Isfet, trying to hide his doubt.

"Well, quit your games, for now. We must meet Mwongo and decide what we must do about a certain being here who can disrupt my plans." The woman in red placed her hand on the locked cell, and red electrical light was released and dispersed along the bars. The cell opened when Jay pushed. Isfet turned and walked away, and he followed.

#

Tree walked into Kale's front yard and sat on the steps, swinging her locs in front of her to the right side. The broken glass from the door remained on the porch, but the main front door was locked. Tree rested with forearms on her thighs and hands hanging off the edge of her knees, closed her eyes, taking deep breaths. She felt sad and worried for Kale and the others of this town who had no idea what forces they were dealing with. The sun's light pierced through the trees' branches, spreading its warmth through Tree's thick hair shaft. She lifted her head, exposing the rays to her face to absorb the light. It had rarely shown through the gloom since she'd been there. She slowed her breathing and began to feel lighter, calmer, centered. Taking a moment of soothing breaths always reminded her to stay focused on her purpose. After about twenty minutes, she opened her eyes and saw Tora sitting in front of her, staring with her head cocked to the side. Tree smiled, leaning her head in the same direction.

"Hello, my beauty, or should I say, warrior? You look well." Tora moved like a silent ninja toward Tree and let her rub long thin fingers behind her ears.

"Kale is doing better. She is weak, but she will live. The sickness she was carrying is similar to the mucus caused by the unhealthy lifestyles lived today, which contributes to inflammation and deterioration, but on a more extreme level. The venom from this consumes the body in weeks or days instead of the diseases one can develop over the years. What made it worse was that she was bitten, receiving contamination directly into her bloodstream. But from my observation, it can also spread like a common cold. You were also affected by attacking the young man, but I easily cleared it from your body because of your size. Honestly, I don't know how I will stop the spreading of this to an entire town. I know it can be done; I have complete trust in the power of the light, but I have to find out how and if I can." Tora sat back on her hind legs and looked back up at Tree as though she was hanging on to every word.

"I will find this place called Garden Pointe to check on Kale's children. But first, I have to find the Mother Oak. She can tell me how to stop this illness. A helpful soul said the oak was in a cemetery not far from here, so I must go the opposite way from before."

Tree rose and walked to the edge of the road to kneel near a patch of dandelions. Tora followed her and watched as she whispered to the plant and placed a hand on her heart. She blew seeds from the stems into the air. They rose like feathers, gliding through the wind, dissolving from sight.

"The dandelion will contact a friend to find me and show me the way. Until then, I will walk. My warrior, I need you to stay here. I have a feeling I will need your strength."

#

Lionel watched the woman walking down the road as ropelike hair swung behind her. Garden Pointe was the apartment complex on the other side of town. Lionel thought he'd do a neighborly thing and check on her children for her instead. His eyes glowed as he stepped away from the side of Kale's house, where he eavesdropped. He had watched Tree since the moment she came upon the porch, sickened by her pureness of heart but observing her to sense any form of weakness. He sensed none. But maybe, he could create one.

Walking to the front of the house, Lionel heard a loud hissing behind him. He turned and saw the bushy, black cat he'd seen before, glaring its sharp teeth. He was tempted to kill it. But he turned away instead, walked out of the yard, going to his own house. Omens followed the one who killed a cat, so it was best to leave it alone. He stepped up on the porch of his grandmother's house, finding the screen door unlocked. When he walked into the living room area, he saw his grandmother on the floor motionless, her complexion gray. The woman in red sat in a nearby chair. Jay was standing over the body and wheezing.

"Did you kill her, Isfet, or is she just suffocating?" Lionel asked unmoved but already knew the answer to his question.

Jay lifted the old woman's hand and watched as it dropped against the floor like a log, "Looks pretty dead to me." He laughed, letting saliva shoot out his mouth.

"I wished you wouldn't have done that. She was a pest, but she cooked wonderfully. My belly hasn't tasted such fulfillment in a long time," Lionel complained with no expression of care.

"Too bad it doesn't fulfill your whole body." Jay laughed.

"Quiet, Ngonjwa! I didn't come here to concern myself about your gluttonous ways, Mwongo. A light being is here, perhaps one of the strongest I've come across probably since the ancient time of Asar. She is a Green One who walks around like a lowly peasant, but she radiates the light of the brightest sun rays. Some part of me feels she doesn't know the level of potentiality she has, and it's our job to make sure she doesn't ever realize it. She can trigger a lot more light beings into the world simply by inspiring them with her presence, and we can't have that," Isfet spoke with calm intensity.

"How can we get rid of her if she's so powerful? I couldn't even get near her with those living antennas flying from her head; I think they sensed every move I made," Ugonjwa said.

"We will have to combine as one to take her on alone. But until then, Mwongo, you will turn the one who trusts her against her. She is an extraordinary returned being, but she is not invincible. Together, we can create enough chaos to destroy her." Isfet smiled.

"I know where to start," Lionel said, returning her smile. "Ugonjwa, I need you to drive the old woman's vehicle to Garden Pointe. Time to check on your children."

Chapter Eight – An Elder Speaks

"Lawd, Perry sick, too? I hear a lot of folks going through it. They say it's some kind of flu thang. All I know is I'm keeping my behind at home," Aunt Niecy stated over the phone. She was sitting on the couch, filling out a word puzzle, binging on the local news, scaring herself with the latest story while the kids played with toys on the floor.

"No, honey. They won't let me see her, not since she was first placed in there. When I called, they said she was doing better cause she's off the breathing machine now. It's probably for the best cause I'd hate to catch that sickness. I sho' hate to hear that about Perry, though. But I'm sure he's going to be fine; Perry's strong."

Hampton looked at his aunt, then rose from the floor to head for the kitchen.

"Shae, let me get off this phone. You know, I'll talk all day. But this nephew of mine 'bout to eat me out of house and home. Okay, all right. Take care, honey. I'm praying for y'all. All right bye, bye." Aunt Niecy placed the cellphone on the end table by her couch and rose to go after Hampton. He was standing with the refrigerator door opened, just staring inside.

"Baby boy, what are you doing? You just ate a turkey sandwich. You still hungry?" she asked, looking at him. He shook his head and closed the fridge. "You want some cold water?" she asked. He paused and nodded.

Aunt Niecy walked past him and grabbed a clean cup from the dish rack. Then took an ice tray from the freezer and twisted it, popping ice out, placing a few cubes in the cup. Aunt Niecy turned back to look at Hampton and saw that he was crying. Setting the ice down, she went to him, walking him back on the couch to sit for a moment.

With an arm wrapped around him, she asked, "You miss your mama, huh?" Hampton nodded before lying against her cushiony bosom. Davis looked up from her toys with sad eyes at her brother and auntie.

"I know, baby. But your mama is strong, and you're strong just like her. Everything is gonna be all right. She was just a lil' sick and needed the doctors to look after her just for a while. But when she gets out, she's coming straight to you and Davis."

"But when she's coming home, Auntie?" Hampton

asked.

"Soon, baby, soon."

There was a light knock at the door. Aunt Niecy and Hampton looked towards it. Aunt Niecy kept her cool so as not to frighten the children, but she was not expecting anyone to visit. *Lawd, who in the world is coming to bother me?* She walked to the door and looked out the peephole. It was a young, familiar-looking boy.

"Auntie, don't open it; it might be Daddy with the red eyes!" Hampton said, running over to grab Davis' hand.

"Baby, calm down. Your mama got you believing that fantasy mess, too? Aw, Lawd, it's just a boney little boy at the door. I think I know who this is." Aunt Niecy said, turning back around to unlock and crack the door open. She peered down at the young teen.

"I know you; you're Geraldine Johnson's grandson, ain't cha?" Aunt Niecy asked, wondering why this skinny little child was all the way over on her side of town. She wanted to offer him a jelly biscuit or two from the leftovers she and the kids had for breakfast but decided not to and find out what was going on first.

"Yes, ma'am, I was," Lionel responded with a smile.

"Was? Whatcha mean, baby? Geraldine passed?" Aunt Niecy asked. She remembered Geraldine as an extremely sanctified and kind lady who could cook her socks off. The meals she sometimes prepared and brought to church had everybody craving for more. But by the looks of this child, it looked as though he hadn't had the luxury of enjoying an ounce of her cooking.

Lionel held his head down a moment and looked back at Aunt Niecy with a crazed look in his eyes. "Yes, ma'am, she at home lying on the living room floor as we speak."

For a moment, Aunt Niecy stared, not believing what she'd heard. Lionel's face dropped in sadness, and undeniable pain filled his eyes. Aunt Niecy stared at Lionel with empathy, wanting to share her naturally caring ways by holding him. But as she continued watching him, his cries turned into wicked giggling.

"What in heaven's name?" Aunt Niecy gave a puzzling stare at a boy who had obviously lost his mind. "Baby, you stay out here. I'm going to call the police. They will be able to help you."

As she was closing the door to get away from Lionel's strange laughter, a hand stopped her from closing it. Her eyes stretched as she saw the source of what blocked her door; it was Jay. His horrid smell caused her to gasp. When she tried to push the door on him, he forced himself in, causing her to let go and back away. Lionel followed in behind him.

"Hey, Auntie, long time no see," Jay said with an eager look in his eyes, licking his bottom lip. Aunt Niecy backed away, giving him a quick distasteful look up and down.

"By the looks of thangs, it's good I haven't seen you in a long time; you could've kept yourself hidden. Now whatcha want? Kale ain't here." Aunt Niecy kept her eyes on him. From her peripheral vision, she could see the kids had moved from the spot they were sitting in before she answered the door. She hoped they'd stay hidden wherever they were.

"Aunt Niecy, you always did have a nice sense of humor. I can't help but feel that you've never liked me."

"Like?" Aunt Niecy forced a quick chuckle then frowned at Jay. "You run around on my niece and act like a damn fool that won't grow up. Don't help with your babies. Do you think that would qualify you to win an award for the most likable person of the year? Mmm?" Aunt Niecy asked, casting a questionable look.

"Oh, you got jokes." Jay sneered. "See, that's one thing I've always liked about you, Auntie."

"I ain't your damn auntie; busting in my house like

this. Whatcha want Jay Bird?" Aunt Niecy repeated.

"I want to see my babies. I know they're here." Jay glared at Aunt Niecy.

"They ain't here! Can't you see that? Now you and your starving Marvin compadre can leave. You stanking up my house!"

"She lies," Lionel spat. He stepped in front of Jay. His jaw dropped open, freakishly low, releasing numerous screaming voices. Aunt Niecy's closed her eyes in fright as her hands shot to her ears to block the sound. Blood slipped through her fingers as she fell to her knees in pain.

"Stop wasting time, Fool, and look in the back for those children," Lionel commanded Jay after reattaching his jaws.

"No, Jay! I said they ain't here!" Aunt Niecy was crying and crawling, attempting to rise from the floor. Lionel's eyes blinked, red instantly filled them. He stood directly in front of Aunt Niecy, now on her hands and knees, blocking her view of Jay. Lionel released a whirlwind scream once again, causing her to collapse back to the floor. He walked away and followed Jay to the backroom.

"Ngonjwa, did you find them?" Lionel saw Jay standing alone in the room with an opened window.

"I think they climbed out and ran. They must've left

as soon as they heard a knock on the door," Jay answered, staring at the window.

"Which means they couldn't have gone far. Let's go after them. Isfet wants them." Lionel's red gaze went to Jay, who still stared with normal eyes. Lionel glared at him.

"Why are you just standing here? Let's go. Or are you getting soft, Ngonjwa? You finally took a body more powerful than yourself. One that you can't fully control?"

Jay spat in disgust as saliva ran down his mouth. "Never!" His eyes gleamed back at Lionel with the same burning red intensity. They left Aunt Niecy on the floor of the apartment and went around the back to where the open window was to see if the children were hiding in nearby areas.

"These ground-level buildings are small, not that much to hide behind. So where could they be?" Lionel asked, walking away from Jay. He gazed back and forth.

"We just have to keep searching around the units until we find them. They are small children; they aren't that smart, it shouldn't take long to find them," Jay answered.

#

Aunt Niecy's dryer door opened, and a halo of fluffy black hair popped out. Hampton's big eyes scanned the room before he climbed, then turned to help his little sister. He left the small closet laundry space near his aunt's kitchen, holding Davis' hand. They tipped into the living room and saw their aunt unconscious on the floor. Davis ran to Aunt Niecy and shook her. But she wouldn't wake. "Auntie," she whispered with tears flowing. Hampton turned to see Aunt Niecy's phone on the side table by the couch and grabbed it. His small finger swiped across the screen, unlocking it, and touched the phone symbol. He saw numbers listed in the recent calls and pressed hospital contact to dial.

"H-Hello," Kale's voice was rough and scratchy, but she sounded a lot better than before.

"Mommy," Hampton called.

"Baby, is that you? It's so good to hear from you. How's Davis? Is she nearby?" Kale asked. She wanted nothing more in the world than to be with them.

"Yes, Mommy. Davis is here. Daddy came here, too," Hampton responded.

"What! Is he there now? Where's Aunt Niecy?" Kale asked with sudden panic. Hampton hesitated for a second. "Mommy, she's on the floor. They hurt her."

Kale jumped out of the bed and started searching for her clothes. "Baby, I want you to hang up and call nine-one-one. Remember how I taught you to do in emergencies. Grab Davis' hand and stay put. I'm coming."

Although Kale was still weak, she untied her hospital gown with the phone still to her ear. "Hampton, you hear me? Hampton!" Kale shrieked, not hearing her son anymore. Someone else responded.

"Hello, Kale. It's nice to speak to you again." A familiar woman's voice answered. Kale paused for a moment, trying to place it.

"W-where are my children?" Kale asked, no longer interested in who this woman was but whether she'd hurt her children or not.

"Do not worry, they are fine. But if you do not give me what I ask for, they will not be."

"I will give you anything you ask. I don't have much. You can have it all—whatever I've saved in the bank and my house. I'll do whatever you need me to; just don't hurt them. They're innocent." Tears streamed down her face. Kale was angry at herself for letting her children come to danger.

"Your worthless material goods hold no use or value to me. You already know what I want. Give up your life for theirs, and they go free."

Kale remembered her nightmare like a light switch turned on in her head. The boy from her neighborhood, Jay, and the woman in red. How did this woman invade her dreams? How did she find her children? How did she even know she had children? She had to have found out from Jay. Kale's cries came through on the phone. "Please, please, I'll give whatever to save them. Please, promise me you won't hurt them!"

"I don't make promises. You will know how to contact me when you want to see your children. Goodbye, Kale."

"Wait! Wait! No! Oh, God, nooo!"

#

Fully dressed, Kale grabbed the rest of her belongings and walked out of the hospital room. Spotting her nurse further down the hall, she took a breath, releasing tension, knowing the nurse would try to stop her. Kale continued anyway to exit the building.

"Ma'am, wait! I know you're feeling a lot better, but it's not time for you to be discharged just yet. Please, it's important for you to get back to bed. The police also want to talk to you about what happened in your room." The nurse called after Kale, trying to stop her.

Kale looked back and said, "My children have been taken by someone I don't know, and my aunt who was watching them may be seriously hurt. Nothing is keeping me here any longer." Kale rushed off, following the exit sign. She ran into the doctor and the police officer who came to her room the night Tree left.

"Wait, Ms. McCray! What's going on? You are not ready to be discharged yet," Doctor Anderson said, stepping into Kale's path. "This is Officer Thompson; he just wants to ask you a few questions. If you can, please, come back to your room."

"No way, man! My children need me. Now, please, move," Kale said, growing angry.

"Ms. McCray, we really need to find out what happened in your room. If you can..."

"I don't know what happened in my room; I was out of it. I had a freaking cough attack, and I can't remember much else. Before that, I felt like I walked across the room after having a nightmare. The vines, I don't know what to tell you, but I'm not staying here. Someone has threatened my children. I have to leave to go to them, and there is nothing you can do to stop me." Kale walked away from the officer and tried to pass the doctor. He placed his hands on her arms, trying to hold her. She gazed into his eyes with viciousness.

"Ms. McCray, please. You're still very sick. Let us help you," he said with genuine concern. He released her arms, taking a quick breath under her hard gaze. "Ms. McCray, what you have seems to be spreading to a lot of people here. Until we know what it is, we'd like for you to stay, please."

"Doc, you've taken all the tests you need from me. If you haven't figured it out yet, then that's on you. My babies need me."

Kale continued rushing past the doctor and officer and followed the signs until she reached the hospital's lobby. Looking around, Kale noticed almost everyone was wearing masks and an unusually large number of people being admitted to the facility. Kale walked outside and crossed through the parking lot, remembering she didn't have her phone and her van was still parked at the house. Aunt Niecy's apartment wasn't too far away, so she'd walked. Her mind was racing with where her children could be and the fact that this woman who took them didn't want money or anything, except her life. Not needing to think about her decision anymore—Kale had already made up her mind.

#

Tahj searched his phone and found the video he had of Tree and the woman in red. Kinte stood beside him, looking skeptical as Tahj pressed play to start. All he saw was Tree standing, staring off into space. He shook his head in doubt at the video, getting visually impatient with Tahj.

"Kinte, just keep looking, man," Tahj said, hoping

Kinte wouldn't turn away.

"Man, she ain't doing nothing. You're wasting my time. I could be…" Kinte's voice trailed off as he saw a woman in red appear then send lightning toward Tree. Tree's hair seemed to absorb it, sending it back toward the woman, but she vanished. Kinte scratched his head as he stared at the phone then looked at Tahj.

"See, see! Man, ha, ha! I told you her hair is alive. Now you believe me? Them joints lifted and flew in the air like, like a weapon or an octopus with twenty feet arms or something!"

Kinte chortled to himself, smiling. "Nigga, let me see that shit again; that was crazy." Tahj handed his phone back to Kinte. "Is this a trick video off on YouTube?" Kinte tried to make sense of what he was looking at.

"Hell, naw, fool! You looking at it from my videos on my phone. But I already uploaded it to my page. That was in westside cemetery a few days ago, man! You should see how many views it has already! You should have seen it in person; it was …" Tahj paused as a breeze blew around the two young men while they stood on Kinte's mother's porch. Kinte held his hand out and saw dandelion seeds blow through his fingers. They listened as faint voices spoke through the floating seeds.

"Sounds like whispers. Like someone calling. Aw, shit! Kinte, this some real spooky shit. Maybe she knows I just showed you this video!" Tahj said with worry spreading across his face.

"Calm down. I don't think you have to worry about that. I think it something else. I think she needs help." Kinte said, speaking softly whispering. "Come on, let's go. I'll call my mom later to let her know I took the car."

"So, you believe me, Kinte?" Tahj asked, grinning.

"All right, you ain't no simp. I got you, bro." Kinte responded, climbing into the car. He cranked it up, and they drove off.

#

Tree crossed over a railroad track and paused. She turned back to see a familiar medium-sized gold car approaching her. The car stopped in the road beside her, and the driver rolled down the tinted window. Tree saw Kinte, giving her a friendly smile.

"Need a ride, my friend?" he asked.

Tree flashed a bright gorgeous smile and walked up to the car. She gave a silent thanks to the dandelions for helping her contact them quickly, so she could move faster to find the Mother oak tree. Tahj climbed out of the passenger seat and called over to her, "Tree, come and take my seat in the front."

Tree nodded and got in. "Thank you, brother."

"No problem, queen," Tahj responded, climbing into the backseat.

They drove further down and made a few turns, looking as though they were on their way out of the city. Kinte realized which cemetery Tree was looking for after giving them the description she had received of it. He hadn't been there since his grandfather was buried there years ago. His grandfather would take him to the farmer's market next to the cemetery to get the best-tasting watermelons the city was famous for.

"Tree, in the summertime, you gotta try a watermelon from here," Tahj said. Kinte gave him a scolding look through the rearview mirror, making him think about what she told them and their family earlier.

"Oh, sh-, my bad. You don't eat watermelon neither, Tree?"

"No, my brother, I do not. But when I used to eat it, I did enjoy it. So, I appreciate your enthusiasm for such a healthy food," Tree said, smiling at him through the passenger side mirror.

"You mind if I ask you something?" Kinte glanced at Tree then looked back to the road.

"You can ask me whatever it is you like, brother," Tree responded, looking back at him.

"Is there some sort of meaning or secret behind your hair? I mean, is it alive?" Kinte asked.

Tahj scowled at Kinte for starting the conversation he was interested in, then glanced to Tree, curious as to what she was going to say. Tree laughed to herself.

"Yes, it is alive." Tahj's eyes grew bigger with the confirmation that he was right. He was amazed that she admitted it.

"So, you have like some sort of magical hair that can move when it wants to, like moving your arm?" Tahj interjected, making Tree laugh again.

"Brother, I have been on a long journey of self-realization, and part of that journey was disciplining my body and unlocking inner keys to my subconscious. As my thought patterns were freed from the waking dream, I began to have abilities that one would say defy normal constraints. I was shocked at first, maybe even afraid, but I knew I had to continue the changes I was going through.

My hair grows tightly, as you can see, and the tighter the spiral, the more the spiritual energy moves through me, literally causing my hair to come alive and move. My hair formed like the branches of a tree, gaining an awareness like a powerful nervous system outside of my body until it could sense all that I felt within and out. I know to others hair is just dead matter, but why is it affected by the nutrients we take into our bodies, why is it affected by the stress or peace we feel, why does it grow? Living things grow, not dead things. I respect other's opinions. But for me, hair is very much alive; and in my case, even more so."

Tree smiled to herself in reflection. "There was a time when I used to be bothered by the things people would say until I realized this hair was a blessing and my crown. It's part of my purpose. Everything about who I am, including this hair that tightens to form little balls along my hairline, is a gift from the stars to protect me, to attune me, and to connect me to the All."

Kinte and Tahj were quiet, listening to Tree's soothing voice. Tahj broke the silence. "Man, and I thought it was just hair."

"It is, brother, and so much more." Tree said.

"That's deep. I know you said your religion is life, but did you learn what you just said from any kind of book, like um, um?" Tahj asked, looking from Tree to Kinte, snapping his fingers as though that would restore his memory.

"What, like the Bible?" Kinte asked, glancing at him.

"Yeah, or like, um, that Indian spiritual book the Bhagavad Gita or the Torah; you know, a Scripture or something," Tahj said.

"No, what I speak, you can feel it and see it in nature. Books are wonderful guides and teachers, but most of what I live by comes from experience, life, and my innate wisdom."

Tahj wanted to ask more, but they passed by the farmer's market. They could see from the road there weren't many vendors at this time of the day. Kinte pulled into the entrance of the cemetery.

"We are here, Ethel Cemetery. What are we looking for?" Kinte asked.

"There," Tree answered, pointing to the far end corner of the cemetery away from the entrance.

Located at the far end of the cemetery was an oak tree with a trunk as wide as the size of a small storage shed. Its massive branches were so heavy that some grew out, almost touching the ground. Kinte drove onto the dirt road alongside the outside of the graves, circling the area where the tree was located. As they came closer, they gawked at the vastness of its makeup.

"Good God, that's a big tree!" Tahj leaned out the back window to get a full view as they drove closer. Kinte parked, and everyone got out of the car.

"It looks like it's gotten way bigger since the last time I saw it; it's like it doesn't stop growing. Tree, is this what you're here for? To see a tree?" Kinte asked.

Tree looked at him with calmness. "Yes," she answered, walking up to the tree trunk. Its size seemed to swallow her as she approached it. She gleamed as she held her head up to take in its beauty. She placed both palms onto the trunk and saw different visions the elder tree had experienced. The visions hit her so strongly that she pulled away for a moment in surprise. She peeked back at the trunk then placed her hands on its bark. She saw native rituals, funerals, families embracing and crying, then bright, beautiful days, and treacherous storms. She saw tortured stolen life hanging from its branches, and she saw a time when there was nothing in this area but untouched green life.

Tree stepped back in silence. Her eyes teared as she looked at the tree. Confused by her actions, Tahj walked up beside her, checking to see if she was okay. She looked at him and answered without him even questioning, "Brother, it's okay. This is an ancient elder, and I must connect with it. She holds heavy memories that even I can't fathom. Please, for your safety, stand back for a moment. I am going to hide us in a sacred dimension so as not to be seen. But you and Kinte must remain quiet no matter what. Do you understand, my friend?" Tree asked, looking back at him.

Tahj nodded, even though he was still a bit cautious. He backed away and then went to stand beside Kinte, who had walked closer to get a better look at what was going on. Kinte furrowed his brows at Tahj, but Tahj just shrugged because he didn't understand what was going on either.

Tree found a spot in between the tree's large roots where she could sit with ease and feel the earth. Removing her sandals, Tree crossed her legs in a lotus position and placed her hands with palms up on her thighs with her thumbs meeting her pointer fingers. Tree took a deep breath and closed her eyes. Elongating her neck and spine, she tilted her chin, concentrating deeply on long inhales and exhales. A light greenish golden glow began to emit from around her.

Tahj and Kinte looked at each other in amazement, then looked back at Tree. After about a minute or so. Tree's long thick locs slithered around her and intertwined with the tree's roots. Tree's skin began to morph into a texture similar to the oak she sat with. Her eyes opened, emitting a green glow. Tahj and Kinte grew nervous and looked around to see if anyone was around them to witness what they were seeing. They were far off from the main road entrance, and they didn't see anyone else in the cemetery. They looked back to

Tree and noticed a spreading shimmer began to manifest all around them like a shield. It was as if small stars filled the air like numerous shiny light bugs. It spread to the tree and out as far as to where they stood, surrounding them. The sky within the shimmer appeared in beautiful shades of pink, orange, and wine, and through the floating stars, it was as though they stood in a light mist. Beyond it, the sky and everything else appeared normal. But within, they could hear unusual noises like voices whispering and see brightly colored insect-like creatures fluttering that they had never before seen. Tahj looked at Tree and saw her still sitting in the center of it all as though nothing had changed.

Tree held her head up and looked at the oak's massive branches. The atmosphere now was dreamlike. She watched the light particles floating through the air for a moment, then glanced back and saw Tahj and Kinte staring at her. She nodded toward them with bright green eyes, letting them know everything was okay. She then began to speak.

"My great elder, I need your guidance. I was told by the green spirits that I could ask you of your knowledge of the fleshless ones that have come to this place. Can you help me find a way to stop the spreading of a sickness the fleshless ones have brought to these dear people here?"

Tree sat and waited; then she heard cracking and deep moaning. Tahj jumped, startled by the loud cracking sound. Kinte frowned at him. He was just as nervous, but he hoped Tahj wouldn't trip out again like before when they first met Tree. They looked back at Tree and the oak. Some of the bark began to fall away, two spaces lifted, and Tree saw large piercing olive green eyes staring down at her. Tree brought her hands to her heart's center in prayer and nodded toward the oak. Tahj and Kinte stared, trembling in shock as a low grumble sounded and more bark fell where a mouth formed into the large trunk. A slow deep, old, feminine voice, like a grandmother, began to speak.

"I—have not—seen—one of your kind—in ages." The old oak muttered.

"My great elder, there are more returned humans like me, rising from the waking dreams every day," Tree stated.

"Yes—yes. But you are different. You are very— very—strong." The oak paused for a moment longer with the spaces between her words, causing Tree to gaze up.

"Yes—you—have a great—great—responsibility being so highly in tune. Through my deep expanding roots— I have experienced many things—some beautiful—some very—painful—but your presence has given me hope—for all life."

"Thank you, my great elder," Tree said. "I've come for your guidance. There are beings here that are trying to destroy hope for all. They intend to control and destroy the balance. I must prevent this."

"The ones you seek, yes—the Africans from the east—to the west—then brought here—spoke of—the Zar— they consume souls of those—they inhabit—and cause destruction—around them. They are darkness—the other side of your light—but unbalanced." The oak fell silent for a moment. Tree sat, waiting, then looked around, seeing the green spirits flashing lights amongst the grass, whispering.

"She will awaken soon. You must give her time, Green One," they said.

"It is fine. I know she is very tired. I am grateful for whatever knowledge she shares with me." Tree smiled. The moaning began again, and Tree saw the oak open her eyes.

"You—In you—I sense a shift coming," the oak said.

"What do you mean, my elder?"

"Are you—forty-three years old?"

Tree was amazed that she correctly guessed. Usually, people incorrectly guessed her age and thought her to be younger than she was.

"Yes, how did you know?"

"I can read—the quality of your skin. Humans in this

day—sometimes hurt themselves—with their fast lives—and stress place upon them. You are actually—aging perfectly. Today—humans think forty-three is old—but that is just the beginning—of scratching the surface—of who you are—your purpose."

Tree nodded, listening patiently.

"The younger plants here—their roots—connect me to all underground—to all of this city—tell me of this sickness—that the Zar spreads. When you experience your shift—you will be able—to plant your roots—connect to all below—and release spores into the air—that will float further than the dandelion seeds—and it will heal all touched—by the sickness. No matter how far it has traveled."

Tree looked puzzled. She had never been aware of another shift she would be going through since becoming a sun traveler.

"Elder, when will this shift occur?" she asked.

"Same as the others you have—experienced—on the reoccurrence—of the time and day you passed through the portal of life—you will be the sacred forty-four—old studies of the mystics—they discovered the shifts—of master numbers in light beings—beginning at age eleven. Eleven is the observer—the heightened intuition—then again at age twenty-two—the builder, the organizer—thirty-three—the elevation of consciousness, true universal love, and supernatural physical abilities—and the last and most powerful—the age of forty-four—complete master state—the energy flow—inside of you—to plant roots further than even I could imagine. You will be able—to contain the darkness of the Zar—without letting it taint your light."

Tree held her head down, thinking. She didn't place much emphasis on birthdays anymore, but she was aware of numbers holding significant vibrations. Tree noticed before how easily she could shift from the spirit realm to the physical realm and see through dimensions at will. Turning forty-four, made Tree wonder of what more power she had within herself. It was an honor to serve and protect humanity, but it was also a great weight. Tree looked back to the oak.

"Thank you, great elder. All I can do is serve the people here until I can contain the Zar. Is there anything I can do for you? You've given me much knowledge to think about and much to meditate on until the anniversary time of my born day."

"All I want is peace—and I know that is your goal—for us all." The Great Oak's voice faded away along with her facial features.

Tree's skin smoothed back to its dark chocolate

shade. She lifted her locs with her hands, tugging them from the tangled roots of the oak, and swept them to her right shoulder. She raised her hands into the air then swept her palms together with one clapped. The sound energy of her hands released a vibration that melted the alternate dimension away. The vibration spread from the oak back to where Tahj and Kinte stood. The two young men looked around, realizing they could now hear the sound of cars driving by the street. Tree placed her palms on the earth, lifting herself to stand.

Tahj and Kinte watched Tree rise; then she walked toward them. The sky was darkening again, and the wind was picking up.

"What was that? What just happened?" Tahj asked.

"Dimension shift. When times call for it, I'm better able to shift and communicate with beings that exist, but the physical eyes cannot see," Tree answered.

"You just spoke to a tree, and it spoke back. And— and—and the sky changed and—I feel like I need to be admitted to a home," Kinte said.

"No, my friend. You are not crazy, and you are always home within your physical body; it's just that there is more to you than the physical you see. Life is everywhere; it is spirit; it is all. And now I know what I must do." Tree said.

"I'm glad because this weather out of the blue just started to look suspect," Kinte stated. "This is just wild."

Tree nodded. She realized them seeing what she allowed them to see was extraordinarily mind-boggling. Still, she didn't have much time and needed to take a chance on having others she felt she could trust. She looked to them, knowing they were good at heart. "Thank you both for your help."

"No problem, Tree," Tahj said in awe. He looked to Kinte and spoke beyond the whispered tone he meant, "Man, I wish I would have gotten that on video!"

Kinte cut him a sharp look. "What?" Tahj responded.

"Come on, Tree. We'll take you to where you live. This weather looks like it's gonna be an issue real soon." Kinte said.

They all climbed back into the car and drove off.

"Brother, can you take me to Garden Pointe?" Tree asked Kinte.

"Garden Pointe Apartments? Yeah, sure," he answered.

"You live all the way over there?" Tahj asked, "it's on the other side of town."

"No, I have family that needs to be checked on."

Chapter Nine – Lost Hope

Kale rode home in silent anguish in the back of a police officer's car. She got out of the car without saying a word and walked away. After sitting on her porch steps and watching the police car drive off, she buried her face in her hands, bawling. She felt something soft rub against her arm, looked down to her side and saw Tora's big green eyes staring back at her. Tora moved closer and rubbed her head against her arm once more. Kale reached out a shaky hand and ran her fingers down Tora's back.

"Tora!" Kale gasped through tears, glad that the old cat was okay.

"Thank you, old girl," Kale muttered. She had to get up and go in the house and wait until she heard from the police for any updates, but she had a feeling they were not going to be able to find out anything nor get her children back. What she was dealing with was supernatural. The woman who stole her babies could invade her dreams.

Maybe that's how she found them. Maybe Kale couldn't blame it all on Jay; it was her fault as well. All Kale knew for sure was that if she didn't find them and get them back, she might as well be dead. Kale couldn't bear the thought anything happening to her children. Why didn't Tree go to check on them like she promised? Maybe she could have gotten them away before anything happened. Now her aunt was the one in the hospital and possibly infected with the same disgusting sickness she had.

Kale had no one to count on. All she had was herself, and she had to figure out what to do. She thought of Lionel, the boy from her dream, and remembered his grandmother lived not far from her. Lionel's grandmother may be dealing with similar issues with her grandson as she had dealt with Jay. So, she couldn't just sit and do nothing. She placed fingers over her eyes and wiped away the lasts few tears, then rose. She looked down toward Tora again with bloodshot eyes.

"Thank you again, Tora, for protecting us and my mama's house. I'm going to find my babies," Kale said, giving Tora a final rub between her ears. Tora purred, pressing her head into Kale's hand.

Kale stepped with her boots cracking onto the shattered glass as she went to unlock the front door. Pushing it open, she entered as if she was afraid someone was inside, but she saw no one. Flashing images of the attack flooded her mind; she snapped her eyes shut to keep from seeing them. Distraught, she hurried back outside and locked the door back up. She went over to her van, climbed in, and cranked it up. Pulling out of the driveway, she took one last glance at Tora in her seated position, staring back at Kale with knowing eyes. Kale pulled off with two destinations in mind, Lionel's grandmother's house, and Jay's old apartment.

#

Kale parked on the side of the road in front of Lionel's house then switched off her van lights. She tiptoed onto the unlit porch in an unsuccessful attempt to minimize the sound of the creaks, which was unavoidable for a house of this age. She could tell by the wood it had been a long time since any maintenance was done. Knocking on the screen door, she waited with no answer. She pulled the screen door open to the front door, found it unlocked and cracked. She pushed it open and went inside. The house reeked of rotten garbage and something else. Kale grabbed a face mask she had in her pocket, then turned her head to the right toward the living room area and gasped, on the verge of puking. Lying in the middle of the living room floor was Lionel's grandmother's decomposing body, still staring with a frightful expression. Kale figured it was the woman in red, working through Lionel. She controlled Lionel just as she controlled Jay. What would happen if she gave this woman her body? Would she really let her children go, or would they be in even more danger, possibly killed? Interrupting her thoughts, Kale heard a sound coming from further back in the house. She looked around to see if she could grab something to use as a weapon because she was not walking away to hide. Nothing was going to keep her from getting her children back.

Kale saw the kitchen area ahead of her and tiptoed toward the doorway, leaning near the counter to slide a knife out of a knife holder. Then crept back to the living room, ignoring the horrid smell, and headed to the back bedrooms. She walked to the first bedroom door and pushed. It creaked open, and she saw a crisply made bed and wooden dresser. The walls were plastered with old wallpaper and a faded framed picture of a pale Jesus. It had a stale mothball smell. Kale deduced it must be Lionel's grandmother's room. She only knew of old folks who still used mothballs and kept a blue-eyed Jesus photo on their walls.

Kale stepped further back and pushed the door open to the next bedroom, knowing it was a teenage boy's room.

Posters of Kobe Bryant, Black Panther, and Avatar Aang were on the wall. Kale walked further in. From behind the door, something swung out, almost hitting her but missing, causing her to jerk back. She almost dropped the knife but then strengthened her grip, holding up her arm, ready to stab whoever was trying to hit her. The person ran toward the window, and Kale stuck her foot out, tripping whoever it was down to the floor. As the person flipped over, Kale lunged down. She was about to bring the knife down to scare more so than kill. The last thing she wanted to do was harm someone, but she would defend herself if needed. She looked under the person's grey hood and saw the wide eyes of a teenage girl. The girl threw her hands up.

"Please, don't kill me! Please!" she screamed. Kale stared at the girl for a moment, then glanced at her hand with the knife. She released the breath she had been holding and came back to herself. Kale lowered her hand and rose.

"What are you doing here, kid? I could've killed you!" Kale snapped, sliding her mask down, trying to calm her breathing from the rush of adrenaline.

"M-my friend Lionel, something is wrong with him. I was only over here to speak to his grandmother, but I saw her on the living room floor...dead. I—I—I was only looking through his things to find anything that could link me to what happened to him." The girl's eyes shifted to the knife Kale held then back at Kale. Kale returned her suspicious gaze.

"I didn't hurt her. I was friends with Ms. Johnson, and Lionel is my best friend! You can ask anyone in our school. If—if –it—they were open!" the girl said.

"Calm down, stop stuttering, kid," Kale said, motioning with a hand to tone down the volume of the girl's shrieking voice. "What's your name? And what happened to Lionel?" Kale already had an idea of what happened to Lionel. It was probably the same possession that had taken over Jay, but she wanted to hear from someone else to further confirm what she saw in her dream. Maybe to confirm so she wasn't alone in all this.

"I'm Iesha," she responded. Iesha hesitated, knowing what she was about to say sounded crazy. But Ms. Johnson believed her, so maybe this lady could, too. "I think Lionel was possessed," she blurted. Kale turned her head and looked down, then gazed back at Iesha, pressing her lips together. Iesha knew this woman was going to think she was crazy now.

"I believe you."

Iesha's shoulders dropped as her mouth released air. "Oh, my God! You believe me?"

"Yes. The same thing happened to my ex. I think they are working together. I believe ..." Kale's eyes became watery, and her voice was stifled by pain. She paused and swallowed, taking a breath; now was not the time for tears. "I know they helped this woman kidnap my children. Somehow, she controls them."

"Oh, my God! So, it is them!" Iesha exclaimed more to herself than to Kale. Kale looked at Iesha, frowning, wanting to know what Iesha was referring to.

"What do you mean? Them?" Kale asked, staring.

"I was doing research, and I found articles online talking about a group of entities, demons, whatever you want to call them, called the Zar, or the Red Eyes. Stories of them have existed throughout the ages, and they only come together as one when a light being, whatever that is, is to become a master. They exist in varying degrees throughout the world in the form of lies, illnesses, and chaos, but they come together as one to destroy the light being that is soon to complete a shift. They take bodies for their use and consume their souls while inside. You will know them by the red glow of their eyes, and it's three of them. Lionel was acting weird, and then I saw his eyes change. It scared me to death. I only figured that maybe if there are three of them, then there must be two other people who would be acting similar. You've just confirmed to me there are!" Iesha said with a weird mixture of excitement and fear.

Kale was quiet for a moment, taking in all of what Iesha said. As much as Tree talked about light, she had to be this master who had caused the Zar to come. If it weren't for Tree, none of this probably would have happened. Further anger rose inside of Kale.

"Ma'am, so, you think they caused this sickness and possibly all this stormy weather we've been getting over the past few days?" Iesha asked.

"You don't have to call me that. I'm Kale. But, yeah, I think so. I was suffering in the hospital from it." Iesha's worried eyes stretched, and she took a step back. Her dad was going to be angry she snuck out of the house and even more so when he found out she had been exposed to the sickness.

"No, I don't have it anymore. I'm not contagious, but you really need to go home. I'm sure your parents would be worried if they knew you were here with what is going on."

"Yeah, I snuck out. One of my classmates, James, he's this … was this bully at my school. This thing inside of Lionel killed him. Everyone thinks it was this sickness, whatever the hell it is, but I saw it with my own eyes. I—I just really want to help. But I don't know if it's even Lionel anymore when I see him, ya know?"

"Yeah, I feel you. Jay, my ex, is the father of my kids; whatever is in him has helped this woman take them, and they hurt my aunt. Look, I don't know what can be done to stop all of this, but what I do know is I don't want anyone else getting hurt. Leave, call the police to come here. I need you to go home and stay safe."

"Kale, you need someone of the Light to stop the Zar. I don't know what that means exactly but look," Iesha said. She pulled out her phone and pulled up YouTube. This is *Mysteries and Myths,* one of those sci-fi shows that talk about ancient stories. They had an episode on the Zar that came out a few years ago, but they talked about these light beings, too. Their details were slightly different, but they were basically saying the same things as those sites I googled. They talked about everyone being made of light and how some humans are born able to activate that light in their lifetimes to its fullest potential. With that activation, they can do all this supernatural stuff. Look at this," Iesha said, pulling up another video. "This was uploaded a few days ago."

Kale grew impatient, but she looked anyway. It was a video of Tree and the woman in red. Kale felt her body tense as she watched Tree look as though she directed lightening with her hair. All Kale ever saw her do was turn into a tree, which was an amazing feat in itself, but she'd never seen her use her powers as a weapon. It made her wonder how she handled Jay the night of her attack.

"This is wild but, I've never seen anything like this. It looks so real; honestly, it looks like that area up near West town. Have you met someone like her?"

"Maybe," Kale said. Iesha's face lit up, and even more questions came to mind.

"Hold on! If this all-powerful light being is really here, this person is the reason my children are kidnapped, the reason these Zar demons are here, and none of this sickness would happen if the Zar weren't after her," Kale said, turning to walk away. She grabbed the doorknob and saw her aura. It was dull and small. She was filled with too much anger to care.

"So, it's a she?" Iesha asked, going after Kale. "Wait! She can stop all of this and possibly get your children back. Is it this woman in the video?"

Kale spun around with hurt in her eyes and commanded, "Iesha, call nine-one-one and go home. Now, before it gets too dark and anything else happens. You're a kid; it's not safe for you."

"But, Kale, light beings help people. It's their job to

serve. Shitty stuff happens everywhere; pardon my Portuguese. But whoever she is, she came here for something good, and these demons are trying to wreck it. Is she your friend?"

"Not anymore! Go home, kid!" Kale walked off the porch and went back to her car. Iesha held up her phone and dialed. As she called to report information about Lionel's grandmother, she watched Kale drive off.

#

"You sure you going to be okay with us just dropping you off? I don't mind waiting," Kinte asked Tree before she got out of the car.

"Yeah, Tree, it's getting late," said Tahj. Tree smiled.

"Thank you, brothers. How about when I find the place I am looking for, I will give you the okay to leave?"

"Cool," Tahj confirmed.

Tree climbed out of the car and walked from the front parking lot further into the complex. She didn't know where Kale's children were located, so she walked onto the curve and kneeled into the grass. Placing a palm into the ground, she closed her eyes. Tree concentrated and slowed her breathing until she began hearing faint whispers coming to her.

"You have a lot of hair!" exclaimed a wispy white-haired elderly lady watching Tree. The whispers descended into the background, and Tree opened her eyes. The elder held a curious Bichon Frise on a lease by her side, staring at Tree with excitement.

"Why are you on the ground, honey? You're gonna get dirt in your pretty hair and stain your knees. You looking for something?" The woman's blue eyes twinkled through her furrowed face, complementing the curious stare of her furry friend.

"Yes, my sister, I am looking for my friend's two small children who were temporarily staying here." Tree replied, standing to face the elderly woman.

"Oh, I hope you're not talking about those children's pictures I saw on the news this morning." The woman's kind eyes saddened.

Tree looked concerned. "What happened?"

"The lady who lives in building twelve-thirty-three over there in the back," the elder said, pointing a thin finger to another building ahead of Tree to the right. "Someone broke in her unit and attacked her and took her grandbabies. The mama was out here with the police looking for them, but they didn't find them. They said on the news they may have been taken by the father who had broken out of jail."

Tree's hand went to her heart, and worry came to her eyes. *Maybe I shouldn't have let Jay go.*

"I felt so bad. I heard the mama screaming and carrying on. I lost a child a long time ago. Well, he was grown when he passed. But there's no pain like the loss of your baby. If I see anything or hear anything, I'd like to help her," the elder said. Her dog barked at Tree. "Calm down, Snowy! It looks like my Snowy likes you. If Snowy likes you, I know you have a kind soul because Snowy doesn't like anybody. Are you family to them?"

Tree gave a forced smile to the elderly woman and her dog. She kneeled and rubbed Snowy behind the ears. Then stood and faced the tiny elder. Not only did their temperaments match, but Snowy's fur color was similar to the elder's hair. It was as though they were made for each other.

"Thank you. Um, yes, I am. I'm sorry. I have to go," Tree said, walking away.

"Oh, honey, it's all right. Take care. I hope they find those two babies."

Tree walked back to where Kinte and Tahj were sitting in the car. She climbed back into the passenger side and sat in silence.

"Tree, are you okay?" Kinte asked. "Did you find

what you were looking for?"

"No, my brothers. My heart is heavy. Two small children I was supposed to check on for my friend in the hospital are missing. They were staying here."

"Oh, man! I heard about that on the news this morning. I had no idea that's why you wanted to come here. We can help you look for them. Are there any leads as to who may have taken them?" Tahj asked.

Tree was silent for a moment then answered, "Yes, I have a lead, but I cannot ask you to help me. I need you and brother Kinte to take me back to the area where you first met me. I must go back to my friend's house and wait."

"Wait?" Tahj repeated. "Why would you wait? We can help you."

"Tahj, the people who have taken those children are pure darkness. They will take your body at will and consume you, and I cannot put you in danger like that. Plus, this sickness makes it even more dangerous for you to be around others. Please, take me to where we met and go home." Tree sounded calm and stern.

Tree could see in Tahj's eyes that he did not like her plan, but he respected her wishes and nodded. "It's that lady in the red from the cemetery, huh?"

Tree took a few moments to answer him. They all

listened to the sound of the car cranking and pulling off before she answered, "She's the cause of it, but I think their father physically took them."

#

They drove back through the town, barely speaking, and noticed how visibly the city streets were empty. It was only after 7:00 p.m. But there were barely any cars out, and most of the businesses they passed were closed. When they reached the area, right before where Tree met Kale, they saw flashing blue lights further up an adjacent road.

"What the hell happened here?" Tahj asked. "Whose house is that?"

"I don't know," Kinte answered.

"My brother, you can let me out here, coming up on the right." Tree directed him, bringing Kinte's attention back to driving. He pulled up into the driveway. Tree turned to look at them.

"I know this is a lot to take in, seeing the oak and knowing of the forces I have to deal with, but it's my way of protecting you. It's my honor and job to serve you and others. Soon, you will understand all I am doing."

"Well, I'll be honest, you're a different kind of person, but you seem like cool people. I just hope your friend finds her children," Kinte stated.

"Yeah," Tahj agreed, "Just call. Do you even have a cell phone?" Tahj asked, switching thoughts.

"No, my brother. I do not carry a phone, but if I need your help, I will be able to contact you," Tree said with a twinkle in her eyes. "Thank you both."

Tree rose from the passenger side and walked around the car to the porch. Then watched them pull out the driveway and head down the road. Tree hadn't thought much of her birthday since her last shift at age thirty-three years old. During that time, she remembered a change within, where her abilities became stronger, and she developed a more supernatural approach. Tree could feel a shift coming closer then, but now she felt nothing. She had never been aware of the forty-fourth shift, but the oak told her she'd be able to stop the sickness from spreading once it happened, as well as contain the Zar's unbalance. So, she'd welcome the change when the time came.

She walked onto the porch and saw the shattered glass still there. She saw Kale's van was gone but decided to try the front doorknob, anyway, and found it locked. She could easily get inside but decided not to. She knew the fleshless ones of the Zar had to have a reason for taking Kale's children, but she wasn't sure why, unless they wanted something from Kale. She sat down on the outdoor sofa by the front door and decided to wait for Kale to come back.

#

Kale pulled into the parking lot of Hadley Grove Apartments and stared at the large crowd of young people partying and doing only God knew what else. It was the weekend, and Hadley Grove was always filled with the most noise then. Kale was just as young as the majority of the people here but the bass was already bringing on a headache. Her mother would always remind her of her old soul. Kale let out a rough breath, questioning why she was even at Hadley Grove. Knowing the police were looking for Jay, she had a thought that maybe there was a chance he had come home, even after the cops told her they didn't find anything here. She got out of the car and mentally prepared herself to head through the crowd.

"Pssss," one guy said as she passed by. "Ah, baby, you ain't gonna talk?"

"Talk about what? How you hissing at me like I'm a snake instead of greeting me like a normal human being?" Kale asked, glaring back at the young man. He was leaning his large body on the front end of a car. She felt a small amount of her Aunt Niecy's feisty tone coming out of her and knew she had to do what she came to do, whatever it was, and leave before she had a run-in with someone.

"Aw, man," he replied, holding his hands out to his sides, shaking his head.

Kale ignored him and continued through the stares and comments to the inside of Jay's apartment building and walked up the stairs to door 9-B. She knocked, but there was no answer. A neighbor, a young brown woman with long beautiful braids, across the hall, cracked her door and peeked outside. She saw Kale, reaching for the doorknob.

"Don't nobody live there." Kale turned around to look at her speaking through her mask. "After they found out he was arrested and spreading that disease, the landlord put an eviction letter on the door. Somebody tore the letter down, but it was cleaned out yesterday. I saw them throw his shit out; it was a filthy mess."

Kale pulled her mask down from her nose to be able to breathe and talk better.

"Have you seen him since they put him out?"

"Naw, I ain't seen him; don't wanna see him. I ain't tryna get sick. You might want to ask them dumb-ass folks hanging outside that don't seem to care if they get sick or not. And the police ain't no damn help. They claim it ain't enough police to handle this shit, so they just try to keep the peace. They got a weird definition of peace. Every weekend I got to hear this noise." The young woman smacked her lips in disgust and lowered her hand in defeat.

"They say that dude ran off and kidnapped his kids. I feel for his little kids, though, putting up with his stanking ass. He ain't used to be so bad; used to be cool people. But lately, he's been a different person. You friends with him?"

"Yeah, those are our children they say he took," Kale said.

"Oh, damn! I'm sorry," The young woman's eyes stared deep into Kale's. "Well, I hope you get his ass or get him some help. I know you going through it. I'd kill somebody over my kids."

"Thanks," Kale said.

"Mm, mph," she responded. "Mama! Mama!" yelled a child in the background.

"Y'all shut up that noise!" The young woman looked behind herself then looked back to Kale. "Take care," she said, closing the apartment's door.

Kale felt alone standing in the hallway. She didn't even know what she expected to find by coming here. She began to feel as though she was just wasting time. And the more time that passed, the more time her children spent in the hands of the woman in red. She released the breath she'd held and looked at Jay's apartment door, frowning. Strangely, the door was cracked. Kale placed her hand on the door and pressed it opened. Her nostrils were consumed with the stifling smell that made her somewhat dizzy. She looked down the hall on both ends, saw no one, then pulled her mask back up over her nose and walked inside.

Once inside, she stepped on clumps of trash and garbage strewn across the floor. The room was dark and unusually cold for an April night. The wind blew in from an open window, and Kale could hear the music and noise from the partying outside. She looked around and saw Jay's phone on the floor with a shattered screen and went to pick it up. She pressed the *on* button, but it was dead. She looked toward the dark kitchen area and saw a shadowy figure in the corner. Her heart began thumping hard against her chest; then pain rose into her throat.

"Is it you?" she asked, whispering. She stepped partly through the living room to see who was standing in the kitchen. She thought it might have been the woman in red, but the figure just stood silently in the darkness. Kale became more uncomfortable as she watched the figure. She couldn't make out who it was; then, she saw two red glowing eyes emerge into view. The figure stepped forward, causing Kale to clasp her chest. It was Jay. Kale breathed so hard she thought she'd release all the air she had.

"Jaybird!" she gasped.

"Hey, baby, you okay? I'm not gonna hurt you," Jay said with a cynical smile. He stepped closer as Kale threw her arms out with fingers spread as though willing him to stop.

"Don't come no closer!"

Jay laughed. "What? You can trust me. No one else is here; everything is going to be all right. You came for those sweet little children, huh?"

"Jay, I'm warning you! Don't come no closer, or I'll nut the hell up on you!" Kale eased herself closer to the apartment door to leave.

"I like it when you talk like that."

Kale watched Jay's red-lit face. His slimy Cheshire cat's smile spread as though a knife had cut his face in half. His shoulder's scrunched with a hump in his back, and he rushed toward Kale as she grabbed and tried to twist the doorknob that refused to turn. The force of his rush caused her to knock the side of her forehead into the door. Screaming for dear life, she managed to raise her knee and gave a powerful hit into his groins. As he stumbled, she pulled out of his reach, running to the dingy kitchen area and grabbing the first thing she could get her hands on. She swung behind her, banging a large pot upside his head. He doubled over for a moment, barely stung. He shot her an evil gaze.

"Damn, baby, you turning me on." Jay's voice was not his; his mouth opened, releasing wicked laughter. Kale stood flustered and on edge, watching him. She wasn't sure of how she would get out of this apartment she was trapped in. Something grabbed Jay from behind and pulled him to the floor. Kale, confused, watched as Jay, in his healthy form, began fighting the sick version of himself. He pulled the sick Jay up then rammed him into the wall. He yelled back toward Kale.

"Kale, wake up!"

"What!" Kale exclaimed. The healthy Jay pulled the sick Jay out of the damaged sheetrock. He swung to hit him again but fell back as the sick Jay rose and lunged on top of him, growling like an animal.

"Shut the fuck up! She don't fucking love you anymore! Stop resisting me cause you didn't do your job for your family. I rule now. You'll never be nothing. I'ma suck your soul til it's dry, motherfucker!"

The sick Jay sunk his teeth into Jay's shoulder, causing him to yell into the air. Through his pain, he looked at Kale. A tear rolled down the side of his face. "Kale, baby! Please, wake up!"

Kale opened her eyes. She spun around, standing

within the hall she had just spoken to Jay's neighbor in. She looked toward Jay's apartment door, which was now locked.

"Hey, you okay?" The young woman said, leaning out her doorway. Kale looked back at her bewildered and nodded her sore head. She felt like she had been knocked in the head with a bat. She placed her fingers on the side of her head, near her hairline, and felt a knot forming.

"I'm sorry; I have to go," Kale said, walking away.

#

Feeling deep stress, fear, and anxiety, Kale pulled into her driveway and sat for a moment with her head low. The pain of her children being gone from her was too much to bear. There was no way she could rest; even in her dream state, she ran the risk of being attacked. Maybe the woman in red was waiting on her to dream her in, to give her what she wanted. She would have to; there was no other way. She noticed Tree sitting on the porch steps with Tora sleeping beside her. Kale felt heat rising underneath the skin on her face; her eyes darkened as she looked away. *She has the audacity to just sit on my porch as though nothing is wrong.*

Kale stepped out of the van, walked to the front door, ignoring Tree as she stood to meet her. Kale fumbled with her keys in frustration until she dropped them.

"Kale," Tree called. Kale snapped out her hand,

stopping Tree from saying more. "Please, Tree, leave," she commanded, voice shaking, trying to keep cool.

"Kale, I am sorry that I was not there in time for your children, but I will get them back. I promised you that," Tree said, stepping closer.

Kale stared down into the space in front of her then looked back toward Tree with fire in her eyes. Before she could stop herself, one hand flew through midair, meeting with Tree's cheek, causing Tree to shift to the side. Tree closed her eyes and let the tears flow. She stood there, patiently waiting for Kale to release her anger. Her shoulders rose and rolled back as she sucked in a deep breath and turned back to face Kale. Normally, Tree's locs would have spread out and grabbed arms, legs, neck, anything to protect, but she knew Kale had hit her from a painful place within. She needed someone to blame, so Tree let it be her.

"You promised me you'd check on them, protect them. The only thing that makes my existence worth living are those two kids, and they've been taken by I don't know who. A demon, a woman, someone like you for all I know! What good is having power, turning into a fucking tree, acting like a freaking monk, speaking all philosophical, if you can't help people! You said you're here for humanity, but you couldn't help two small children, my babies! My babies are gone! Anything could be happening! So, I will do what you can't! I will get them back!" Kale stood, shaking, turning her head away, catching her breath so she wouldn't do anything she'd regret. She leaned over, wincing at the pain her forehead was in and grabbed her keys. She shoved them into the lock, opening the door.

Tree looked back towards Kale. Her gaze softened as she stared directly into Kale's eyes.

"Kale, I had to find an elder to help me understand what I was up against and how I can stop this. I am here to help you and all of humanity, but I am not perfect. I went to where your children were, and found they had already been taken. A resident there told me that you and the police had been there looking for them. Kale, I know it is not too late. I can get them back. And I will."

"Please, just go back to wherever it is you came from. If it weren't for you coming here in the first place, no one would be dealing with this sickness and this gloomy weather. I know about these people you're after or who's after you. Some kid was friends with one of them before he was possessed like Jay. She wanted to help him, but I told her there is nothing anyone can do. She showed me a video post of you and that woman in red in a cemetery."

"Kale, you don't understand."

"I think I understand perfectly. This is all your fault. It's all on you!"

"Kale, please, listen."

"Leave!" Kale snapped," I have a way to get my children back! I don't need your help any longer."

"I came because of Linda." Tree managed to say between Kale's outbursts. Kale glared at her.

"I never told you my mother's name? Are you invading my dreams, too? Maybe you're in it with the woman in red. How did …"

"Your mother was my friend," Tree interjected, "a really good friend. But that was a long time ago. This was before you were born."

Tree backed away from Kale and leaned on the porch railing. Tora circled her feet and hopped into the cushion of the chair beside her, curling into a bushy black ball. Kale watched with curiosity, wanting her to continue. Even though she was upset with her, hearing that Tree was a friend of her mother's, reminded Kale of how much older Tree was than her. She was still in awe that a woman Tree's age could be so youthful-looking and mesmerizing.

Tree didn't talk much of her past because she felt it was a lesson learned and a time that no longer existed. The present was all there was and what she concerned herself

YOUNG /A WOMAN CALLED TREE / 249

with, but she felt Kale would want to know the main reason she came here.

"I was and am a creative at heart; I'd sing songs and easily write lyrics since I was young. Your mother, a painter, of course, I remember her work. She was an exquisite artist. Her paintings gave so much life, and the colors were so vibrant. She sketched me once. I don't know what happened to it or if she ever finished it. I can be quite a wanderer, always moving." Tree paused, thinking back to her past. Kale listened, smiling inwardly about her mother because she thought the same as Tree about her artwork. But to hear Tree was a singer gave her more insight into the life of this enigmatic woman.

"I was young and in a toxic relationship, but highly intuitive. It was just a confusing and lost point in time for me. I didn't completely trust myself in life. Doubting myself but being extraordinarily sensitive to knowing things, was not a good combination. But back then, it was in my music where I was completely free." Tree wiped the tears from her cheek, where Kale hit her, and the twinkle in her eyes came back to life. Her locs moved around like being underwater as they sensed the joy of her memory.

"I met your mother at an arts festival. I stopped to look at her work after a singing performance, and we just clicked as friends. I was young at the time, around nineteen or twenty. Your mom helped me with a place to stay when I didn't have anywhere to go, and she gave me time to stand on my own. This was a short while before I met my teacher. Your mother, in a way, was like a great teacher with her love and encouragement. She was like the older sister I never had. At the time, I think she had grown tired of the city because she talked a lot about moving back home, here. Before she left, she told me she was pregnant with you. You were her dream. She had suffered quite a few miscarriages. For some reason, she knew you were different. She was only showing a bit then. I touched her belly. And even at that time, I could feel your light radiating within her womb. I wasn't completely aware of what I was sensing, but I knew you were a special being."

Kale looked away and closed her eyes. Tears rolled down her cheeks. "Your mother eventually left and came back here to raise you, but we kept in contact by writing letters every few years or so. Then the letters stopped coming until I received one over a year ago. Your mother asked me to come check on you to see if you were all right after she left this physical plane. She told me that you had many things in common with her and what I was going through when I was young. She knew you were special and not just because you were her daughter. So, I promised her when the time came, I'd come here for you."

"Yeah, well," Kale said, sniffing back tears. Her ego still didn't want to let go of the anger she felt. "She didn't know what drama would follow you here and that her grandchildren would go missing."

"Kale, the darkness was here before I arrived. Darkness is everywhere, just as light is. You cannot have one without the other. It is only when darkness becomes out of balance that things start to become out of control. The darkness makes us forget the light inside of us, and we become identified with the lies we see on the news, the hardness of life, the obstacles placed in our way, the negative things people say and do to us. We think those things are real, and I'm not dismissing those things. But sometimes, we close ourselves off or think we are alone. The All never leaves us; it is always there. It is us. And the great truth is nothing can truly ever touch us. The real us is infinite and eternal."

"And I'm not talking about the eternal you reach after you die; I'm talking about you now. You, your children, we all are divine expressions meant to express light through our own versions of heaven. Your children will not be harmed yet. I can feel their light still going strong. But they are being blocked. I cannot see where they are because of the energy that is surrounding them."

Kale wiped back her tears and opened her front door. "Follow me."

Tree followed Kale inside to the first room and switched on the light. Kale went to her closet as Tree stood by the entrance, watching her fumble through clothes and plastic bins, looking for something. She pulled out a canvas and turned it around. It was a colorful painting of Tree with her hair as it was in all its locked glory surrounded by a golden glow and numerous flowers. Tree walked up to the painting and smiled.

"So, this is what she did with that drawing; my roots were just forming then," Tree said, referring to her short locs in the painting.

"Yeah, I forgot about this painting until I heard your story, and I knew you seemed familiar when I first met you. It's because I had seen you through my mother's work as a child. I don't think I've seen this painting since then." Kale handed the painting Tree.

"You can take it if you want. Maybe she did it for you," Kale said.

"No, my sister. Keep it here in this house. I have a feeling it's needed here. Thank you for listening. And I will find your children."

Kale nodded and set the portrait down, leaning it on the wall behind her. She held her head down then looked back into Tree's face. "I'm sorry for hitting you. I guess I just feel so much anger for her leaving me so soon. I wasn't ready for this."

"Your mother hasn't left you. The flesh you knew of as your mother is no longer. But she is still here, within you. It hurts because our flesh lingers to theirs. But your spirit can feel she is free; I miss her, too. She was a good friend, a real lifetime one. But I see her in you strong."

"Thanks, I needed to hear this. I don't think I've cried this much before; it's embarrassing. I'm usually strong and can handle things."

"Kale, you shouldn't be embarrassed to feel. We are divine beings, but we have human experiences. We feel; we make mistakes, we fall, we rise, and we learn. It's just all a part of living. It becomes a problem when we let all these things define who we are when we are so much more than this human body and its mistakes."

Kale turned her head away, coughing, placing her hands over her mouth. She sat on the bed, stopped coughing after a few seconds, and cleared her throat. Holding her head where the knot was, she realized it had increased in size, then placed her hands on her knees.

"I have a continuous rumbling in my chest. I had such a realistic dream when I went to Jay's apartment. He attacked me again."

"The Zar is getting stronger. I pulled most of the sickness out of you. But until I go through my last shift, I won't be able to pull it all out. But I can help you with your head." Tree placed a warm palm on Kale's forehead. She closed her eyes and let her glowing hand shrink the knot, willing the pain away. She took her hand down to reveal a smooth spot. Kale, no longer in pain, brought her hand to the corner of her forehead, feeling the knot gone. She looked at Tree with beaming eyes.

"You must rest so that your body can become stronger," Tree said, nodding, accepting Kale's facial expression as a thank you.

"So, when will this shift happen for you?" Kale asked.

"Tomorrow at 1:35 p.m.," Tree answered. "Kale, please, rest."

"Tomorrow? Why then at that time?" Kale asked, concerned, sitting on her bed. "And not to be so nitpicky, but I've never seen you with a cellphone or a watch. How would you be able to keep up with the time? You can estimate time by the sun?"

"Actually, yes, I can." Kale widened her eyes in amazement. "Tomorrow is the anniversary of the day and time I came into the world. My birth time adds up to the number nine. Nine is the number of responsibility, finality, and completeness. The numbers of my birthdate add up to the master number eleven, April 19, 1977. Eleven represents doorways, intuition, and spiritual wisdom. There's more that goes into a birth chart that you can study later. It is like a vibration you are born with that gives you the right tools to help guide yourself through this physical realm, and no one has the same vibration. An elder told me for my forty-fourth anniversary that I would be powerful enough to contain all three of the Zar as well as stop the sickness from spreading." She walked to the entrance of Kale's room, leaving her to rest.

"Tree," Kale called, and she turned around. "How can you stop this and get my children back?"

"I don't know the how, but I know the will. Sleep well, Kale." Tree left out of Kale's room and walked outside into the night. She kneeled into the cool ground, and her locs fell around her as she held her head down, placing her hands into the dirt. She looked up toward the moon then closed her eyes.

"Be with me, fill me, move through me. I surrender. Ase." Tree opened her glowing green eyes toward the moon and lowered her head. She concentrated on all the goodness and love she felt within, blocking out the small tinge of worry that tried to creep inside of her. She rose from the earth and walked back into the house. She passed by Kale's bedroom, seeing she had finally fallen asleep with Tora faithfully watching her at the edge of her bed. Tora looked back, glanced at Tree, then climbed down and went to the front door for Tree to let her out.

"Meow," Tora purred before walking out. Tree placed her hand on her chest and nodded. Then Tora was gone into the night.

Tree sat on the living room sofa and relaxed her shoulders, taking a few rounds of deep breaths. The sofa was soft and a little too cozy for her. After merging with trees for so long, the feeling of stretching and sleeping on a sofa or a bed felt foreign. She went inside her shoulder bag, pulled out the earth-colored cork yoga mat, and unrolled it across the wooden floor. As Tree reclined, her long locs sprawled across the mat then molded around her body for further comfort. As she lay at ease, she soon surrendered to the night.

Chapter Ten – The Shift

Awakening with a jolt, a sharp pain drove into Tree's chest, causing her to grasp the painful area and rise from the floor. She looked around, bewildered, trying to source if something had hit her, but she was the only one in the living room area of Kale's house. The morning sun rays shining through the sheer curtains told Tree she had slept much too late. She started to walk toward Kale's room when the jarring pain rammed through her chest again, causing her to fall to the floor. Someone was dying. Someone of great energy connected to her was being tortured and crying out, and Tree could feel every ounce of the pain. She pulled herself up again and staggered to Kale's room, only to see that Kale was gone. Tree walked to the front door, which she found unlocked. Walking outside, she found Kale's van still parked in the driveway. This put her in a state of even more worry. Tree looked around and saw Tora climbing down from one of the pecan trees. Tora leaped from the tree to the earth and came toward Tree with a noticeable limp. Tree bent down to examine her. Tora hissed as Tree tried to touch her back leg.

"What's happened, my little warrior? Where's Kale?" Tree asked, scooping up Tora despite her hissing to place her in a chair cushion on the porch. Tree waved her hands over Tora's pain area, releasing heat from them. Tree closed her eyes, then opened them, placing her hands on Tora. "You will be okay, my friend. I eased some of your pain, but you must stay here and rest to fully heal. I'm going to find Kale. I will return."

Tree left Tora and walked around the house, still not seeing Kale anywhere. The sharp pain stabbed within her chest. She leaned against the brick wall and scraped her arm. Someone came up behind Tree and caught her from falling. She looked up to see Kinte.

"I got you, Tree," Kinte said, assisting Tree to stand. She noticed Tahj standing behind him.

"Thank you, brother. When did you all come? I asked you to stay home. What I am confronting will be dangerous," Tree said, looking at them. She looked down at the outside of her scraped forearm, watching her flesh mend back into smooth dark skin.

Kinte and Tahj glanced at each other to confirm they were witnessing the same thing, amazed that her body could heal so quickly.

"That was amazing, Tree! You are an immortal," Tahj stated.

"So are you. My spirit is forever immortal. But my flesh is human like yours, just returned to a pure, highly charged state."

"You can die? But healing the way you just did and all the things you do, how can you be just a simple human?" Tahj asked.

"Brother, being human is no simple feat. It is a revolutionary act just to be. Even without all of the special acts one does, the human body is a powerful, intelligent entity within itself and coupled with the power of the mind and the fuel of the spirit, to be human is to be a walking phenomenon." Tree's gentle smile and words reminded Tahj of his own worth. He returned the smile and nodded.

Tree doubled over, holding her chest and breathing through another wave of pain. Kinte and Tahj went to stand on both sides of her, helping her to rise. They glanced at each other with trouble written across their faces.

"What's happening?" Kinte asked when Tree rose back up.

"Something I've connected with is in great pain. I must go to the source of where it is coming from. Since you all are here, Kinte, can you take me back to the oak?" Tree asked.

"Yes, let's go."

#

Fiery lightning struck the Mother oak several times before her cries of pain stopped sending signals for help. Her trunk was split open with flames bursting from the inside. Several large limbs fell to the ground around her. The whispers of the green spirits went unheard as they tried to connect with her, but she was gone. Lionel, Jay, and Kale's children stood away, watching with dull eyes as the fire destroyed the strongest, oldest roots in the area. Roots that could connect Tree to sacred earth knowledge to be able to heal this place. There was no way the woman in red was going to let that happen. The people lived in fear, plenty were sick, and many lay dying. As soon as they were done draining what life they could, they would watch it spread as far as they could go.

A car approached, causing Lionel and Jay to look around.

"Take the children, Mwongo. Their souls will be consumed when we are done here. If this takes longer than expected, break their little necks, and enjoy, 'kay. It looks as though your emaciated body could use an extra meal," The lady in red joked.

"Yes, Isfet," Lionel said, rolling his eyes. He began

to walk away, and like zombies, Hampton and Davis followed.

The woman in red saw the car stop and then turned back to the burning tree. Jay stood beside her, still watching the car.

"Stop here," Tree said. Kinte did as she said as they watched, appalled by the enormous tree burning to ashes. A woman stood before it with flowing red fabric draped around her with a red turban crown. Her fabric flowed through the wind as though she and the flames were one. Kinte recognized the guy standing near the woman. As he thought it, Tahj, as usual, acted and blurted it out.

"Man, ain't that the dude Jaybird that owed you that fifty? Man, he's messed up!"

"Yeah, he looks rough. He can keep that money! I don't want nothing he's touched. I'm going to call nine-one-one to get the fire department out here." Kinte said, pulling out his phone.

"No, I don't want others harmed." Tree opened her door.

"Wait, what are you going to do?" Tahj asked, looking worried.

"End this." Tree replied, looking back at him. She got out of the car and walked toward the flames.

#

Officer Thompson parked his car on the side of the road in front of Kale's house and stepped up to Kale's porch to knock on the door. He wanted to let her know they hadn't found Jay and reassure her that he was still looking for her children. He was about to knock when he heard a hiss behind him and spun around to see a black long-haired feline in one of the furniture chairs.

"Hey, kitty, not tryna scare you," he said, extending a hand closer to her. Tora executed one of her famous lightning swipes, causing the officer to pull away just in time.

"Man, you're a vicious little thing! All right. All right. Just trying to be friendly." He leaned back and stared at Tora for a few seconds. "Where is your master?"

Tora leaned her head to the side with attitude. Officer Thompson chuckled. He could have sworn this cat was offended when he said the word master. He shook the silly thought from his head and turned back around to knock on Kale's front door. No answer. He left Tora on the porch undisturbed, walked to the side, where Kale's car was parked and went on to the back. He looked through a window, but he couldn't see anything nor anyone. He walked back to the front and was about to get in his car when he looked to the sky.

It was still cloudy and dark like it had been for days, and he felt the first few raindrops began to fall. Looking off into the distant sky, he saw strange red lightning appear. But instead of seeing it coming from the sky, it appeared to be coming from something on the ground shooting out into the sky. He decided he'd check on Kale later when she was home. For now, he was curious as to where this red lightning was coming from. He saw Tora peeking over the chair she was in, and her green eyes shone before she looked away, reminding him of the night something broke into Kale's hospital room. He stilled wondered what happened. He hopped in his car and drove in the direction of Ethel Cemetery.

#

Tree's eyes glistened as she watched the oak disintegrate into the flames. She felt the rain beginning to fall and hoped it would soon extinguish the supernatural fire. She called out to the Mother oak within her mind, but she heard nothing beyond the painful whispers of the green spirits. Their voices were on top of each other in a frenzy. She still stood a short distance away from the woman in red and Jay as she kneeled to touch the earth.

"Oh, Green One, she is gone. The Mother has been

destroyed! The fleshless ones are here to destroy you before your shift happens!"

"I know it is to happen soon, but I cannot wait any longer. They must be stopped. Too many more people will suffer if they are not contained."

"But you cannot hold the darkness without corrupting yourself. You must kill them if you are to win. Are you willing to do that?" the green spirits asked. Tree glanced toward all three members of the Zar. A tinge of doubt crept within her.

"I do not kill. Life is what I treasure above all else." Tree's sad eyes looked at the green spirits, seeing glimpses of their light flashing within their realm. "I-I will find a way to end this. If I have to sacrifice myself, then so be it."

Tree stood away from the earth, ignoring the frenzied whispers of the green spirits. She released a deep breath and inhaled, pulling her shoulders back and widening her chest. She boldly faced the woman in red and began walking toward her.

Jay's vibrant red eyes lit within his sickly face as he watched Tree approaching. His hungry grin beamed with anticipation, eagerly ready to attack. He glanced to Isfet, who stood still, watching the oak burn.

"What are you going to do? Just stand and watch that

burning tree burn like Moses, or shall I stop her?" he asked, wheezing.

"I'm waiting. Do your job," Isfet said.

Jay spat, disgusted at Isfet's arrogance, then charged toward Tree like a crazed silverback. She stopped walking, stood her ground, extended her arms out, and spread her fingers wide with palms forward. Then Tree spun her palms downward into a warrior mudra, pressing her fingertips into the air, commanding roots to rise out of the earth and take hold of Jay's feet. He slammed into the earth, screaming, then glared at her with his twisted unnatural smile. Tree walked up to him and saw the vines crawling up his body, containing him. He laughed as she kneeled to touch his forehead with her middle finger.

"Balance is the true nature of all. Release this body, or I will have to force you to." Tree said, looking at Jay.

"No, there will be no releasing today." Isfet spun around, releasing red lightning-like torpedoes from her hands toward Tree. Tree lunged to the side, away from Jay, dodging the lightning's flames, landing on her hands and feet as smoothly as a lynx. She looked up with dread as her locs moved back. The woman in red looked at her through Kale's eyes, releasing a hearty laugh at the shock written on Tree's face, then walked closer as though she wanted Tree to have a better look.

"Yes, a new me," Kale said, striking a pose with both hands on her hips. "You like? No?" She asked when Tree didn't respond. "Is this body familiar to you? It's amazing what a mother will give up for her children, huh?"

With Tree's concentration interrupted, the roots loosened enough for Jay to slip through them and stand.

"I think she's become as silent as the trees." He chortled, standing near Kale.

"Well, maybe, I should burn her, too. It'll be one less sun being in the world, and no one has to hear righteous speeches on love, peace, and humanity."

Kale's eyes filled with blood as she brought her hands up, crackling with red lightning.

"Let's set this bitch on fire!" she hissed, pointing all ten of her fingers with crackling fiery rage directly at Tree. With lightning-speed reflexes, Tree morphed her entire body, from her toes to the tip of each loc, into the texture of thick vines and drilled her body beneath the soil of the earth, dodging billowy flames flying right over the area where she vanished.

"Where did she go?" asked Jay. Kale and Jay stood looking around for a moment, trying to locate where Tree disappeared to.

"There," Kale said, looking at the ground surface, crumpling upon itself. They were prepared to attack, but the ground's surface became still. "Look, she went back under!" Jay pointed to another area where a burrow was being made underground. They kept their eyes on it until it, too, became still.

"She's moving through the ground!" Jay exclaimed.

"Don't worry! We will get her," Kale stated.

Tree moved with extraordinary strength and speed, winding through the dark ground like a southern black racer. She could feel the vibration from where Kale and Jay stood and moved around to further confuse them. Jay and Kale stood for a moment without being able to locate Tree. Behind them, the ground exploded open, and numerous large roots torpedoed into the air with Tree gliding in the center, wrapping around Jay and Kale, constricting every limb on their bodies.

"Kale," Tree called but continued to hold on. "I know you are still in there. The same energy you used to see your blue aura, call on that now to rise to the surface. This entity is not more powerful than you."

Kale began to smile. "Oh, you miss your poor friend. Well, you two will soon be in the same place. Now, Ngonjwa!"

Jay widened his mouth before a vine could grab his neck and hold him back. He opened his huge jaws and slammed them down onto Tree's forearm. Annoyed, Tree wrapped a vine around his head, pulling his mouth away from her mucus-tainted arm. She didn't want to kill him, but he was making it tough to keep him alive. Within, she felt the souls of the original hosts from a lost place, waiting to be released. Her bitten flesh shifted back into normal smooth skin, and the sickness Ngonjwa spread visibly moved through her arm. She had to stop and eject the sickness from her body, but she didn't want to let them go.

On edge, Kinte and Tahj sat in the car, watching the battle between Tree, Kale, and Jay.

"We have to find a way to help her!" Tahj snapped.

"How, man? She doesn't want me to call the cops or the ambulance, and we can end up dead messing around with that lady shooting lightning out of her hands and that sick ass dude." Kinte stated. He was just as worried about Tree as Tahj was, but he knew they did not have a chance in the world.

"Look!" Tahj said, seeing another vehicle approach.

"What! Who called the cops?" Kinte asked, seeing a cop car approach, then looking toward Tahj.

"Don't look at me! I'm the last person to ever call a cop. It looks like it's only one." Tahj said, watching the car as it approached. They looked back to Tree and the two she was fighting.

"What happened to the other little guy? I forgot about him," Kinte asked.

"That little boney kid! Not long after we arrived, I saw him taking those missing kids into the bushes off into the far right, past the oak. Come on!" Tahj commanded.

"Man, what the hell you think you're doing?" Kinte asked, but he had already gotten out of the car.

"Damn!" Kinte cursed. He jumped out of the car to follow Tahj.

"Freeze!"

Kinte and Tahj stopped in their tracks.

"Turn around slowly!" The officer commanded. The two cousins did exactly as he said.

"Really? Now!" Tahj whined, eyeing the gun the officer pointed at them. Officer Thompson stood behind his opened car door, watching them and trying to decipher what was happening further across the field.

"Shut up, man! Stay calm, or this trigger-happy fool is gonna do something crazy," Kinte said.

"What's going on here?" Officer Thompson asked.

He looked toward the fire that was dying out, leaving a damaged tree. But what blew his mind was the red lightning that drew him there was coming from something that women in red held in her hand. She looked familiar, but he couldn't get a clear look at her face.

"Officer, if you look over there, we were just trying to get away from being killed," Tahj said, directing his gaze toward the woman in red and Jay.

"So why didn't you just drive off, huh?" The officer asked, getting ready to reach for his radio.

"Officer, the two children that were reported kidnapped recently on the news were taken by those people," Kinte said. "Their other partner has taken the kids into the woods, and we didn't want to leave them."

"Oh, really?" Officer Thompson glanced from Kinte to Tahj with skepticism. He leaned forward, grabbing his radio from the car. "This is Officer Thompson, assistance needed. I need back up, suspicious activity at Ethel Cemetery on Highway 41."

The rain slacked a bit, and Tahj peeped at his cousin with a look Kinte did not like. He breathed harder, looking intense, hoping Tahj got the message not to do anything crazy. Tahj looked away, pressed his lips together, and stared at the officer. They all heard the sirens from the police cars close by. As soon as Officer Thompson glanced back at the approaching vehicles, Tahj took off, with Kinte following close behind.

"What the hell? Stop!" The officer fired a few shots, but the two men had jumped beyond the thicket's edge out of his sight. He cursed himself and waited for the other police cars to pull up near him.

#

"You a crazy fool!" Kinte snapped, trying to catch his breath. "You know they are gonna roast us alive when we come out of here."

"Not if that woman in red don't roast them first. Don't worry 'bout that now; we got lives to save. Tree's been looking for these kids, and this is one way we can help her while she deals with them fools out there," Tahj said, turning to find somewhat of a path. He paused a moment to feel the right side of his body. He held his shaking fingers out, and they were stained with blood. "Damn, Kinte!"

"Oh, shit, cuz! Let me see!" Kinte said, stooping to look at Tahj's wound. "It's just a graze, thank God. You'll be all right."

"Okay, okay. I thought that was the end. Kinte, you really do love me, cuz, don't you?" Tahj asked, holding his wound to relieve the pain.

"Tahj, shut up, and come on, man." Kinte chuckled, then got up to walk deeper into the wooded area. He was frustrated dealing with Tahj and his wild ideas, but he did care for his cousin. He had to admit to himself that Tahj had balls when it counted. He just wasn't in the mood to get all soft at this moment.

They saw the two missing children staring off into space through the entangled vines and tree branches, oblivious to any danger. Kinte and Tahj approached closer and saw what they were staring at. It was the slim boy Tahj saw that led them there. His eyes glowed, holding them in a trance as he moved in closer. He stood first in front of the little boy then his jaw dropped open. Tahj and Kinte watched, shaken by the facial disfigurement, and the older boy began to suck the life out of the small child.

No longer able to stand by and watch, Tahj ran like a maniac into Lionel, tackling him and tumbling over. Lionel fell, slamming his head into the ground. Kinte grabbed a child in each arm and began to run with Tahj close behind him. Lionel, coming to his senses, rolled over, then rose from the ground. His body tensed as he lowered his jaws, releasing a horrid scream.

#

The police cars and fire department drove up to Officer

Thomas. They watched the dying flames rising from the oak and what appeared to be a woman in a violent confrontation with two others. A powerful sound of dissonance moved from the trees, causing numerous birds to scatter throughout the sky.

As the policemen drew their weapons, Tree couldn't let them kill anyone. She debated within her mind whether to stop the cops in case they began shooting or holding on to Kale and Jay. The sickness spreading within her was another hindrance that stood in the way of performing at full capacity. It couldn't kill her, but it weakened her abilities. As soon as she decided to let go, Kale struck her with lightning. Tree screamed and fell backward.

"Stand down! Or we will be forced to shoot!" Officer Thompson shouted at the woman in red. Kale stood straighter and spun around. Officer Thompson's eyes stretched wide in shock as he watched crackles of red lightning surge up her arms. She held her hands up and wiggled her fingers, showing that she had no weapon in her hands.

Kale laughed and swung her arm out, electrifying a police car, laughing at the explosion.

"Fire!" another officer ordered. Bullets began to fly toward Kale, Jay, and Tree. Within range of the first flying bullets, Tree lifted her arm with fingers spread and held it in the air. The atmosphere around the three of them contracted, bringing them within a separate parallel dimension. The bullets flew through thin air.

"Cease fire!" The officers look confused. "What the hell is happening, Thompson?" another officer asked. He shook his head, just as stunned as the rest of the officers.

Tree held up her hand until Jay leaped to attack her. Once in range, her locs grabbed him and slammed him to the ground. Tree could see the venom he released into her, rising up her arm, reaching her collarbone and chest. Kale, giving no mercy or time for her to heal it, released another round of lightening. Tree rose from the ground, flipping back out of harm's way. She stood ready for another round of red lightning with her locs flying behind her, glowing palms out in front of her as though she held an imaginary basketball emitting a green glow. Kale's lightning flew in. Tree caught it, holding it within her palms before sending it back toward her. Kale pivoted to the side, dodging it.

"You think that just cause you shifted us here that you can save us?" Kale asked, looking Tree up and down. She glanced around at the orange-tinted atmosphere, frowning at the whispers she couldn't distinguish. "You're weak. And you don't want to kill me. Isn't that sweet?"

"It's not you that I'm worried about," Tree responded, her eyes glowing, watching Kale and Jay as he was becoming conscious.

"Oh, you don't have to be so blunt. But you do need to be worried about yourself." Kale's gaze went to Tree's arm. The venom appeared like worms crawling underneath her skin. The atmosphere expanded and then contracted. Tree couldn't continue holding the dimension shift to block them from the police bullets for long with the sickness moving within her. Still, she needed a moment to rest to pull it out.

The officers began to see an image appear before them like a video screen trying to clear. Then their target fully appeared before them. But before anyone could respond, Kale released a fiery lightning wave toward the officers and the fire trucks, extending to the area surrounding their location.

"Get the hell out of here!" Thompson yelled, rushing to get inside of his car with others doing the same. They all retreated, realizing they were worthless against this supernatural situation.

Tahj and Kinte stood with Hampton and Davis, watching in excruciating fear for Tree as the woman in red released a title wave of lightning fire. They remained hidden behind nearby bushes and trees, unable to get safely back to their vehicle. They didn't want to run and risk the chance of being caught in the crossfire of attacks with the children. Tree knew there was a chance she'd have to sacrifice herself to save everyone else, but it was a chance she was willing to take. It was her duty. She ignored the poison spreading within her and curled her hands into tight fists, then took a stance, grounding her feet into the earth. She slammed the tops of her fists together and released a powerful battle cry. On command, a wall of force blocked the path of the lightning wave, stopping further damage among the retreating cars and throughout the cemetery.

Tree was exhausted and dropped to her knees to catch her breath. Lionel came up from behind her, emitting dark voices to further disrupt her already weakened state. He tried to pull her energy from within her but could not. Tree was on all fours, resisting his pull, breathing, holding herself together.

"Damn, even weakened, she's strong as hell!" Jay exclaimed. Kale's eyes cut into him, causing him to shrink then look back at Tree. She walked up to Tree and kicked her in the head. Tree fell back, sprawled out on the ground.

#

Tree opened her eyes, squinting in a bright all-white room.

Feeling dizziness, she rose from the floor and gazed around. Her head ached worse with every movement. There was no direction or pinpoint for an exit. She stood in slow motion, wincing at the pain her body was in, and looked down at her bitten arm. It still held the sickness within it.

"Hey, sis," a female voice beside her said. She turned to see Kale, giving her a proud look. Tree responded with a weak smile.

"I knew you heard me. I need you to come back to the surface," Tree said.

"I've been trying, Tree, but I can't find walls here— let alone a door to leave this place. It's endless in this deathly white place." Kale looked around, holding her hands out in defeat. She looked at Tree's bruises and bitten arm, then looked down, feeling guilty. "I'm sorry, Tree. I left to take her bargain. I just couldn't wait while my children were in danger. I was too afraid for them. Forgive me; I-I hate you're handling this all on your own."

"Nothing to forgive. I would have done the same if it were my children. Love drives you to protect your loved ones against the unthinkable in any way imaginable. What other way is there for a parent to be?" Kale looked at Tree, soaking up her words. "It's a struggle, though, trying not to physically harm your form until I can separate it from Isfet, especially with the others of the Zar and this." Tree held up her bitten arm. "But I will."

"Even in the state you're in, you are so freaking confident and sure; it's ridiculous. You don't know any fear, do you?" Kale asked.

"Honestly, I do. I feel fear more than you know. But I breathe, and I remember who I am and what I stand for. Then I act; I don't dwell on thinking. There's a time for that. But in acting, I see that fear is just a mirage in my mind. And I'm at an age where the belief in my mind's mirages doesn't last that long, so I seem fearless."

"I hope to get to that point one day."

"It's possible to be that way now. Just be." Tree smiled. "Come now, sit, and chant with me. The time of my birth is here, and I feel the light calling me."

"How will you make it back? There are no doors?" Kale asked.

"If there are no doors, then I will create one."

Tree sat in lotus position on the floor, and Kale sat across from her in an easy seat. Kale felt a hand on her shoulder and turned to see Jay looking surprisingly well. He squatted to sit beside her, and across from him, Lionel came to sit. Jay smiled and held out his hand to Kale. She looked in his eyes and somehow knew he had her back. She took his hand. Then she took Lionel's hand with her other one, and Lionel took Tree's hand until they were all joined. Tree closed her eyes and began chanting.

"Be with me. Fill me. Move through me. I surrender. Ase." Then the others joined in, forming a synchronistic rhythm of voices on top of each other until it sounded as though their voices had multiplied. Tree began to feel wind circling all around her as though she was being lifted upward by the ancestors, still chanting her mantra. She opened her eyes when she returned to her body. Pain ravaged her as the red lightning scorched her further. Kale laughed in hysterical joy as Tree screamed in agony. Tree managed to roll over on her right side and attempt a fetal position, but she stopped moving.

"Ase," she whispered as she surrendered, then closed her eyes.

All of the Zar walked around Tree's body, giving each other satisfied smirks.

"Is she dead?" Lionel asked.

"Hell, yeah, she ain't breathing," Jay answered. "She was a tough one to take down, but Isfet, you are stronger in that light being's body."

"Yes, a sun traveler is always more powerful than a regular fearful human. We have accomplished what we set out to do." Kale looked at the old oak, no longer threatened by the wisdom it could share. The fire upon it died out, and the police and firefighters retreated. The sickness was continuing to spread across the city and moving beyond to nearby cities as well. Kale/Isfet felt ready to conquer another place weakened by corruption to further tip the balance towards the darkness.

The Zar heard a car cranking up across the field near the cemetery. They looked and saw Kinte and Tahj trying to leave.

"It's the ones who took the kids," hissed Lionel.

"You let someone take them? I told you to consume them!" Kale snapped.

"Let's enjoy them now," Jay suggested, his wide lips watering and dripping mucus.

#

"What the hell is going on, Kinte!" Tahj yelled.

"Man, I don't know! The shit won't crank!" Kinte panicked.

"Oh, shit. Why now! Why are those crazy-ass demon folks coming over here? Did you remember to put gas in?" Tahj said, panicking, looking back at Hampton and Davis in the back seat, holding one another. Seeing them made him calm down enough not to think of his own fear.

"It's gonna be all right, okay?" Tahj said, trying to comfort them as well as himself. Hampton just nodded. Davis buried her face in her brother's embrace.

Kinte continued turning the key in the ignition and pressing the gas, but the car still stalled. He turned it off for a moment, then lowered his gaze and whispered, "Please, God."

"Try—try—try it again, man!" Tahj yelled, watching the Zar approaching. Kinte blew out a frustrated breath of hot air then turned the key in the ignition one last time. It sputtered as though it was going to stall; then it kept sputtering until it cranked. They yelled with joy as Kinte pushed the gear into drive and stepped on the gas. Only something from the back held the car from moving. Hampton leaned up, looked out the back window, and saw his dad's distorted face staring back at him. He screamed then sat back in his seat, crying, grabbing hold of his sister. Jay held the car from the rear, licking his lips with bulging eyes shining at Kinte through the rearview mirror.

"Press it, Kinte!"

"I'm pressing! I'm pressing!"

Kinte floored the gas pedal as the car slung from side to side, but they could not release from Jay's grip. Kale and Lionel stood on opposite sides of the car and watched Jay have fun terrorizing the passengers.

Tree's eyes fluttered back open, releasing tears running across her nose, dropping to the earth. In pain, she pushed her tortured body over onto her back, trying to catch her breath. She felt as if she had been drowning and was now able to finally breathe. Coughing up blood, she turned her head to the side to release it. The sickness now covered her neck and half of her face. She straightened, focusing in the direction of the sky. The rain had ceased, a sliver of light peaked through the dark clouds, hitting her, and began to expand commanding the clouds to move away. She took a deep breath and exhaled through her mouth, letting the breath move through her body with steady repetition. Her brown eyes closed, knowing it was time as the light filled her with strong heat, causing her body to heal itself. Her face cleared and bruises faded; she stretched out her bitten arm, allowing the sludge parasites to crawl out of the puncture holes Jay created. As they were released, they died, drying out in the sun's light. Tree's bite wounds sealed up fully intact as she sat up with her glorious nappy locs draping behind her.

Tree floated up, levitating into a standing position a few feet from the ground while her body radiated a golden-green light. Her locs levitated behind her like sea serpents fully in tune, sensing all energy around. Tree opened her eyes and lowered herself back to the earth, fully healed and ready to share her light.

Jay guffawed as Kinte, Tahj, and the children screamed inside the car. He glanced across the field and saw Tree walking toward them. In a state of shocked, the car slipped from Jay's grasp and sped ahead out of control toward a tree. Tree held her right hand out, willing the car to stop before it crashed. Kinte and Tahj looked around in bewilderment until realization crept through them. They looked at each other and started screaming and hugging, happy to still be alive.

"Tree!" Tahj called.

Tree gazed at him, then spoke to his mind.

Go, now, and take the children to safety.

"Kinte, go!" Tahj yelled as Kinte pressed the gas pedal, spinning around, speeding out of the field and past the cemetery grounds.

Kale's twisted grimace focused on Tree, not at all impressed but ready to destroy. With her regal red crown raised, she stood even higher in her stance, with Lionel and Jay both at her side. Her eyes grew dark red, contrasting with Tree's sun gold shining gaze. Kale's hands curled in, pulling earth energy into her body, then she thrust it forward, releasing an unstoppable fiery force toward Tree. One side of Tree's lips curled mischievously. Then she willed the surface of her chocolate brown skin into the blackest shade of the universe. Light moved throughout her form, appearing back and forth underneath the surface of her marble-like skin, glistening like stars across a night sky. She held her arms open, welcoming Kale's force to come toward her. Tree let it reach her shimmery skin. Allowing the flames to penetrate into her flesh.

Kale's eyes gave way to a sliver of doubt as she watched Tree absorb the force like a vacuuming black hole. She threw out two more rounds of power then watched as Tree pulled them within her form.

"Get her!" Kale yelled to Jay and Lionel. They both ran toward Tree. As Tree commanded black roots to rise from the ground, Kale, thinking she was distracted, manifested a ten-foot-long spear of lightning within her hands and shot it at Tree's heart. It absorbed into Tree's flesh upon contact. The roots Tree called, caught and wrapped around Jay and Lionel, creeping up their bodies, immobilizing them. The roots harden, only leaving their faces exposed. In a blind rage, Kale screamed, rushing toward Tree, releasing the deadliest lightning energy within her. Tree braced herself, bringing her hands together, aiming them forward shooting a force of light, meeting Kale's energy blow on contact. Tree's green light energy pushed closer until Kale's red energy force was pushed back and consumed her. Kale collapsed.

Tree walked up to Kale unconscious, then willed roots from the ground to wrap around Kale's wrists, ankles, and neck. Tree kneeled beside her and touched her forehead with her middle finger. Tree's green aura traveled from her to Kale's body, consuming Isfet's red aura. Kale awakened with a start and began screaming in defiance.

"You nappy-headed, black bitch! You think you've won! You can't destroy me! You're nothing! Nothing, you hear! Walking around with your scruffy clothes and holier than thou act. I will invade your fucking soul!" Kale yelled, twisting, trying to release herself from bondage. But it was too late. Tree stared at her and then moved her hand, placing it onto Kale's cheek.

"Isfet, you are the other side of me, and I, you. You're right; I cannot destroy you. But I can contain you. I care nothing about winning. I care about balance, harmony, and doing what is right. To you, this world, I may seem like nothing, but I know I am a part of everything that was, is, and will ever be. Go with grace and rest with the All." Tree smiled with kindness.

The fearful glow from Kale's eyes faded, returning to their natural brown color. A red force of energy pulled upward from Kale's chest cavity, leaving and entering into Tree's marble black skin. Once all of Isfet's energy was contained, Kale lay quietly, breathing, and slowly opened her eyes to see Tree's sparkling form.

"So beautiful; the perfect black," she whispered. Tree smiled, then walked over to Jay and Lionel. Mwongo and Ngonjwa screamed in agony as their escapade of wrongdoing was being put to an end. Their fleshless energy dissolved into Tree's flesh. Jay and Lionel remained unconscious once they were freed from the evil entities within them. Tree willed all the roots and vines to release all three of them. Jay remained sickly looking with numerous unhealed wounds and abscesses. Tree kneeled over him and placed her palm on his heart. Her green glow engulfed him, causing his body to mend. The sores dissolved, and his color returned to its normal caramel shade. He opened his eyes to see Tree already kneeling over Lionel. Tree looked up at Jay and nodded. He was in awe of her shimmery black skin and mouthed the words, "Thank you." He looked around to see Kale rising from where she laid. He got up to help her.

Tree stood after healing Lionel and walked a few feet away from him, Jay, and Kale.

"Tree, is it over?" Kale asked.

"No, I have one last great healing. Please, stand back."

All three did as Tree commanded. Tree glanced back at the destroyed Mother oak's mutilated stump and then took a long deep breath, looking down at the earth ahead of her. She closed her eyes, allowing a glow to encapsulate her body. She began to change form, similar to when Kale first saw her merge with another tree, but she grew larger, forming into her own separate entity. Once again, her dark skin became the roughness of tree bark, and her locs lifted, forming endless branches with leaves appearing all over. Tree's feet and legs merged creating roots that drove deep into the earth. As she grew taller, all traces of who she was faded away. Her roots spread beneath the surface of the ground, leaving the cemetery and spreading as far out as she could reach. She connected with other roots below, into a natural underground network system; helping her to spread healing even farther. Kale and the others looked in awe at the larger new oak before them. Its branches spanned at least two hundred feet. Kale ran up to it, placing her palms along its huge trunk, hoping to still feel Tree's energy. She smiled back at the others.

"I can still sense her!" Kale exclaimed.

Suddenly, black flower buds began appearing all over the field. Once through the ground's surface, the buds opened their petals releasing shimmery spores into the air upon Tree's command.

"What is this?" Lionel asked, trying to catch some of the spores in his hands.

"Amazing," Jay said watching the spores move through the air.

"It's beautiful. It's her! All of this is her!" Kale said, pulling away from the tree. She looked towards Jay. "We all need to go. I have to get back to my babies."

Chapter Eleven - Like the Wind

A determined steady wind blew through the city, filling the air with a shimmery star-like haze. It covered buildings, homes, cars, and other plant life blowing beyond the city limits. Neville still appeared more ghostlike than usual as most remained tied to their homes for fear of the unusual immune-deteriorating sickness. Now there was this mysterious shimmer adding to the numerous issues Neville was dealing with.

Kinte and Tahj, with Kale's children in the back of their car, pulled into the hospital's parking lot. Kinte parked as they watched everything around them become coated with shimmer. The small amounts of the star-like particles began to come inside through the car vents. Davis looked at Hampton and whispered, "Pixie dust."

"Where is this stuff coming from?" Tahj asked, fanning sparkles from his face. "If I were in better shape, I'd film this."

"Man, don't worry about that now. You need to go

on in and get patched up. You're gonna need stitches. That thing could get infected," Kinte said, referring to Tahj's graze wound.

"What if they try to say we kidnapped these kids, man? I can hold off until we hear from Tree," Tahj responded.

"Man, are you crazy? You don't know how long that's going to be." Kinte shook his head in awe, thinking about what he had seen. "She saved our lives. It's like she died and came back. Look, she wanted us to get to safety, and if anybody says anything, we'll just tell the truth. Well, part of the truth and leave out the weird stuff, but you need help. Come on!"

Kinte got out of the car and opened the door to let Hampton and Davis climb out. The shimmer began to coat the top of his head and shoulders. Hampton squinted his innocent eyes then looked up at Kinte. Hesitating, he looked as though he wanted to say something but declined.

"You okay, kid?" Kinte asked. "We are good people, friends of Tree. You know her, right?"

Hampton nodded.

"Then we are on the same side. My cousin here is hurt and needs help. But I'm gonna wait inside with you and your sister until we can contact your family, okay?"

Hampton nodded again. "I'm hungry," he muttered.

"Okay, let's get you guys something to eat," Kinte said. He lifted Davis into his arms, and Hampton followed closely beside him. Davis held one of her little hands out, catching the shiny star-like flakes.

"Kinte, you're gonna get them that cafeteria hospital food? Well, maybe we are in the right place. After eating this stuff, we are gonna each need our own doctor. And I hope you're right about this, Kinte. I can't go to jail. I don't think my sanity can handle it. And you light skin, too, bro. Did you see that old blaxploitation movie, *Penitentiary*?" Kinte shook his head and ignored Tahj's griping as they all entered the hospital.

#

Kale, Jay, and Lionel hopped off the back of a battered old blue truck one at a time by the side of the road near her home. Luckily, Jay had an uncle coming from the farmer's market who wasn't too afraid to offer them a ride so long as they stayed on the back. Jay didn't dare walk up to his window. He waved a peace sign. His uncle nodded, lifted his cap brim, and drove off.

Kale had already hurried into the yard, leaving Jay and Lionel. She grabbed a hidden spare key she kept behind an African mask her mother hung over the door years ago and unlocked the front door. Kale entered, looking for the cellphone she'd lost. She remembered her aunt's phone she had on her dresser. She dialed the hospital connecting to her aunt's room. Jay and Lionel walked in, watching her from the doorway.

"What! Okay, I'm on my way!"

"Where's Hampton and Davis?" Jay asked.

"At the hospital, the two guys who brought them in are being held," Kale said, snatching the red headwrap off. She walked past Jay, grabbing her keys. "Come on, and turn the lock when you walk out!"

Lionel hesitated to get into the van with Jay and Kale. Both looked at him, sensing the worry on his face.

"My grandma; I need to see if I have family looking for me," he mumbled.

"Lionel, come with us, just come with us to the hospital. My children are there. Maybe we can find out if other family has been searching for you, too," Kale suggested. Lionel nodded, trusting her and climbing into the backseat.

#

Kale pulled into the parking lot of the hospital and saw the parked police cars. She noticed one car on the end of the curb had passengers in the back. She walked to the entrance with

Jay and Lionel at her side. The attendant stopped them as soon as they entered, giving them masks and asking them to check-in.

"I'm looking for two children, a boy and a girl, brought in with two guys," Kale stated.

"Yes, please, place your masks on, and we will …" Kale didn't even hear the rest of what the attendant had to say. Her eyes locked on Hampton and Davis being walked out by Officer Thompson and another unknown officer.

"Mommy!" Hampton yelled, breaking free from the officers. Kale caught Hampton in her arms, kneeling lower to take better hold of him, and held out her other hand for Davis.

"See, my babies, I always come back to you," she said, holding them tighter, never wanting to let go again. Jay, with tearful eyes, watched Officer Thompson walk up to Kale and the other officer walk toward him and Lionel.

"Ms. McCray, you have some explaining to do." Officer Thompson said. Kale looked up at Thompson and inhaled a deep breath to stand and face him. Nodding, she slowly exhaled.

#

After a few weeks, news broke that the sickness was slowing down. There were reports of numerous people recovering, some claiming they were feeling better than before. The shimmery spores still moved through the air but at a much lesser amount. Aunt Niecy was now home, obsessing over the news like she usually did, talking over the phone, nagging Kale about taking care of herself and the kids.

"Are y'all staying in? They said this weird sparkling pollen in the air might be what's helping people to get better. Can you believe that? Mmph, regular pollen 'bout to kill me, having these sneezing attacks, but this pixie dust is an immune booster."

"Yeah, Auntie, it's crazy. Are you coming over?" Tree asked, rolling her eyes and smiling.

"Chile, please, and you inviting other people over, too. I don't want to get sick again! No ma'am."

"Auntie, for once in a long time, the weather is nice outside, and you can wear a mask as well as stand a few feet from others for extra protection. But I think things are getting better with this shimmer." Kale said, sounding hopeful. "It's not even in the air as much as before. Honestly, the sparkles are kind of pretty. Don't you think so?"

"Yes, it's pretty like when I just so happened to be visiting your mama that one time in Atlanta, it had to be covered with snow and ice, freezing my glorious behind off. 'Oh, it's so pretty,' she said, 'it's never snows down here.

Ain't it pretty Niecy?' Uh, naw. So, to my niece, my heart, baby girl, my spirit is with you, but my body is glued to this sofa. I'm 'bout to watch my show, relax, and stuff my face. But you have fun, tell everybody I said hey, and kiss those babies for me, okay?" Aunt Niecy responded.

"Okay, Auntie, bye." Kale laughed while hanging up. She realized her aunt felt more comfortable bringing stories up about her and her mom more often. It honestly felt good because it gave Kale more of a sense that her mother was even more so with them.

Kale placed her cellphone she found a few days after the Zar incident into her back pocket. She had been without it since the night Jay attacked her, and it felt good at times to do so. It must have been the type of freedom Tree felt, not being tied to phones and emails or constantly responding to every beep she heard. Kale heard a knock at the door and walked out of her room to look out the front window. Lionel and his friend, Iesha, were standing outside. She opened the door, flashing a bright smile.

"Hey, y'all. How's it going?" she asked, hugging Iesha.

"Good," each one responded. Kale could still see the pain in Lionel's eyes. Lionel was not only dealing with the loss of his grandmother and living with other family members, but he held deep guilt regarding the death of James. He had talked with Kale about the anger he felt from not controlling his body when the entity was within him. Even though it was not his fault, Lionel couldn't shake his guilt. It was something only he carried. But as long as he did, Lionel felt comfort in knowing that Iesha, also knowing what happened, stood by his side in support.

Kale's eyes softened reaching to give Lionel a nurturing hug. After a few seconds, his body stiffened, then relaxed and he lifted his arms to return her hug. Lionel looked towards her then shyly took his gaze down, nodding slightly, confirming he was ok. No child should have to carry that weight, Kale thought.

"Come on! Everybody is out back," Kale said, waving a hand toward the hall.

Kale and the teens walked through the house and out the back door. She had decided to have a small get-together in honor of Tree. No one had seen her since the cemetery incident, but Kale had a strong feeling she was all right. She looked at Hampton and Davis, playing with Jay. He tossed a ball to Davis, then Davis would throw it with all her might to Hampton, only for the ball to end up flipping out of her hands, rolling toward him. It took a few days for them to accept that their dad was back to normal. And even then, they were having nightmares. It was just something Kale knew would take time to heal.

Jay laughed, then looked at Kale and smiled. She returned the smile and nodded. Even though she decided to work on forgiving him, she also decided not to take him back. He was disappointed but respected her decision and wanted to keep the peace. Kale still thought of him as part of her family, just in a different arrangement. Aunt Niecy wasn't feeling it, but she'd get over it.

Kale walked over to Tahj and Kinte, hearing one of their numerous passionate conversations they seemed to always have since she had known them for the past few weeks.

"Man, I'm still tripping out on how all the charges were dropped!" Kinte said to Tahj. "I know we didn't do anything, but it's weird. Usually, it's …"

"It's a brother going to the big house," Tahj interjected. "Catching the short end of the stick, getting …"

"Okay, Mouth," Kinte said, stopping Tahj. "You're right; I was just thinking what kind of explanation they took to let us go."

"I gave Thompson the truth. After that, I asked him did he really want to take that to his superiors and that he'd be smart to manipulate the story enough to make enough sense for them. No one would believe what his eyes saw as well as the other officers who were there."

"Damn!" Tahj and Kinte exclaimed in unison. They gave each other knowing glances then looked toward Kale.

"He took that?" Tahj asked.

"Strangely, yes. I'm just as surprised as you guys are about how my words influenced him. But that doesn't matter; all that matters is you guys are free, and I will always be indebted to you two for protecting my babies. It's the least I could do."

Tahj and Kinte nodded.

"Just trying to do the right thing, sis," Tahj said.

Kale looked toward Kinte. "Did Jay set you straight?" she asked, referring to the fifty he was owed. Kinte laughed.

"Oh, we've already settled that, sis. Don't worry. I think ya boy Jay is turning over a new leaf," Kinte said.

"Have you heard from Tree?" Tahj asked Kale. "What I wouldn't give to hear that smooth philosophy she be spitting on. How she say it, Kinte?" Tahj asked.

"Life, brothers, life," Both Kinte and Tahj said in unison in a calm persona. Kale chuckled at their mystical interpretation of Tree.

"No, but I feel like she's still here," Kale answered,

missing Tree's presence as well. Looking at her hands, she could still see her shining blue aura. It was much brighter than the last time she noticed it. It was as though it was growing. She didn't understand what her mission in life was, being what Tree called a sun traveler. All Kale had done since she and the kids settled back into their life routine was take care of mundane things and head back to work at the same annoying job as before. But she did so with a notice to the changes within her. Kale became aware that while at work, others didn't push her buttons so deeply now. There was a strong sense of ease within herself that began to reflect outwardly. Kale also noticed others couldn't get deep enough to rock her world in a negative way. This ease she felt made her so comfortable in her skin that she celebrated by shaving off all of her hair. Kale was surprised that she really liked the shape of her head and the lightness of being her simple self. She even began watching videos and learning to add yoga poses and breathing exercises to her routine in the morning and at night before bed. Even her food choices changed by adding healthy alternatives to her diet. Tree had truly inspired her. But she still couldn't figure out what her gift was or how she was supposed to share her light.

Davis came up behind Kale and tugged on her pants leg. "Mommy, I want a story," she demanded, gazing up at her.

"Now, baby, we have guests over. Don't you want to finish playing ball with Hampton?" Kale asked, trying to deter Davis.

Davis had also been more verbal in her requests lately, which was another positive change. Kale guessed right; all Davis needed was time. The kids had become insistent on hearing Kale's made-up magical stories. Kale didn't think that much of them. But every day, she had been coming up with weird, fantastical ideas, splicing together unheard-of creatures and creating worlds for them to imagine. Their ears consumed every word she spoke and would light up with each character voice she brought to life. Gazing down into Davis' serious-looking, large brown eyes, she paused for a moment.

"Mommy, Mommy?" Davis called. Davis' lips moved, but it was another voice Kale heard. *It is in our childhood that we sometimes discover the call of what we must do. We forget that call as we age, needing that innocence to help us remember. Be quiet and listen.* Kale could have sworn she heard her mother talking directly to her through Davis.

"Mommy?" Davis called again, bringing Kale back to herself. She blinked her eyes and smiled at Davis.

"Yes, baby. Let's sit on the steps and tell a story," Kale answered, swooping Davis onto her hips, tickling her belly. Davis laughed, trying to block and push away Kale's hand. Kale sat and began another creation, smiling, realizing what her gift was and how she would share her light. Hampton dropped the ball he and his dad were playing with like a hot potato and ran to his mother's side to listen. Afterward, others gathered around, lost in the trance of a fictional world.

#

The leaves awakened from the soft cool breeze maneuvering through the branches on the newly formed oak. The base of the trunk made a loud crack as pieces of bark fell to the ground. Part of the trunk split and began to peel forward, separating, pulling away from the main body of the tree. Shaped like a woman, the wooden figure tumbled to her knees, opening her mouth, taking in a deep breath of air. She peeled her eyes open, looking around into the darkness before dawn, while her skin shifted into smooth dark chocolate. Bald as a newborn, spirals of hair began to twist from her scalp, curling around itself like a vine growing in rapid motion. Her newly fluff black halo began to merge into sections, transforming into ropes that swelled, growing down her back until the tips grazed the grass she knelt on.

Tree stood, swinging long locs behind her, then leaned toward the tree, and closed her eyes. Within her mind she saw Kale and the others and knew her work here was done. A tone of sadness ran through Tree, but her work was not limited to one place. It was her job to share her light wherever she went with anyone she encountered. Tree rubbed the bark and gave a silent thanks, then willed leaves from her flesh, covering her sacredness. Welcoming the early sun's light, Tree walked out of the cemetery alone.

#

Kale woke up early, intending to sit alone and enjoy a quiet meditation before it was time to get the kids up and head off to work. She walked into the living room area and glanced at Tree's cork yoga mat and green shoulder bag on the floor in the corner of the room. Kale kept her things in the spot where Tree had left them, hoping she would return. She had returned to the cemetery wondering if Tree shifted back to human, but all Kale saw was the extraordinary new oak Tree had become. Kale went up to the mat and knelt, running her fingers along it, feeling its grainy texture. Her gaze went to the shoulder bag, leaning against the wall. Temptation called her to look within it. What could it hurt? Kale was curious about what kind of magical things a sun traveler as powerful as Tree carried around.

Kale grabbed it and pulled it open. Inside, there were extra pieces of clothing, a lavender-colored t-shirt, a beige sweater, and some handmade gray pants similar to the brown ones she wore all the time. Kale felt a stick-like object and pulled out a small bamboo flute. Maybe she would get Tree to play it whenever she saw her again. Kale placed the flute to the side and reached in deeper, feeling something hard and smooth, hearing light clinking. She pulled out an indigo blue star-shaped crystal, then an oval-shaped purple stone with white streaks and other small stones. Kale also found a pen and a small notepad with scribbles of rhyming lyrics. There was no wallet or identification of any kind to know who Tree really was. There wasn't even any cash or other means of finance. It was like she completely renounced her past. A knock on Kale's window caused her to jerk up. Embarrassed, Kale turned to see Tree gazing back at her holding her bag. Kale placed it back down on the mat and went to the door to let her in.

"Tree!" Kale exclaimed. Tree's hair hung around her, shielding her body with the help of the leaves. "How did you get here? You walked here like that?"

"Yes, sister. My original clothes were destroyed after I shifted. I had no choice but to come like this." Tree answered, walking past Kale, heading toward her shoulder bag. Tree retracted the leaves within her body as she knelt to grab her items, then stood and slid her clothes on. Tree pushed her long locs back and smiled at Kale, happy to see her again. Kale, for a moment, was at a loss of words just looking at her. Kale couldn't believe this strange, beautiful woman and all she could do and had done. At one point, Kale was annoyed and angry with her; now, ironically, Kale was grateful for their friendship.

"Kale, you look different. You cut your hair." Kale rubbed the back of her scalp and grinned.

"Yeah, it was time. I wanted my kids to know how beautiful they are and there's nothing wrong with their natural hair texture. And how am I supposed to do that with me trying to hide mine? I actually like it, and it's low maintenance. I don't know if I can grow locs as glorious as yours, but I'll be feeling a cute little afro when it grows out." Kale's said, beaming.

"You don't have to have hair like mine to have glorious hair. Your whole being is glorious because you are fully comfortable with yourself from within. I think your haircut is beautiful. I looked similar many years ago. Although I adore my sacred locs, I enjoyed the fresh start of beginning new and watching my hair form on its own. Sometimes new growth is needed as a reminder of the everchanging of life."

"Speaking of life, thank you so much for saving me and saving my family. You've risked your life for this place I complain about sometimes," Kale said. She looked down with glassy eyes then rushed to squeeze Tree. "I'm sorry for hitting you, and I—I didn't mean to go through your things. I wasn't sure if you were coming back or if you permanently became a tree, but I could feel your energy hadn't left."

"Kale, it's all right." Tree pulled away to look at Kale. "It was my duty. I love you and the children, my sister. I love this earth, and all I want to do is my part while I'm here on it. I thought about staying within the tree created. It was so peaceful, but my calling is too deep. Also, I don't have much in my bag, so it's no bother if you were curious." Tree giggled. Kale smiled with relief.

"I saw a flute with your things, and I remembered you said you were into music at one point. Can you play something, please?"

"I used to play during my school days as a youth, and it's something I not too long ago picked up again. So, I'm honestly very rusty, but I will try a few lyrics from a song I wrote. Is that okay?"

"Wow, um, yes! That would be amazing!" Kale's face lit up.

Tree smiled, then sat on her mat, crossed her legs, then grabbed her flute. Following her steps, Kale sat across from her and watched. Tree closed her eyes and seemed to go into a different state of being. She sucked in a deep breath, rolled her shoulders back, then opened her eyes before casting them downward. Her golden-green aura illuminated as she brought the flute to her full lips and blew. The melodic notes she played moved smoothly from one note to the other. Tree swayed as her fingers moved amongst the flute's holes. The sound brought Kale back to the dream, where she found herself in a forest and saw her mother. She watched in admiration as Tree played with such peace. Tree blew a long note at the end, lowering the flute, then began singing a song corresponding with the energy of the melody she played.

"I've chosen this life. I'm one who comes and then goes—a wanderer born free. But I must share what I know— no attachments with me. So, I have more room to love. Some don't grasp the mystery. But it's a nature we're all a part of." Tree brought her flute back up to her lips and began to play once again.

The joy Kale felt witnessing Tree's music was absolute magic. The chills she felt moving through her were so intense that Kale thought she'd jump out of her skin. Soon, Tree brought the flute down, then looked into Kale's eyes and smiled.

"That is all I have written with that melody. But it's one I deeply enjoy. Maybe one day I will write more when the words come." Tree chuckled, placing her flute in the bag.

"That was utterly spellbinding. Why are you not like doing something with it? I mean, I know you said you were before, but that was just so beautiful! And we had a small get-together in your honor yesterday. You could have shared that. I wish you were there. What you do is extraordinary. And people, from what I've seen and heard on the local news, are getting better from the flowers and the tree you grew." Kale spilled her words out with so much uncontained passion that she could barely help herself. "People should really know about the work you do and how you care so much."

"I am just glad the work is done, and I can share. The people of Neville are healing, and the light will spread, starting with you. Then others will join you. I sing now for just the joy of it. I don't need nor want recognition. I enjoy my unknown-ness," Tree said, placing the rest of her things back into the shoulder bag.

"I kind of thought you'd say something like that." Kale chuckled, thinking of Tree's mystical sayings. "I think I now know how I can contribute to humanity as a sun traveler," Kale said, beaming with light in her eyes.

"Yes, yes. I knew you would. There is always a way to live your purpose no matter what circumstance your life is in." Tree said.

"I'm a storyteller. I've never thought too deep about it before; I think my children made me realize it. Looking back on other situations, telling stories seemed like an ignored gift I'd use but not really value. Also, another clue was my aura. So, I looked through that chakra book I told you my mother left, and I learned blue deals with self-expression, communication, and speech. I've been a storyteller since youth, but I didn't realize it. Lately, I'd been so angry at life, working a job I hated, seemed like I wasn't getting anywhere, taking care of the kids alone, my issues with Jay, and most of my hurt came from my mother dying. I just couldn't deal with anything. I needed a break from life. But I remembered telling my mother a story. I was a little kid then, but the amount of joy I felt and how it made her light up was like healing for both of us. I would create stories after she became sick with cancer, but it wasn't with the same pure light I had as a child. It's amazing how the answers to healing yourself are already within you. And just creating these stories for my kids has been powerful healing for me. So, I've been writing them down so I can get to a

point where I can share them with others beyond my family."
Tree beamed, watching the blue aura glowing around Kale
as she spoke.

"Wonderful!" Tree exclaimed. She hugged Kale then
pulled away to look at her in awe. "You will be able to
continue bringing a lot of good to this place as well as to the
rest of the world through your power of words. I am so happy
you have discovered this magic within yourself!" Tree
kneeled to roll up her mat. She slid it inside her bag. Then
placed the bag over her shoulders and stood back to face
Kale.

"It is now my time to go. I feel the call to leave and
help others who have a hard time seeing the light within
themselves, so I must share mine."

"Wait, we still need you here! Neville still needs a lot
of help! I can't do this yet by myself." Kale felt the bad taste
of loss rising within her. She wasn't ready for Tree to leave.
There were still many questions she wanted to ask.

"Kale, think about what you just said to me about
healing. That the answers to heal yourself are already within
you." Kale took a deep breath, listening to Tree speak. "If
you have the power to heal yourself, you have the power to
bring healing to the world. And it's through your healing that
other sun travelers will awaken to their light within, and the

cycle will continue. We may seem alone in this world, but we are never truly alone. Spirit is everywhere around you and within you, and we both are made of this same spirit. Therefore, I am always with you."

Tree went to the door and walked outside. Tora was on the porch, waiting when she saw Tree and crept up to her, circling, then rubbing her head against Tree's leg. Tree kneeled to give her one last rub. Kale followed outside behind Tree and watched her through sad eyes.

"No need for worry, Kale. Learn to be more like my old warrior friend here," Tree said, scratching behind Tora's ears. "Walk with grace, be fierce, love true, and know that the forces of the universe are within you."

"I will miss you, Warrior." Tree said, running her fingers through Tora's thick fur. Tora looked up at Tree and purred.

"Continue to protect this family and take care of yourself, Tora."

Kale looked to Tree with teary eyes, beginning to burn; still, she managed to smile. "You didn't want to say goodbye to everyone else?" she asked, trying to convince Tree to stay longer.

"I don't say goodbye. I say I will see you later or bid you good day," Tree responded, standing. Tree's eyes became watery then she smiled.

"Kale, no need for sadness. One spirit, remember? So, goodbyes, separations, death—they are all illusions. Don't be fooled by form. Form can make your mind believe something is over, or that something is just gone, but go deeper to that eternal. That's the real you and me, and then you'll know you will never truly lose anything or anyone. Love is the eternal nature of us all, and it can never be broken by form. Okay?" Tree asked, placing a hand on her dear spiritual sister's shoulder. Kale nodded and blinked as tears streamed down her cheeks. She knew Tree was as solid, calm, and powerful as the trees in human form. But in spirit, she was the wind, and how can you contain the wind?

Tree wiped a tear away from her spiritual sister's pecan-colored cheek and smiled. She nodded and walked away the same as she had first come down the road with her large magnificent locs swinging behind her. Kale watched her walk away, not caring if she was running late for work. She watched until Tree disappeared down the road.

The End

About The Author

Carmen Liana Young is a natural born artistic and mystical soul, who finds joy in self-expression through life within the forms of singing, songwriting, painting, acting, and creating handmade items. She is a lover of nature (especially trees), astrology, numerology, fantasy, crystals, and metaphysical subjects. And often finds that daydreaming, spending time in quiet reflection, and following her intuition leads to positive results.

Carmen is a musical artist who released the album *"Who I Am"* under the name Carmen Liana through Lotus Records. She has a bachelor's degree of Art from Albany State University. And received her yoga teaching certification through Homegrown Yoga Studio.

When Carmen is not writing she is often found moving like the wind on an adventure with her family. *A Woman Called Tree* is her first novel.

Made in the USA
Las Vegas, NV
24 September 2021